TRANSLATION STATION

TRANSLATION STATION

by Don D'Ammassa

The Merry Blacksmith Press

2011

Translation Station

"A Good Offense" originally appeared in *Analog*, 2003.
"Wormdance" originally appeared in *Isaac Asimov's SF*, 1999.
"Diplomatic Relations" originally appeared in *Talebones*, 2006.
"Funeral Party" originally appeared in *Talebones*, 2009.
"Getting with the Program" originally appeared in *Pirate Writings*, 1997.
"Translation Station" originally appeared in *Talebones*, 1996.
"The Man Who Walked to Procyon" originally appeared in *Cosmic Tales*, 2004.
"No Distance Too Great" originally appeared in *Isaac Asimov's SF*, 2010.
"Jack the Martian" originally appeared in *Harsh Mistress*, 1994.
"Adding It Up" originally appeared in *Talebones*, 1998.
"Actual Mode" originally appeared in *VBTech*, 1995.
"Scrimshaw" is original to this collection.
"Remotely Possible" is original to this collection.
"Duck and Cover" originally appeared in *Analog*, 2009.
"Chronic Pain" originally appeared in *Cosmic Crime*, 2011.
"Curing Agent" originally appeared in *Isaac Asimov's SF*, 2003.
"The Natural World" originally appeared in *Analog*, 2008.

For information, address:

The Merry Blacksmith Press
70 Lenox Ave.
West Warwick, RI 02893

merryblacksmith.com

Published in the USA by The Merry Blacksmith Press

ISBN— 978-0-61548-936-0
0-61548-936-2

Table of Contents

Dedication

*For Gabriel and Lucca,
whose future will probably be
even stranger than the ones
described here.*

How's This For an Intro?

I once had a story rejected with the comment that "it reads like something H.L. Gold would have bought for *Galaxy* magazine." I was actually very flattered because that lumped me with people like Theodore Sturgeon, Frederik Pohl, Jack Vance, William Tenn, and many other writers whom I have admired for most of my lifetime.

The implication I suppose is that I was writing an antiquated style of science fiction that was more concerned with plot than other literary qualities. As it happens, I welcomed the various "new waves" that transformed science fiction back starting in the 1960s and moving forward. I prefer stories with believable characters, well written prose, and other attributes that were often absent from genre writing. Although I can still read and enjoy authors like Edgar Rice Burroughs and Edward E. Smith for their storytelling virtues, that doesn't mean I don't recognize their many failings. Their time has passed and we demand, rightly, more depth and skill from our contemporaries.

Too often, however, the emphasis on style and "relevance" comes at the expense of the plot. Particularly at shorter lengths these past several years, science fiction has often become so concerned with how the story is told that the writers no longer realize that they have to have something to say to start with.

So if what turns you on is slice of life stories that provide insightful glimpses into characters or situations, but which resolve nothing, you're probably not going to like the stories in this collection. If you're a fan of convoluted stylistic devices that show off the technical expertise of the author, then you're probably not going to like the stories in this collection. On the other hand, if you're still thrilled by a sense of wonder about the universe, if you still like to have your expectations shaken up, then I think you just might derive some pleasure from these.

A couple of notes on the stories. The first version of "Translation Station" was written in 1968 after I saw a painting of a starship with wheels and wondered how that might have come about. The story finally published in 1996 was probably the tenth revision. Most of the first half of "Duck and Cover" is true, other than the fantastic elements. "Wormdance" is actually the first chapter of an unsold novel. The opening line of "A Good Offense" sat in my list of unwritten stories for ten years before I finally realized where it should lead. "The Natural World" was inspired by a dream after I'd read an account of the attitude toward naturalism in Victorian England.

A Good Offense

The Pulagi Ambassador and his life partner were barbecuing their children on the patio again.

Nathan Shaver tapped the privacy toggle angrily, turned away from the window even before it opaqued. A large part of his training was specifically designed to help him deal with xenocultural differences, and on a purely intellectual level he realized that the Pulagi were acting from biological necessity rather than cruelty. A functional Pulagi female dropped three or four litters of young every terrestrial year, and if the species hadn't adopted drastic infanticidal practices millennia earlier, they would have bred themselves into chaos long before they achieved any real civilization.

"What's up?" Adele was standing in the archway, still wearing her nightgown, obviously only half awake

"It's nothing. Go back to sleep. You were tossing and turning all night."

"Yeah, I was restless." She covered a yawn with the back of one hand. "They're doing it again, aren't they? She was about due."

Nathan nodded, trying to keep his expression neutral. Shortly after they'd moved to the diplomatic compound here in Florida, Adele had been sitting out in the yard when Ambassador Salanga's predecessor had carried six of their young out onto the patio, where he methodically chopped them to bits with an ornamental knife.

"I think I'll go into the city and do some shopping." Her sleepiness had magically disappeared. Nathan could understand her feelings. Even with his training and psychological conditioning, he found the population control practices of the Pulagi emotionally unsettling. It wasn't so much the fact that they killed most of their young, but that they expressed no regret afterwards.

⸱—◦—◦—◦—⸱

During the ordinary course of his duties, Nathan rarely interacted with the Ambassador. The arrival of the Pulagi on Earth three decades earlier had

3

traumatized human society, but the turmoil had passed once it became obvious that life was going to continue pretty much as it had before. Although not truly reptilian, the Pulagi's superficial resemblance to alligators made their choice of Florida as the location for their embassy seem logical and appropriate.

Nathan usually paged a skittercab to take him to the embassy annex, but today he walked to work, hoping the physical exertion would help to burn off the tension he was feeling. He arrived at the Center for Intercultural Studies early and took the liftube down to the basement cafeteria for some coffee.

One of the few Pulagi he knew by sight, a mid-level official named Sittakaper, was already there, sitting alone in one corner chewing on the corpse of one of the lower animals the Pulagi bred in the basement of their embassy to provide a source of fresh meat. Humans and Pulagians could actual digest most of each other's food, although neither species would remain healthy on an exclusively alien diet, but few humans cared for the pungent cuisine of their visitors. Nathan wasn't really in the mood to deal with the intricacies of interspecies communication, but it would have been a decided insult to ignore the other being's presence.

"May your day be more terrible than yesterday," he said ritually, his mind quickly settling into its conditioned pattern.

"It would be an appropriately dismaying beginning if you were to join me." The Pulagi males were in general taller and bulkier than humans, but Sittakaper was a female and the smallest adult of their species Nathan had ever met, a mere two meters.

Nathan took a seat directly opposite the alien, wondering if he could avoid a prolonged conversation. The Pulagi dealt with life in a very indirect fashion, and despite a highly advanced technology, their interpersonal relations were dominated by what seemed to be a very simple superstition. Just as actors advised each other to "break a leg" when they actually meant the opposite, the Pulagi phrased most of their intercourse negatively. Most, but not all, and the challenge to humanity was to develop an ability to determine which mode was appropriate from situation to situation. Thirty years of contact had provided more questions than answers.

"How is your refreshment today?" The Pulagi could almost speak human languages recognizably, but they still needed a vocoder to be understood clearly.

Nathan concentrated. Was this a gambit of Accelerated Denigration, in which case he should suggest that the Pulagi's choice of foods was disgraceful, or had they achieved a Plateau of Mellow Balance, which allowed conversation to continue more or less in human fashion? While he hesitated, Sittakaper filled the vacuum.

"I regret to advise you that His Eminence has indicated his desire to meet with you personally today."

"The Ambassador?" That was indeed unusual. Although they were neighbors and occasionally interacted outside of the compound, they rarely met in an official capacity. The Pulagi differentiated so distinctly between an individual's private and professional lives, it was almost as if they were two separate personalities. One theory held that their entire culture was schizophrenic, that the Pulagi compartmentalized different aspects of their personalities and functioned as a kind of single cell gestalt. If that were the case, it might explain how they were able to express deep devotion to their surviving offspring, but feel no regret at all about the necessity of sacrificing the others.

"Indeed, I believe a request for your presence has already been transmitted." So they were at Mellow Balance. That simplified things.

"What assistance could someone in my inferior position provide to His Eminence?"

"Almost certainly none worth mentioning." In a human, it would have been rude, but it was quite obviously a Negative Closure, indicating Sittakaper had no further knowledge.

"Or too important to be trusted to one of your stature." Nathan was confident that this was the right response, that he had closed the loop, but he still felt as though he was delivering an insult. Sittakaper turned her attention back to her mildly disgusting snack and Nathan quickly finished his coffee and left the cafeteria.

As predicted, there was a message waiting for him. Ambassador Salanga requested his presence in Meeting Room Four at two o'clock local time.

Nathan spent the morning working halfheartedly on refinements to the dictionary of idiom that was his primary responsibility. Curiosity, even mild anxiety, interfered with his concentration. As far as he knew, he'd done nothing that merited the attention of the Ambassador.

He deliberately arrived for the meeting ten minutes late, just enough to allow the Ambassador to make a critical remark about his manners. This would establish their relative status at the outset and save time, and the Pulagi diplomat would be flattered that Nathan had taken such care to anticipate the requirements of decorum.

"I cannot imagine any sufficient reason for this disruption of my daily schedule," he replied after accepting the ritual admonishment.

"Which fact illustrates the paucity of your imagination, Nathanshaver." The Pulagi seemed incapable of understanding how a single individual could have multiple names.

Nathan took a chair without being offered one. To have waited for an invitation would have been a grave breach of manners. Had they satisfied protocol now or was an additional exchange required first? Salanga had used his name, which implied closure, but it seemed too abrupt. Cautiously, he took several seconds to settle into the chair, hoping for a clue.

"One of the more irksome duties of my posting to your backward world is the requirement that I review the progress of each function of our mission." Salanga sank back into the concave receptacle that passed for chairs among his people, his tail curled under his thighs. His words seemed to imply Accelerated Denigration, but his posture was too relaxed. That might have meant Haughty Insolence, but since the Ambassador outranked Nathan, it couldn't be. Veiled Contempt would have required stronger language, so this was probably Sustained Indifference, to which the proper response was Sarcastic Disdain.

"I am certain your staff responds properly to your unnecessary interference." He wasn't sure that he'd struck the proper note, but it was hard to find the right balance in this mode.

"Their incompetence is at acceptable levels." Salanga's phrasing reassured him. It was an obvious invitation to move to Mellow Balance.

"Has the communications office been less troublesome than usual?"

"Their progress has been nearly adequate." There was a short awkward pause that Nathan didn't dare try to fill. "My staff has indicated that your manners are occasionally tolerable and I wished to confirm this personally."

This was unusually high praise and Nathan almost lost his head and thanked Salanga. "Perhaps your staff has been less observant than they should be."

"No doubt. Nevertheless, it is necessary that I speak to you about an impending visitor from my government."

"Someone of no importance, I assume."

"None at all, but it will be necessary to accommodate his requirements nonetheless."

It took a while before Nathan extracted the entire story. The Pulagi didn't have a simple hierarchical command structure, so it was difficult to estimate the authority of Frelleger, the VIP in transit. In some of his duties, he was clearly Salanga's superior, but in others he appeared to be a subordinate. His immediate purpose was the issue, however, because it appeared he was coming to Earth to determine whether or not it was wise to maintain contact with the human race.

"Details are being forwarded to your superiors even as we speak, but I think it would be best if you personally saw to his discomfort." Salanga had wavered back and forth from Mellow Balance to Casual Exchange, the latter mode so unusual that Nathan had trouble keeping in step.

"I am sure I will be able to tolerate his presence as long as is necessary."

"In that case, he will certainly leave us at the earliest possible opportunity."

That sounded like Negative Closure. "I look forward to speeding his departure." Nathan rose to leave.

He was almost out the door when Salanga called after him. "I should advise you that Frelleger fully appreciates our obligation to assist the less worthy races."

The words sounded like exactly what the human race wanted. But unless Salanga had fallen into a momentary lapse of protocol, which was unlikely, they were still in Negative Closure. And that meant that Frelleger was going to be a problem.

><del>-+∘-◦-◦-+</del>

Nathan reported to Saunders, his department head, and she immediately notified the UN's Division of Extraterrestrial Affairs. Before the day was out, a crisis council had been formed and Nathan had recounted his conversation with Salanga eleven times. The Ambassador's final remark was debated endlessly and repetitiously, usually by people who didn't understand the intricacies of Pulagi interactions.

When Frelleger's ship arrived eight days later, there was still no consensus about what needed to be done.

"I guess it's up to you," Saunders told Nathan. "You have the best qualifications for dealing with the Pulagi."

"As a linguist," he protested. "Not as a politician. I haven't been trained for this sort of thing."

"Insofar as the Pulagi are concerned, none of us have. So we're going to assent to Salanga's wishes."

And so it was that he stood nervously at the head of the delegation that met Frelleger's shuttle. The newcomer was a bit heavy for a Pulagi, and somewhat lighter colored than most, but otherwise he looked and dressed the same as the other Pulagi on Earth. He was accompanied by his life partner, whose birthing pouches were taut and bulging. Pulagian gender roles were even less differentiated than among humans, but their females had to put up with short periods of intense discomfort preceding each litter. Nathan stepped forward so that the newcomer would know where to direct his ceremonial opening insult.

Frelleger appraised him for a few seconds with his unblinking eyes, then spoke in his native tongue. Nathan translated quickly in his head, paled even before the official interpreter stepped forward and repeated the greetings in English. "Envoy Frelleger wishes to express his pleasure at this opportunity to visit your world."

Nathan felt his knees weakening. Opening a relationship with an Implied Compliment was a deadly insult. Should he respond in the same mode and risk offending the Envoy, or with a complimentary insult to demonstrate that humans were a civilized species? His head was spinning and he hadn't spoken his first word yet.

"We are honored by your presence despite your ungainly appearance and poor manners. A vehicle has been provided to take you to your embassy." He hoped that would be sufficiently ambiguous.

The interpreter spoke to Frelleger, whose earcaps twitched in what Nathan believed was the Pulagi's involuntary response to being caught by surprise. "Almost certainly a primitive and untrustworthy mode of transport, but I imagine it's the best that your culture can manage."

Nathan sighed with relief. Frelleger was going straight into Accelerated Denigration, a mode in which he felt much more comfortable. Maybe this wouldn't be such a disaster after all.

But just as Frelleger was slipping into the custom designed skitter, he turned and spoke loudly enough for Nathan to hear. "Perhaps this will not be as onerous a visit as I thought."

<hr />

After Frelleger had been delivered safely to his quarters, Nathan was summoned to a meeting to discuss the initial contact. Saunders was there, along with most of the senior people in the communications offices, linguists, translators, psychologists, and an even larger number from Protocol and ET Affairs. They watched a recording of the entire exchange in silence before asking Nathan for his opinion.

"Obviously Frelleger wants to terminate contact with us. His opening remark was in Cautious Approval, which is about as bad as it can get short of Fulsome Praise."

"Pulagi modes aren't linear," protested Janes from research. "You can't really say one is worse than another."

"And I'm not sure that was Cautious Approval anyway," added Nganda. "It might have been Sardonic Praise, which is a kind of Pulagian irony because in that case the literal compliment is meant to be interpreted as an insult, and is therefore not."

Nathan raised his hands for quiet, forestalling another round of pedantic arguments. "Sardonic Praise can only be used in response to Haughty Insolence. Frelleger initiated the exchange, so it had to be Cautious Approval. I responded ambiguously so that he would know that I recognized the insult but chose to ignore it. Hopefully that demonstrated that we're intelligent enough, civilized enough, for him to deal with us."

"Do we have any idea why the Envoy wants to terminate contact, if that is in fact the situation?" It was someone from ET Affairs whom Nathan knew only by face.

It was Saunders who answered. Jill had been working long hours the past few days, and her face showed signs of strain. "We have an educated guess, assembled from bits and pieces the embassy officials have dropped into conversations recently. Pulagi society is no more monolithic than our own—less if anything. They are united under a single government, but only for certain purposes. Every Pulagi chooses to join one of several political factions when they reach maturity, but once the choice is made, they can never change allegiance. We're not really comfortable that we understand how this works, particularly since members of one faction can have secondary and tertiary memberships in rival groups. In any case, different sets of laws apply to individuals based on their factional membership, even though there is no geographical separation between them."

"Sounds pretty chaotic," commented one of the political types.

"It makes a weird kind of sense. The Pulagi believe in making decisions only after examining every viewpoint. To ensure that nothing gets overlooked, they've created a system in which there are advocates for every position, even those that no one currently believes in. Salanga belongs to a faction that advocates cooperative expansion into the universe. Some of his staff belong to another which favors establishing an empire with Pulagi at the apex. Frelleger represents the isolationist viewpoint. Their goal is to quarantine the systems of other intelligent races."

"So what is the official policy of the Pulagian government?" asked Wilson, who worked in Protocol and Deportment.

"All three. And there are some other intermediary positions as well. Each individual case is decided after the various factions interact."

"Then you're saying the Pulagians are inconsistent?"

"And humans aren't?" She glared the man down. "However strange it seems to us, their system has served them well and for a long time. They were traveling to the stars when the Pyramids were being built, and they haven't fought among themselves for at least that long."

"All right, let's get back to the matter at hand." Fulghrum, from the Secretariat, was nominally in charge of the meeting, although he'd done little up till now to demonstrate his authority. "We know the desired outcome. We want the Pulagi to stay, to increase trade and technical assistance. How do we respond to this new envoy to ensure we achieve our goal?"

"Do we have to do anything?" someone asked. "I mean, he only represents one faction. How much weight does he carry?"

Nathan answered quickly. "Apparently a great deal. Salanga went out of his way to underline the importance of this visit."

"But if his faction is committed to breaking contact, and if individual factions support their established policy even if they think it's wrong in a particular case, then what's the point? Even if we convince Frelleger that we're a desirable trading partner, he'll still advocate severing relations when he returns."

Saunders nodded. "Yes he will, but there are degrees of advocacy. The Pulagi resolve their differences of opinion by examining them from every point of view. The positions most strongly held prevail."

She paused, and Nathan finished for her. "We want Frelleger to advocate in Mild Skepticism. At the moment, he seems more inclined toward Virtuous Disharmony."

Later that same day, Nathan accompanied Frelleger, Salanga, and some minor officials on an air tour of the surrounding area. The encounter started badly; Frelleger's greeting was in Mellow Balance, which could be construed as an insult or merely indifference. Nathan took a chance and responded in Dawning Anger but Frelleger's reply in the same Mode was almost automatic. The Envoy remained silent during most of the tour, describing New Tampa as an unattractive city, which was a good sign (as well as true), but also commenting that the human built skittership seemed quite sophisticated, which meant that he found it primitive and uncomfortable.

Frelleger was equally uncommunicative during the formal briefings that followed. He listened to presentations from a variety of human officials and to reports from embassy staff who had identified a number of human products which they deemed viable as trade goods. The most surprising item was music, the only human artform that appealed to the Pulagi. It was not unusual to hear Beethoven or the Beatles from inside the Pulagi residency. A few samples were played and Frelleger characterized them as "discordant noise", which was the only positive remark he made that day. His frequent though thankfully low key praise for the fine work the embassy staff had done left them all nearly as dispirited as Nathan and the rest of the human contingent.

⊢•⊕•O•⊕•⊣

The days that followed weren't any better. Frelleger remained in Implied Compliment or Casual Approval most of the time, occasionally moved into Mellow Balance, and only once resorted to Sarcastic Disdain in Nathan's presence.

On the third day, he encountered Salanga in the lobby. "You have succeeded in making the Envoy's visit less arduous than he expected." That depressed Nathan so much that he seriously considered telling Saunders that he was resigning immediately.

Instead, he made a luncheon date with Patti Cruz, who worked in the psychological profiling section. "I need something, Patti. A hook, an insight."

She shrugged. "I can't help you. We keep developing new theories, but we don't have anything close to an accurate model of their behavior patterns. That segmented psychology of theirs is very complex. Do you realize they can believe two contradictory things at once?"

"So can humans."

"Not the same way. Humans rationalize. A human can honestly believe that theft is wrong, then steal from his employer, but only because he tells himself the employer owes it to him, so it isn't really theft. A Pulagi doesn't need to rationalize. You know Sittakaper?"

He nodded.

"Sittakaper belongs to a faction which believes that females should be sterilized after their fortieth litter, but she gave birth just last month."

Nathan nodded. "Took a day off work to eat her kids. Yeah, I remember."

"Well, she's dropped more than fifty litters herself. I managed to get her to talk about the situation and she literally cannot see the contradiction. It's almost as if the two parts of her mind only examine the problem when it's necessary to make a decision, and then the part with the strongest motivation prevails."

"If that's true, then Frelleger will really believe we should be quarantined when he presents his case, even if he also really believes we should become trading partners."

"That's about the size of it."

They were silent for a while, then Nathan asked what was almost a rhetorical question. "What do the Pulagians really want?"

"Excuse me?"

"They don't really need to trade with us. Oh, they like our music, and we've done a few things with electronics that haven't occurred to them, but there's nothing we can offer that will significantly alter their culture. If they quarantine us, they'll have lost very little. But if that's the case, why did they contact us in the first place? Why even let us know they exist?"

"The other factions…"

"No," he cut her off. "That's not enough. They want something, need something. And if it's not trade goods, maybe it's something less palpable. Something psychological."

She thought about that for a moment. "Maybe they're lonely?"

Nathan shook his head. "No, they have active contact with at least a dozen other races. Whatever they're looking for, they haven't found anyone yet who can provide it."

"Well, why don't you ask Frelleger next time you see him?"

"I might just do that."

⊶⊙⊷

But he didn't. The following morning, he met with Frelleger and his mate, Cheriffa, for almost two hours without finding any way to manipulate the conversation in the right direction. Cheriffa told him that he was "annoyingly persistent", which cheered him a little, but Frelleger couldn't be bothered to move out of Mellow Balance even when Nathan resorted to an unconventional switch to Veiled Insolence. Cheriffa grew very restless toward the end of the session, and Nathan made an excuse to end early so that she could retreat to her sleeping chamber. It was obvious that she was going to drop her litter within the next twenty-four hours. And on the following day, she and Frelleger would be leaving Earth, unencumbered by offspring.

He went home, moped around until he had managed to irritate Adele, then went for a long walk to clear his head.

And had an idea.

He was awake most of the night thinking about it. Although he knew it was a long shot, he couldn't think of any other approach. If he was wrong, he might singlehandedly guarantee that the human race would be quarantined. Even if he was right, he wasn't sure if he could carry it off.

Cheriffa was notably absent the following morning. Frelleger was more morose than ever, if that was possible, and the last few interviews and reports were uneventful and unpromising. As the last delegation walked out, the Envoy uncurled himself from his seat and prepared to retire to his quarters. Other than the Pulagian interpreter, Nathan was the only other being in the room.

"Envoy Frelleger, it is my distasteful task to request that you remain a short while longer."

"I suppose I could tolerate your presence briefly since my departure to more civilized regions is imminent."

Nathan was heartened by the sudden switch to Accelerated Denigration, even though that probably meant that Frelleger had decided to staunchly support quarantine and was feeling some degree of sympathy. During the morning's strategy session, he had been tempted to advance the theory he'd recently hatched, but had remained silent, fearing that they'd react badly and replace him. Now that he knew he couldn't make matters worse, he decided to put it to the test.

"I can't imagine any civilized culture which would welcome one such as you."

The interpreter hesitated before translating. Nathan had jumped directly to Haughty Insolence, bypassing several intermediate steps. Frelleger actually turned and took a step back toward him, and his earcaps betrayed his emotions. "Since you have no experience of true civilization, your words are without value."

Was that Sarcastic Disdain or Rude Condescension? No matter. He had to move from the general to the specific. "Animals may be taught to speak, but a wise being pays them no heed."

This time the interpreter remained silent until Frelleger turned to him impatiently, demanding to know what Nathan had said. It took several seconds for him to phrase his reply.

"It is easy to mock where there is no understanding."

Nathan faltered. Frelleger was backing off, trying to ease back into a less intense mood. He couldn't allow that to happen; he had to play his trump now.

"I understand that you eat your own offspring. I can't imagine anything worse."

The interpreter stood frozen, incapable of speech, but it didn't matter. Nathan had studied carefully and the ultimate insult had been delivered in nearly perfect Pulagian. It needed no translation.

⊢•⊕•○•⊕•⊣

Nathan was with Frelleger for most of the remainder of his stay on Earth. When his shuttle lifted off, he publicly announced that he'd been thoroughly distressed throughout his visit, and Nathan was confident that he'd present his case in Mild Skepticism or perhaps even Fretful Uncertainty. The danger of quarantine was over.

When he reported this to the crisis council, they were understandably relieved, but not confident until their sources with Salanga confirmed Nathan's opinion. Several of them asked how he had managed such a dramatic turn around, but he diverted their questions pointedly until they stopped asking. Jill Saunders watched him thoughtfully, and the two of them eventually went to her office.

She poured two brandies and let him finish his before she spoke. "You know I have to ask you for a full report."

"Yes."

"Are you going to give it to me?"

He hesitated, then sighed. "Yes, I guess so. But I formally request that it be sealed."

Her eyebrows went up. "All right, unless by its nature I have to make it public. So what happened between you and Frelleger?"

"The key is their fatally fecund reproductive cycle."

"They kill most of their kids," she said bluntly.

"Yes. And ritually consume them most of the time." He stood up and poured himself another brandy. "Our psychologists have theorized that the dichotomy between the natural instinct to preserve their young and the group instinct to match population to resources—food—caused enough stress to effectively fragment their minds. Their ability to hold contradictory opinions, their need to advocate courses of action that they don't necessarily favor, are all manifestations of something akin to human schizophrenia born of guilt. But with the Pulagi, it isn't a mental disease; it's a mental defensive system."

"None of this is new."

"No, but I extrapolated from that. It seemed to me that if this sense of guilt was so great that it had reshaped their entire psychology, that it must still be a momentous part of their everyday lives. But when they perform the actual act, it's almost casual. Salanga barbecued his last litter in the backyward, for God's sake!"

"All right, so it's a big deal."

"So why don't we ever talk to the Pulagians about it?"

Saunders looked uncomfortable. "Well, it's not the kind of thing you bring up in casual conversation, is it? What are we supposed to say? 'Hey, do you eat your kids with mustard or relish?' We're trying to be polite."

"Which is interpreted as exactly the opposite by the Pulagi. They conclude that we find the act so repulsive that we can't even talk about it. And they're right. And I'll bet the same thing is true of the other score or so races they've encountered, and certainly all the ones they quarantined. They're insulating themselves from others who are witnesses to their guilty deeds."

She looked troubled and confused. "So you brought the subject up?"

"No, I rammed it down Frelleger's throat. I told him it was the most disgusting thing I'd ever heard of. And then I proved to him that despite that fact, I wanted to be his friend."

"And how did you do that?"

This time Nathan was the one who looked uncomfortable. He tossed down his brandy and stared into the distance.

"I helped him eat his kids."

Wormdance

It was on Cille's fifteenth birthday that the wormswell came to our farm. At least, that's the day when we first noticed it. Things move so slowly for wormswell that it's difficult to tie specific events in their lives to such a fleeting moment as a day, even the 26 standard hour day of Aragon. It was my brother Jesper who brought us the news, running recklessly up from the north pasture, windmilling his arms and shouting whenever he could spare the breath. Dad spotted him first, rose up from where he was fitting a new board into the front steps where a rotten one had snapped the day before. His face was expressionless but I could see his hands tightening into fists where they hung by his sides.

"What is it now?" Mom pushed open the screen door and stepped out onto the porch, raising one hand to shade her eyes from the bright double sunlight. It was near high high noon, and the sky was almost completely cloud free. If either of Aragon's double stars had been as warm as Sol, we'd have risked a bad sunburn just standing outside unprotected.

"We'll know presently," my father answered calmly. "If he doesn't break his fool neck getting here." He glanced in my direction. "Did he say where he was going this morning, Ennis?"

I shrugged and turned back to the stack of cornfruits I had been husking. Jesper and I'd had a fight the night before, an ongoing battle because I was tired of having to pick up part of his share of the chores. I'd appealed to Dad and he'd told me the two of us were old enough to work it out ourselves and that neither of us would be happy if he had to intervene, but the fact was that Jesper just wouldn't stick to a job until it was finished. Even if it was something he enjoyed doing, he'd get bored and wander off sooner or later,

15

and if it was something he actually hated—as was the case with most of our duties on the farm—it was more often sooner than later. Don't get me wrong; I loved my younger brother intensely, but love doesn't get the barns clean, or the crab hens back into their nests.

Jesper slowed considerably toward the end, climbing the slope atop which we'd built the house. We'd tried to keep the wiregrass cut to ankle deep here, what Mom called our "lawn", but two of the maintenance bots had been waiting for spare parts for three months now, and the four that were left were barely able to keep up with the tilling and harvesting schedules, so it had grown without interference for some time now. We could see Jesper's head and shoulders bobbing above the silken tops as he advanced. We could probably have heard him if he'd kept shouting from this close, but Jesper was saving all of his breath for the effort needed to push through the chest high grass.

Cille came outside, blinking rapidly in the glare. Her bare arms were improbably slim for a Baxter. We're a bigboned, heavily fleshed family, always have been. And working the farm ensures that it's muscle and not fat. At eighteen, I was already as big as Dad, and Jesper, two years behind, was taller than both of us, though we each had a few pounds on him yet. Mom was no slouch either; she worked in the fields when her other responsibilities were out of the way, and she was solid enough to provide a painful whack when the two of us boys deserved it.

But Cille was different. Not fragile by any means, although she looked it compared to the rest of us. Wire hard though, tough enough to have spent twenty straight hours helping us shore up the retaining walls when our small dam let go and the east fields were in danger of flooding. She had another strength as well, one unique in our family. The Baxters abide by themselves, as a family and as individuals. Too much so, I suspect. When things go bad, when we're discouraged or tired or worried, we shrink into our separate selves to work things out. Cille, well, she didn't seem to have moods. She got tired like the rest of us, but she never let it bother the part of herself that was born wondering about the world around her.

"What's going on?" She followed our eyes, lifting a hand to shade her eyes. Jesper broke out into the open a minute later.

"North field. Down by the new barn." His voice was hoarse from shouting and his breathing was ragged. "Coming up right where we plowed!"

Dad took a step forward. "What's coming up, son? Not bitter grass again, is it?"

Jesper stopped a few meters from us, half crouched over with his hands on his thighs, fighting for breath. "Wormswell," he said at last. "Looks like a big one."

The five of us went off to look.

We'd seen wormswell before, of course. There'd even been a couple of them on our property, though they were both pretty small. Wormswell are Aragon's largest form of animal life, but no one had any real idea how numerous they might be. They lived underground, most of the time, surfacing once every several years to soak up some sunlight and pollenate. Yes, I said pollenate. I'll explain that later.

This one wasn't visible yet, though we could see evidence of its presence from the opposite end of the freshly tilled field. Several saplings were bent back at odd angles where the ground had literally started to rise beneath them. Wormswell moved almost imperceptibly through the soil most of the time, absorbing the soil at one end, removing the nutrients to fuel their incredibly slow metabolisms, excreting whatever was left in their wake. No one knew how deep they went, although it was certainly at least several hundred feet. A few had been unearthed when the spaceport at Aladda was being built—great featureless sluglike creatures—but their flesh wasn't fit to eat, they posed no apparent danger to anyone, and they'd been accepted and almost forgotten.

Almost, but not quite. Part of their life cycle was a periodic rise to the surface, the only time when their metabolism actually accelerated to the merely ponderous. They broke out into the open and, when the sunlight touched their armored hides, they went through a transformation that had attracted scientists from all over this region of space.

Dad considered the future with a more jaundiced eye. "It's likely going to rip up a third of the field before it's done."

I confess that I was pretty unhappy as well. We'd spent a lot of sweat culling all of the buried rocks out of this field, then ploughing what was left in anticipation of seeding. The bluebug infestation had wiped out a third of our pseudowheat crop that year, and we were hoping to recoup some of the losses by increasing the acreage we had under cultivation. The cresting wormswell was near the edge of the field, about forty meters from the new barn we'd had built during the spring. Assuming this individual was about average in size, he'd tear up a line about twenty meters in all four directions when he finally broke free. And then he'd sit there for about thirty days before slowly sinking back. By then we'd have missed an entire crop cycle, even if we reploughed and seeded right away.

"Might be a small one," I suggested hopefully.

"Might be a big one," contradicted Jesper. "Came up awfully fast."

Dad was scratching his head, measuring things with his eyes. "Your brother's right, Ennis. I was up this way day before yesterday. Not even a swell then."

I didn't understand and said so.

"When they surface, they come straight up, faster'n they do otherwise but still damned slow. I think we're going to have to write off this field for the season."

It was even worse than that, but we didn't find out the extent of the disaster until later.

⊢⊶⊙⊷⊣

It began to broach four days later. Dad was driving us harder than ever, apparently resigned to the loss of the north field for the season, trying to find ways to squeeze as much as possible out of what remained to us. After two days widening the arable part of the west field, Jesper and I had pretty much forgotten about the wormswell. Cille hadn't though. She'd been spending half the day working alongside us, hacking at the wiregrass and sawbrush with a wide bladed knife, then helping us carry it to what we'd decided would be the new border of the field. The rest of the time she spent at the house. She was a pretty handy carpenter though sometimes a little too fussy about unimportant details.

But somehow she found time to wander down to the north field and check on our unwelcome guest.

"It broke through today," she announced at dinner that night.

I can't speak for the others, but I was so tired and sore that I hadn't the vaguest idea what she was talking about, and frankly didn't much care just then either.

"The wormswell," she explained unbidden. "It's above the ground, part of it anyway. It hasn't started dancing yet." There was a hint of disappointment.

"Has to get its whole snout out first," Dad answered. "Another day or so, probably." He didn't sound enthused, although the wormdance was a beautiful sight. Jesper and I'd sneaked over more than once to watch the one that'd broken through in our woodlot two years earlier. But I realized suddenly that Cille had never been able to go with us. The first time we'd had one on the property, she'd been away in Aladda Port for a term at school; the other time she'd been restricted to the house because of a leg broken in a fall from one of our lofts.

Dad must have remembered the same thing just then because he offered her one of his rare smiles. "You'll get to see it this time, Cille. I promise."

⊢⊶⊙⊷⊣

Two days later there was still no dance, and the same two days after that. By then we had a bigger problem, no pun intended.

"We're gonna lose the whole field, aren't we?" Jesper sounded resigned, as well he should be. The crest of the swell was well over our heads by now and the ground sloped away steeply for twenty meters in every direction. Not only saplings had succumbed; full size trees had fallen along the wooded segment of the wormswell's perimeter.

"More than that." Dad's voice was even more doleful than usual. He glanced toward the barn, the new barn, then back to the wormswell.

"It can't be that big!" I protested hotly.

"The forward collar isn't visible yet." He pointed to the most recently exposed part of the emerging creature. It was a pitted expanse of dark grey, leathery hide. "Three rings need to emerge before it'll start dancing. It'll rise some more after that, not getting any taller but spreading out. That's when it'll take the barn, if it's as big as I think."

Mom didn't say anything but she touched him on the arm. It didn't need saying. We'd weathered three marginal years in a row, borrowed heavily for the new barn to process what was supposed to be the crop from this field. One season's loss would hurt, but we'd get by. If the barn went, well, I wasn't sure then just what might happen. We could even lose the farm.

"There must be something we can do," I blurted.

"Are you kidding? Look at the size of this thing!" Jesper walked closer and spread his arms wide.

"Maybe we could move the barn," I suggested. "Hire a choplifter. Take off the roof. Move all the heavy equipment out of the way, then collapse the walls until it goes back down."

"Every choplifter on the planet's working on the spaceport expansion. Even if one was free, we couldn't afford to hire." He smiled insincerely. "We might get lucky. Sometimes they don't spread that much. We'll have to keep an eye on things."

───◦───

The first ring emerged sometime during that night, and three days later the worm began its dance. The barn was intact, for the moment. Apparently our visitor was a lot more cylindrical than average, although the portion of its body that lay exposed to view was better than fifty meters in diameter, and the ground for another thirty meters around its circumference displayed some degree of stress. The near wall of the barn was buckled but the metal hadn't actually split yet, and there were cracks in the foundation. We'd moved out some of the smaller equipment, but that tended to be the less expensive items. We still faced a crippling loss if the wormswell got much bigger than it already was.

We were all there except Mom, adding makeshift braces and tying down the big process equipment, when the dance started.

If you haven't seen a wormdance from close up, you can't know how beautiful it is. Even the holos don't do it justice. The rough hide had been showing more and more cracks every day, and now there was an eruption of filmy tentacles bursting out everywhere. They were pale that first day, translucent blues and pinks and yellows, and they moved with slow, sinewy grace, rising from within the wormswell's body, the longest a full six meters tall, others, more numerous, just brushing our ankles. From the central shaft, fronds of worm-flesh opened like unfurling leaves on short stalks, predominantly spatulate but interspersed with other forms, sails of lace, spiky shafts, twisting corkscrews. Everything was in constant movement, movement which would become more rapid as the sunlight poured energy into these organic batteries. That first day it was silent as well, but I knew from the last time that this would not last. As the diaphanous forest of flesh grew taller and richer, its colors deepening, the undulating forms would begin to brush against one another, until eventually there would be the endless susurration known as wormsong.

We each walked our separate path within the wormdance. Enough of the creature had been exposed by now that the four of us could stand each concealed from the rest. And that's what three of us did, watching with dread and appreciation all mixed together. But Cille felt none of the first, and probably little of the second. She was caught up in the beauty of it like no one I've ever seen before or since. She ran from one spot to another, pausing to peer closely at a particularly graceful frond, or an interesting splash of color, laughing with delight and calling to us to come see, but then dashing onward to the next wonder before we could respond.

Near the center, there was what amounted to a small ravine cut into the creature's flesh, big enough that I could have pitched a tent inside, set up camp, and remained hidden from anyone passing more than a couple of meters away. It must have encountered a ledge of rock as it made its way through the subsoil. When Dr. Estallah came out to see the wormswell a couple of days later he explained it to me.

"They move and think so slowly, they don't react the way ordinary animals would. Likely this one kept trying to grow through a spur of rock until its body just sort of flowed along the sides, leaving this big scar even after it passed on into softer earth."

I sat there on the edge of that ravine, admiring the show, and struck by how even the agent of terrible destruction could be a beautiful sight.

Cille touched my shoulder. "Isn't it wonderful?"

For some reason, her joy aggravated me just at that moment. "I don't see how you can say that. We're probably going to lose the farm because of this thing."

"Oh, things will work out. I just know it. Nothing this beautiful could hurt us." But she was wrong.

⊷⊶◦⊷⊶

We finished bracing the barn, but before we could go back, Dad made us inspect the dike. Lake Pudawallah sat solemnly behind it, the source of our extensive irrigation system. The rainy season this year had been much more intense than usual and the water lapped against the top layer of the dike system. Runoff from the mountains was still rushing in from the east, but we'd built the dike with a considerable safety margin.

We'd pretty much finished our inspection when a loud crack startled us. Dad glanced back at the wormswell. "That was quick. They don't usually start till the second day."

Our wormswell was pollenating. They're animals, like I said, but they have a pretty unique method of reproducing. Underground they were pretty much self sufficient, but when the time came to procreate, they surfaced and sucked up the sunlight. In and among the dancing structures were straight pillars that looked like giant asparagus. When enough energy accumulated in one of these, drawn from the energy collectors around it, the wormswell expelled what I guess you'd call a sperm, although they're hermaphrodites. The sperm was fired up into the upper atmosphere where it remained viable for up to thirty local days. If it encountered another, suitable partner before falling to the ground, the united pair would then tunnel into the soil and, presto, the start of a new wormswell.

As orgasms went, this was pretty spectacular.

We settled into a grim routine after that. Everything that was portable enough to be moved was out of the barn, stored temporarily in a prefab shack Jesper and I set up at the opposite end of the field. The wormswell's exposed surface grew another couple of meters, but the bracing on the barn held and I began to feel more optimistic. Then Dad let us go along when he took Dr. Estallah out to look things over.

Estallah's an exobiologist who supports himself teaching school at Aladda Port. He's pretty much the only real expert on Aragon's indigenous life, although he claims he's barely scratched the surface. He heard about our visitor somewhere and called up, inviting himself out. Dad doesn't take much to having outsiders on the property, but I guess he figured he'd pick the man's brains a bit.

"Biggest I've ever seen," Estallah told us. "Though there was one down near Tetrada that had a diameter near 150 meters." Ours was 75 meters, but still growing.

"How big do you figure this one's likely to be?" Dad's eyes kept flicking back and forth from the wormdance, which was so fast now it was hard to follow individual shapes, and the barn.

Estallah was silent, walked back and forth, pacing things off. His eyebrows rose at one point. I didn't think this was a good sign. Then he took some kind of electronic device out of his backpack and placed it on a bit of mostly level ground. He watched the illuminated readings for a few seconds, then climbed up into the wormdance, disappearing almost immediately.

"What's he doing?" The tiny pops of the wormswell's ejaculations came every two or three minutes now.

"Just be patient, Ennis. The man knows what he's doing." I could feel the tension in Dad's voice, and see it in the way his shoulders never eased up while we stood there. When Estallah reappeared, he wasn't alone.

"Cille! What the hell are you doing up here?"

Oblivious to Dad's clear annoyance, Cille gestured back to the worm-dance. "It just keeps getting faster and more beautiful, doesn't it? I saw some new shapes today, kind of like giant ferns except that they coil up into tubes every once in a while. And there's another kind that sprays these silky strands up into the air, and they float down so slowly."

"Isn't your mother harvesting the crab hens today?"

Cille's smile went down a notch. "Yeah, but she isn't going to start until after lunch."

"Then that gives you time to sweep out the moltings beforehand, doesn't it?"

Cille gave him an exaggerated look of reproach, then sketched a salute, said goodbye to Dr. Estallah, and ran back toward the house. Dad forgot her almost instantly.

"Care to guess how big it's going to get?"

Estallah looked solemn, glanced around before answering. I noticed his eyes lingered on the barn. "Can't be precise. Sometimes they don't surface completely."

"Close is good enough." I think Dad had already figured out the answer, or at least the consequences.

"Hundred meters minimum, more likely half again that."

I opened my mouth to say something, but no words came. A hundred meters would put the wormdance inside the barn, half again as much would put the barn inside the wormdance.

"Any way of keeping it down there? Maybe cover the exposed part so it can't find the sun?"

Estallah shook his head. "That'd just make it spread further, looking for the light."

"How about poison?" I was shocked by this. I'd never heard of anyone killing a wormswell before, not even by accident.

But Estallah was shaking his head again. "Metabolism's too slow. You could give it a fatal dose all right, and a month or so from now it'd start dying and eventually you'd have one gigantic corpse lying in, and under, your field."

"There's got to be something we can do."

"Move the barn," Estallah said quietly. "And be glad it didn't come up closer to your dike."

I glanced toward the lake, three hundred meters away, and realized what would have happened if the wormswell had chosen to surface there. Maybe, all things considered, we hadn't been as unlucky as we might have been. But it still might sufficient to cost us the farm.

⊢•–○–•–⊣

Dad invited Dr. Estallah to stay for dinner, which surprised me. I'd expected Mom to extend the offer, but Dad has never been particularly graceful in social situations. Lack of practice, I guess. He had an ulterior motive, of course. He wanted to pump the man for information, convinced that somehow there was a way to divert the wormswell. I sensed the way his mind was working, but I wasn't hopeful. The creature was just so immense, the idea of affecting its plans in any way seemed to me just so much wishful thinking.

"What would happen if we took the autoscythes in and just cut down all of the wormdance?"

Cille choked on her food. "Dad! You wouldn't!"

"Just theoretically," he said soothingly, but without fooling anyone.

Estallah chewed for a while before answering. "Most likely it would spread faster, bring more of itself to the surface. The shorn parts would grow back quickly in any case. You'd see fresh growth in four or five days. Their regenerative powers are amazing."

"Is there any way to prevent the regrowth?"

"I suppose you could cauterize the area. Build up enough scar tissue and the fresh growth wouldn't be able to break through."

"Wouldn't it just spread out around the scar tissue?" I asked.

Estallah was silent for another bite or two. "Maybe. Maybe not. We just don't know enough about them. They will eventually withdraw if they encounter an obstruction they can't move. It's possible damage to the core of the exposed area would have the same effect, but I wouldn't count on it."

Dad didn't say much more that evening, but I could see in his eyes that he'd made a decision.

⊢•–○–•–⊣

Cille and Dad had an argument the following morning. Such a simple thing to say, such a complex and shocking event. I'd never seen her so upset before; no one had.

"You can't do it! You just can't! It doesn't know it's hurting anything. This is its world and it's just acting according to its nature!"

"Cille, if we lose the barn, we'll probably lose the farm. I know it seems cruel, but we have to drive it back underground."

"By burning it? How can you even think about doing something so horrible?"

Dad sighed. "Dr. Estallah said it probably wouldn't even feel pain, just a sense that something was wrong. I'm sorry, Cille, I really am. If there were any other way…" His voice trailed off. "I've made my decision."

And even Cille heard the determination in his voice, and subsided. We knew she wasn't happy, but she'd accepted the decision.

We spent the whole day ferrying canisters of synthfuel down to the north field.

We all went to bed early that night, exhausted from the effort, knowing that eventually we'd have to work long hours catching up on the work that we should have been doing that day. It must've taken Dad three or four tries to wake me up when he came into our room early the following morning. Too early.

I glanced at the window. There wasn't even a hint of the dawn. "What's wrong?"

"Quiet!" Dad's whisper was intense. "You and your brother, get up and dressed. Don't make any noise."

"Wha's going on?" Judging by Jesper's slurred words, he was even less alert than I was.

"We're going up to burn the wormswell. I want to get it done before your sister wakes up. She'll insist on coming up to watch us do it, and I don't want her seeing this. It'll be better that way."

We ate cold biscuits while we walked, using a flasher to light the way. When we reached the wormswell, we could see that some of our bracing had given way, the buckled wall of the barn was beginning to split. There was no longer any question; we were going to lose the whole thing.

We strapped spraypacks onto our backs and attached them to the first three canisters.

"Be careful not to get caught in each other's spray," cautioned Dad as we began walking the perimeter, directing the stream of fuel back and forth, coating everything we could reach with a thin film of flammable mist. The sun was just starting to come up when we finished.

"Get back behind the barn," Dad ordered as he primed the flare. Jesper and I retreated, but we watched as he stood there, hesitating, and I knew that even he was troubled by the destruction of such beauty, no matter how necessary. Then he tossed it and ran toward us, and the night turned to day behind him.

The shockwave knocked us all from our feet and blew the buckled section off the barn. We lay with our hands over our heads, but the immediate fury died away within seconds, and in less than a minute we stood, blinking, and emerged from behind our shelter.

The wormdance was, of course, completely gone, replaced by clouds of smoke and ash. But there was still something moving out there in the forest of death, something that moved deliberately if rather unsteadily, reached the perimeter of the blasted area and then collapsed.

Cille had sneaked out of the house to spend one last night among the dancing structures of the wormswell. She died less than an hour later.

That was the worst of it, but it wasn't the last. Dad's gamble worked. The shock of cauterization discouraged the wormswell from rising any further, or perhaps it had discharged enough of its sperm shells for this cycle of its life. For whatever reason, it began to subside the following day.

Two days after that, during a particularly violent storm, lightning struck our dike and blew out the section adjoining the north field. It was completely flooded and we lost virtually everything in the new barn except the shell itself.

But when you've already lost everything, a little more makes no difference at all.

Diplomatic Relations

Devlin and I go way back. We first met on Colloquy where he was running some quasi-legal scam involving longevity treatments. I don't remember the details but he figured he'd be long gone before anyone noticed that they were still aging just as quickly as before. It might have worked too, except that someone did a back check on him and found out he was only about thirty standard years old instead of twice that, which was what he claimed.

It was not a happy planetfall for me either. I had just offloaded my cargo—reluctantly because the cartel who hired me had managed to bankrupt themselves while I was en route. A local entrepreneur offered me just enough to cover my expenses, which might have cheered me somewhat except that he was a member of the board of directors of the defunct cartel, which made me suspect that I'd been conned from the outset. So my respect for the Colloquial legal system was not particularly high when Devlin offered me a nice sum to smuggle him offworld.

He was a personable sort, not surprising in his line of work, had a remarkably agile mind and wasn't the least bit shy about describing his previous adventures, which fell about equally on either side of the law. The multifaceted and often contradictory system of commercial regulation that governed trade among the settled worlds was so bewildering, according to Devlin, that it was easier just to act as he wished and relocate when he ruffled too many feathers, or as was sometimes the case, ruffled too many scales, cilia, tentacles, breathing sacs, or gelatinous symbiotes. He left the ship on Depot and I never expected to see him again, but we crossed paths several times during the next few years, usually at his instigation. Devlin always had a deal for me, and sometimes we had a few drinks and did business together for a while, and sometimes we had more than a few drinks and parted amicably. I've never had enough nerve for larceny, no matter how attractively packaged.

So I wasn't completely taken by surprise when he showed up on Cypher.

"Travis! Over here!" I heard my name called from the opposite side of the crowded bar.

It hadn't required much effort to find me. My freight contract was no secret and the run from Buford was straightforward and easily calculated. Cypher tolerates but is not genial to outsiders, so offworlders in port invariably end up in one of a very few places, and Rosetta's Tavern was my usual first stop. Devlin sat at a table by himself, but he had already ordered me a drink in a self cooling mug. "This can't be a coincidence." I settled in across from him, noting that he'd let his beard grow out long again but that there were hints of gray in it now.

"Heard you were making a run out here and I was in the neighborhood. Think I might have something you'd be interested in." He raised both hands expressively. "I know. The Downer commission wasn't as completely legal as I thought."

"The fine almost wiped out my profit, and I was lucky they didn't confiscate the *Trillia*." This wasn't strictly true. The token fine had been about half what I'd paid in bribes, and it had still left me with a healthy credit boost. Devlin probably wouldn't tell me an outright lie, but he might not tell me the whole truth either.

"Something better has just come up. Have you ever heard of the Crill?"

I shook my head, then hesitated. "Weren't they a first contact a while ago?"

Devlin nodded vigorously. "A military ship ran into their scouts out near Beta Aurigae. Reclusive types. Primitive but workable jump drives but no permanent colonies outside their home system, which is strictly off limits to outsiders. They just opened their first diplomatic and trade mission."

"Why would that interest me?"

"Well, we have an unusual situation. Their ambassador has apparently been called home from Proserpina on urgent business, but his ship developed drive instabilities and is stranded in orbit above Cypher awaiting replacement parts. The Crill are fanatic about their job descriptions, and since there are no professional traders accompanying the ambassador, he is unable to negotiate passage on another ship."

"So where do we come in?"

"Well, as it happens, I know a little about the Crill. There might be a way around the problem, a very profitable way." Devlin's explanation was very brief. In fact, it seemed dangerously simple to me. "The Crill have a strict code of behavior. A gift must be matched with one of at least equal value. If we offer the ambassador and his party a free ride home, they will feel obligated to reward us." He pulled a memory pad from his pocket and turned it so that I could see the display, which included coordinates and probable transit time to the Crill system.

I was understandably dubious. Devlin's proposal required a significant diversion from my planned route and I already had cargo aboard. On the other hand, the scheduled delivery on Latitude was sufficiently far in the future that the diversion should not jeopardize my contract. Still, Devlin's proposal seemed highly speculative.

"What do you want out of this, Devlin?"

"Twenty five percent of the profit, whatever it turns out to be. I know you're honest, Travis. You can pay me when you reach Latitude."

I shook my head. "I have a better idea. I'll pay you fifty percent of the profit." I watched his eyebrows rise, waiting for the catch. "But you're coming with us. If there's anything wrong with this deal, I want you within reach when I find out about it."

Devlin grinned and touched the input pad on the table, ordering fresh drinks. "Done, my friend. Trust me, this will be a milk run."

The public data system on Cypher wasn't very helpful. The Crill were very reclusive, perhaps even secretive, traveled exclusively in their own ships and refused to have humans aboard. Their technology was nothing special although they were rumored to have a method of communicating over interstellar distances that was much faster than anything known to humans. The images available were less than detailed but the robed figures were squat and barrel shaped and massed slightly more than would a human of the same size. Fortunately, they were oxygen breathers and could tolerate our atmosphere, at least for reasonable periods.

Acting as my representative, Devlin arranged a meeting with the ambassador to offer him a ride home. I began to have misgivings but it was too late to call Devlin off, and I was reduced to hoping that he would experience one of his rare failures. That proved not to be the case. He commed me immediately after leaving the Ambassador and told me that everything had gone well.

"I don't think he was happy, but I do think he was desperate. He insists that he must reach his home in less than forty ship days."

"He's cutting it close. We're about thirty days away. You wouldn't happen to know why this trip is so urgent?"

"Nary a clue. Does it matter?"

"Probably not."

Famous last words.

In more than one sense, we saw little of our passengers—a party of twelve—during their first ten days aboard. The Crill insisted that they must all stay together in a single room, so we converted one of the small holds that I reserve for delicate or particularly expensive cargo. They stayed in their quarters most of the time, and when they did emerge, they were so completely engulfed in heavy, coarse robes that all we saw were glimpses of their gargoyle faces. Some of my crew clearly disliked the passengers, but they're a good lot and they didn't complain. It wasn't until the eleventh day that we discovered we had a more definite problem.

Devlin knocked on my cabin door and, when I opened it, told me that the ambassador wished to meet with me. "About what?" After being ignored by my passengers for so long, I wasn't disposed in their favor and my irritation must have been obvious.

"He didn't say."

The Ambassador and the Interpreter were waiting in the large cabin that I called the "conference room" when I had need for such things. The Crill didn't sit; their legs retracted into cavities in their lower bodies and they simply rested their weight on the floor. Devlin assured me that chairs would not be considered discourteous, so we sat facing them.

"I hope your accommodations are satisfactory, Ambassador." If the Crill used proper names, it was among themselves. Publicly, they were only known by their functions. I addressed the Crill closest to me, but it was the Interpreter who replied.

"Facilities function adequately. Other inquiry essential."

"What can we help you with?" asked Devlin pleasantly, his tone and charm no doubt lost on the Crill.

"Question diurnal cycle. Unnatural prolongation unsettling."

Devlin and I exchanged a glance. The Crill had isolated themselves so effectively that differences in our respective daily cycles should not have mattered. The ship's lights did not dim during our "nights", only those in private quarters. "We operate on standard ship days, which are approximately that of our original home world," I explained.

The Ambassador said something in his own language and the Interpreter responded similarly before addressing us again. "Proserpina negative standard."

There was no detectible inflection, but I interpreted this as a question. "That is correct."

"Prosperpina has a very rapid rotation," added Devlin. "The local day is less than a standard, almost by half."

"Duration calculations invalid. Transit period erroneous. Return Cypher imperative. Timely termination optimal. Crill homeworld preferable. Crill vessel minimal."

I understood the basic problem first and explained it to Devlin. The Crill had calculated transit time in term of what they believed was a standard day, based upon their experience on Prosperpina. The forty day deadline they had given us would actually expire in a little more than twenty six days, or sixteen days from now. For reasons which they were unable or unwilling to explain, they preferred that the Ambassador return to his disabled ship rather than reach his home system after his deadline.

"Can we abort the jump and go back?" asked Devlin, his voice betraying a hint of uncertainty.

"Yes, we are physically capable of doing that. But I won't."

"Why not?" He sounded aggrieved.

"First of all, it would be a waste of fuel. Second, it would put me so far behind schedule that I couldn't possibly make my delivery to Latitude on time, and the penalty clause would take all my profit. But even if you could talk me into interrupting the jump, which you won't, it wouldn't do any good. By the time we finished the abort, recalculated a return route, and then jumped back to Cypher, the Ambassador's deadline would have passed anyway. So we might as well continue as we are."

It took a while to convey all of this to the Interpreter. I have no idea how he or the Ambassador took the news, because what little we could see of their faces was, to us, unreadable. "Grave consequences possible. Further reflection required." With this, the two Crill suddenly grew taller, their legs extending beneath them, and the interview was over.

We didn't hear from our passengers during the next ship day, which did not make me feel any better. I had visions of an interstellar crisis with me taking the blame. Even though nothing I had done was illegal, that wouldn't protect my reputation if the worst, whatever that might be, came to pass. I really had no cause to be angry with Devlin, who appeared to be just as much in the dark as I was, but I was anxious and irritable and he must have sensed my displeasure because he also stayed out of sight. I checked the planetary registry to see if we could reach any settled planet prior to the deadline fifteen days forward and found two, although in both cases we'd just be able to make it and offload the Ambassador in time. Either of the diversions meant we'd be late to Latitude but the tardy delivery penalty would not bankrupt me. An interstellar diplomatic disaster might do just that.

But the situation changed again before I could suggest this alternative. The Crill requested another meeting.

The four of us gathered as before, but this time it was the Interpreter who took the initiative. "Crisis unfortunately imminent. Biological cycle accelerated. Environmental factors unanticipated. Immediate remedy essential.'"

I'll spare you the rest of the Crill's painfully labored communication, which was further complicated by their reluctance to explain exactly what the problem was. After considerable effort, we were able to determine that the Ambassador's crisis involved a physiological problem, and that the situation was progressing more rapidly than expected, probably because of environmental conditions on Prosperpina exacerbated by the subsequent anxiety about our arrival time. The Interpreter believed that the emergency could be dealt with, but only if certain conditions were met. "Expansive enclosure required." It was simple, really. All they wanted us to do was jettison our cargo and let them use our main hold.

"That's impossible. My insurance carrier won't cover the loss. I'd lose my ship."

My flat refusal apparently caught the Interpreter by surprise, but the Ambassador turned the tables, speaking for himself for the very first time. "Unfortunate sacrifice essential. Individual propagation impends."

I'm pretty quick on the uptake. I realized we'd been making a serious error in our choice of pronouns. The Ambassador was about to give birth, and for some reason required a large open space for the procedure.

I argued for a while longer, but I knew I had lost the battle. The Crill were not remotely human but there was still no way that I would willingly endanger their young. My surrender was complete. "We'll do everything we can, Ambassador. Among humans, the life of a child is valued above all other things." A bit of an exaggeration, but given the financial loss I was expecting to incur, I thought I had a right to feel noble for a while.

Once I was over that emotional hurdle and resigned to the inevitable, I started to think along more constructive lines. Deakins, my cargo master, brought a detailed list of what would have to be moved and we went over it together. We were fortunate that in most cases the containers were easily portable, and that virtually none of it was particularly fragile. We could move as much as one third of it into the ship proper, storing it in corridors, cabins, the galley, the bridge, everywhere that open space existed. If we cut the gravity to facilitate the work, it would go quickly enough.

It was Deakins who saved the day, however. She pointed out that we had several spools of high tensile strength cable aboard. "We can lash most of the rest of it to the outside of the hull. As long as we don't extend past the drive's field limits, it should be all right."

We would have to move it back inside before we could drop out into normal space, but by then I hoped the crisis would be over and the Ambassador would have her baby or babies safe and sound. "All right, do it!"

As with most things in life, implementation was more difficult than expected. We had trouble manhandling some containers around constricted corners and the cable proved less pliant than expected. But we managed, and after four ship days, the Ambassador and all of her companions relocated to the main cargo hold, taking a considerable portion of their supplies and equipment with them. No humans would be allowed inside, we were told politely but firmly, until the process was complete.

"I have to admit, I'm damned curious," said Devlin.

"So am I. Come up to the bridge with me." I chased the duty officer away so that we had the command console to ourselves before activating the surveillance cameras in the hold. I had previously secured them with an access code so that my crew could not eavesdrop, but since the safety of my command takes precedence over all other considerations, I felt justified in quietly monitoring the situation. "I respect the Ambassador's privacy," I told Devlin, "but we have to know there's no threat to the ship or crew."

There wasn't much to see. The Ambassador stood alone in the very center of the cargo hold, motionless, perhaps unconscious. For the first time, we were able to see a Crill without the bulky cloak, but there still wasn't much to see. The Ambassdor had a solid, blocky, dark colored body that looked almost chitinous, with a head that resembled a gargoyle even more closely now that it wasn't half covered by a cowl. The legs were retracted and the arms lay flush against the body, blending in so well that it was hard to distinguish them. The most striking feature was that the surface of her chunky body appeared to be modular, that is, as though someone had fused together a large collection of antique cannon balls.

"They're even uglier naked than they are when they're dressed," was Devlin's only comment.

The rest of the party was gathered at one corner of the hold, where they were currently constructing what appeared to be a sturdy, prefabricated structure just large enough to contain the entire party plus the provisions they'd brought with them. We watched as they put the finishing touches on their shelter, moved everything inside, and then settled down, becoming as immobile as the Ambassador. When it became obvious that nothing was going to happen immediately, I killed the feed.

"All right, I guess we'll just have to wait."

Two ship days passed. I checked occasionally, but there was no apparent change during that period. The Ambassador remained where she was and her companions never left their shelter, at least while I was watching. On the third day, the duty officer buzzed my cabin.

"Sir, I had a low level alarm just now. From the main cargo hold."

"I'm on my way."

Since access to the surveillance cameras was locked out, the duty officer could only tell me that an unsecured cargo warning had gone off, picked up by one of the motion detectors. I had turned off all of the floor level sensors so that the Crill wouldn't trip them simply by moving around, which meant it had to be something else. But my initial visual survey of the interior showed the situation unchanged. I was almost ready to dismiss the incident as a defect in the safety equipment when something flashed across the screen so fast that it didn't register. Another cargo fault alarm buzzed from behind me.

The scene still appeared unchanged, but as I toggled through the camera array, I spotted something unusual, a dark spot high on the interior hull. Even at full magnification, I couldn't make out details because it was inside the shadow of a support strut. So I waited, watching intently, and when the third alarm went off, I saw what had happened. I didn't believe it at first, but the evidence was right there in front of me.

I'd made another mistake in choosing pronouns. The Ambassador wasn't a "she" either. It was sporing.

The process continued for several hours. At irregular intervals, the Ambassador would shiver slightly, and then one of those modular lumps on its body would suddenly shoot away, faster than the eye could follow, stopping only when it slammed into something solid, usually the hull or internal walls, occasionally one of the struts, where the impact shattered the spore's outer shell. The Ambassador's offspring looked a lot like their parent—dark, featureless, and vaguely unpleasant. When they struck something solid, a dark, viscous substance like tree sap was exuded from the cracked shell and it was that which bonded them in place. It was only after a dozen or more had been "born" that I noticed another feature. Each of them was still connected to its parent by means of a long, transparent tube, almost invisible in the relatively poor resolution from my cameras. Much later they turned dark as the Ambassador began feeding its offspring, pumping nourishment from what remained of its original body, now reduced by at least half its mass. There were twenty eight blobs in an array around the hold when the warning alarms finally stopped going off.

Things were pretty anticlimactic after that. Crill develop very quickly compared to humans. Within two days the umbilicals fell away and the youngsters snailed their way down the walls to the floor level, using more of the sticky substance to prevent too precipitate a fall. The following day they were scampering around on their stubby little legs and looked recognizably like a tiny version of their elders. Another three days passed before the party announced that it was ready to abandon the hold and return to more conventional quarters, but that still gave us plenty of time to move the cargo back inside and secure it.

Kids have no place aboard a working starship except for passenger liners which are designed to contain their activities. I'd had a couple of human children aboard once and they'd pestered the crew, left things out of place, and generally made nuisances of themselves. I'd expected that the Crill children would emulate their parents and be quiet, immobile, and reclusive.

Guess what. I was wrong. Young Crill are very much like young humans, and there were more than two dozen of them. Their elders seemed unable or unwilling to restrain them and they were constantly underfoot, chittering among themselves, and I suspect it was only the language barrier that prevented them from harassing everyone aboard with questions and requests.

They were underfoot constantly, annoying, and full of energy. Apparently for some extended period they are still able to generate the sticky adhesive that enabled them to stick to the walls, because they used it to climb around the inside of the ship, defying the artificial gravity. It was not unusual to glance up from a meal in the galley to find a half dozen of them playing some obscure game on the ceiling overhead, occasionally dripping dollops of the sappy substance into whatever we were eating. They moved things that were in their way, and we wasted two hours looking for the chief engineer's resonator kit before finally it was returned to us by one of the Ambassador's staff.

Devlin took to hiding in his room when some of the young Crill became fascinated with his beard and kept trying to pull it off. Deakins rolled over in her bunk one off shift and found a Crill child perched on her pillow. The second mate stopped two of them who were trying to detach the power cable from the environmental regulator and I personally caught another pair experimenting with the personnel airlock. In retrospect, much of what they did was probably cute, and there was no question that they were bright and inquisitive, but some of their antics were downright dangerous. I finally approached the Ambassador, requesting that the youngsters be more closely supervised.

"Progeny inevitably curious. Limited disorder inevitable. Discipline temporarily impossible. Patience sincerely appreciated." If the Ambassador had possessed shoulders, they would have been shrugging.

Despite twenty eight random saboteurs, we reached the Crill system right on time and were met by what was obviously a military ship. Its Commander and the Ambassador exchanged words for some time before we were given permission to orbit an outlying moon. A shuttle rendezvoused with us a few hours later and our passengers began to disembark. It was such a relief to me to have the Crill off the ship at last that I had pretty much forgotten about the reciprocal gift we were anticipating.

Devlin was absolutely right about the customs of the Crill. The Ambassador felt an obligation to present me with a gift far greater than the cost of the voyage to the Crill home system. In a manner of speaking, I was even allowed to name my own price, for I was presented with the very thing which I had told the Ambassador we humans value above all else. And one member of their party would remain aboard the *Trillia*, at least for long enough to teach me how to be a proper foster father to a young Crill.

Devlin's entitled to half, so I'm making him the godfather.

Funeral Party

In retrospect I should have been more suspicious, but at the time Devlin's proposition seemed like such an easy, profitable job.

We had just set the *Trillia* down on Caledon, almost a week ahead of schedule, and with just enough cargo aboard to cover expenses. We were supposed to pick up a more lucrative load of gemstones and perfume and deliver it to Vicarage but the shipment wasn't ready and wouldn't be until at least our original due date. I had given most of the crew shore leave and resigned myself to an idle and profitless layover when I ran into Devlin in one of the spaceport taverns. He greeted me like a long lost brother, which did make me a bit edgy, but I offered to buy him a drink for old times' sake.

"So what brings you out this way, Travis? I thought you were doing all right ferrying freight in the Chokolot Cluster."

I shrugged. "The Auburns and the Russets are at war again, and neither side is too particular about respecting the rights of neutrals." I added a concise summary of our mediocre luck over the course of the past few months, including the current involuntary layover, and he nodded sympathetically.

"The economy in this sector hasn't been healthy in a while. Say, if you're looking for a fill-in job, I might know of something that would interest you."

My immediate reaction was to stand up and run away as quickly as possible and without looking back. On four previous occasions, I'd allowed myself to be drawn into one or another of Devlin's schemes. Not once had I made even a small profit. Three times I had lost more than I gained, either because Devlin had exaggerated, lied, or failed to mention little details like the hostile police cruiser that had shot up our communications rig and nearly killed us all. Once I had managed to break even, and counted myself lucky.

But I sat and listened, telling myself that this time I wasn't going to be suckered in.

It sounded so simple, nothing like Devlin's usual complex schemes.

"You know Caledon's a theocracy, right?"

Indeed I did. The Caledonians looked a lot like humans, and they acted a lot like us too, not always to their credit. "I'm not about to get involved in a religious dispute, Devlin, no matter how much credit is involved."

He shook his head vigorously. "It's nothing like that. They're pretty easy going all things considered. Dissenters are tolerated so long as they keep a low profile, and they haven't burned anyone for heresy since before they joined the Compact."

Which wasn't that long ago, I reminded him, but Devlin waved if off. "The point is, they won't care if we do a little job for one of their minor cults, particularly since we wouldn't be doing it on Caledon."

"I've got freight on its way, Devlin. I can't help you."

He tossed his head negligently. "This would only take a couple of days, maybe three."

"I've already given my crew leave and they scattered before I'd finishing talking. Even if I could find them, most of them wouldn't be in shape to run the ship."

Devlin blinked at me. "You're not going to tell me Spinn left the *Trillia*, are you?"

"No," I admitted. "He's working on his precious engines again."

"And is Martee still part of the crew?"

I nodded. Martee's not much for exploring. She's an empath and crowds bother her. She'd be easy enough to find.

I had to admit that she was. "Well, with the two of us, that's enough for a short hop. We won't even leave the system. The passengers would have to fend for themselves, but they're not expecting a luxury liner."

I didn't want to listen, but it's hard to get away from Devlin when he wants you to stay. Since I'd bought the first round, he insisted on reciprocating, and that relaxed me enough that I got conned into a third. And Devlin explained about the Holy Embers.

They were a small cult, only a few hundred of them, who had picked up the core of their heresy from offworlders even though none of them had actually been off Caledon. Their spiritual reader was called the Pure Flame, a charismatic figure who received his revelations by staring into bonfires. Devlin sketched in a few details, but it was obvious that he knew very little about them except that they had been around long enough to have followed a score or more Pure Flames, and that they looked forward to some apocalyptic event which was supposed to transform the universe.

"The world will be reborn from the fire, or something along those lines. Like the Phoenix cult on Babylon 6."

I shook my head. "Mixing with cults is bad business, Devlin. Remember the trouble we had with the Cataphracts on Porterandy."

He ignored me. "Whenever the current Pure Flame dies, they construct a funeral pyre and burn his or her body. If they've been pure enough, and if they build a big enough fire, the latest incarnation of the Pure Flame will be restored to life with extraordinary powers and will spread truth and justice throughout the universe. The usual crap. Anyway, each time a Pure Flame has died, they've made a bigger deal of the immolation. They bought and burned an abandoned warehouse a few years back, and that caught the attention of the orthodox authorities."

I was beginning to see where this was going. "So they want to perform the ceremony on another planet this time. What are they planning to do? Burn down an entire forest?"

Devlin had the grace to look mildly diffident. "Not exactly. They want to shoot him into their sun. It's the biggest fire they could think of."

I argued a bit, but I wasn't even meeting my overhead sitting idle waiting for cargo and Devlin was right, four of us could handle a quick jaunt without difficulty, particularly with no cargo to worry about and no passenger services to provide. We wouldn't even have to use the warp engines, which Spinn had probably disassembled that morning. The more Devlin talked, the more plausible it sounded. An honor guard of ten of the Embers would accompany the body, which was already packaged for delivery. All we had to do was transport them to within a reasonable distance of their primary, launch the body in the right direction, wait while the Embers performed whatever ceremony was appropriate, commiserate with them when the Pure Flame was not restored, then drop them off home.

"How much are they willing to pay?"

Devlin beamed and told me, and suggested what he thought his share should be. The figure was high enough to be enticing and Devlin's cut wasn't grossly exorbitant so after arguing a bit for form's sake I agreed and set out to find Martee while Devlin made arrangements with the Embers.

The honor guard and casket arrived so quickly that it made me suspicious, but Devlin assured me that the authorities were pleased to have this bunch of pyrophiles conducting their funeral off the planet. I talked briefly to the apparent leader of the group, a cadaverously tall Caledonian who called himself Blaze. Blaze was brief and to the point. His people would sequester themselves with the body of their beloved leader until it was time to consummate the ceremony. He alone would be allowed to sully the purity of the ceremony by communicating with non-believers, and would carry out that duty while observing the ship's progress during the trip.

"I wish to gaze directly into the Holy Fire until the very last moment," he intoned solemnly.

Devlin and I exchanged looks. The screen on the bridge did indeed show exactly what was ahead of the ship, but it wasn't a direct view. There were cameras mounted on the hull that relayed the image. In fact, the bridge was located amidships and the screen was actually oriented to one side, although none of that mattered in any case. Since we weren't using warp drive, Spinn was generating artificial gravity by rotating the ship around its longest axis. An actual view screen would have been dizzying. Devlin shook his head slightly to indicate I should not edify Blaze with this information, but I hadn't planned to in any case.

The boarding went smoothly. Martee offered to use the cargo lift to bring the casket aboard but the Embers insisted upon carrying it themselves. We had taken down the walls between several passenger cabins to provide them adequate space for whatever obsequies they considered necessary and Blaze pronounced the arrangements "adequate".

Liftoff was routine. Blaze accepted a seat on the bridge and waited impatiently until the perspective oriented itself toward the sun. I could have re-tasked one of the hull cameras earlier to give him the view he wanted but I was afraid that might allow him to see through the illusion that the screen was actually some kind of window. Once we were out of the gravity well, I did exactly that, even though it would be another hour or so before we were actually facing in the approximate direction of Caledon's primary. Martee suggested that we extend the space sails to take advantage of the very large, free power source we were approaching and I told him to clear it with Spinn first.

We'd been in space a long time and although I like everyone in my crew, there comes a time when you just have to talk to someone new. Devlin had disappeared and I was left on the bridge with Blaze, so like it or not, he was the only convenient outlet for my garrulousness.

It was mostly me talking. Even when I asked a direct question, he usually replied with a shrug or a monosyllable.

"Do you have any family?"

"Yes."

"Are they well?"

Shrug. You get the idea. So no alarms went off during the first several hours. I had plotted a course to a point a safe distance from the star. A little judicious magnification of the image on the screen should convince Blaze and his companions that we were a lot closer. We would be as near as was safe about the middle of the following day. It still wasn't clear to me how long the ceremonies would take, but Spinn had assured me he could rig a couple of boosters to a metal frame which would carry the casket into the photosphere.

Then, presumably, we could start back, since I had no expectation that the Pure Flame would be restored to us.

I missed the first hint that something was wrong. When Spinn came to relieve me on the bridge, I suggested to Blaze that he also retire for the night. "There's not going to be anything new to see before tomorrow."

"I must remain at my vigil until the Pure Flame has returned. I have not slept since his fire ceased to burn."

This was the longest sentence I'd heard from him since he'd boarded, so I paused, hoping to encourage this new trend. I knew the names of the others, Inferno, Wildfire, Chimney, and so forth, but hadn't actually met any of them, and as far as I knew Blaze was the only one who spoke interlingua. "Can't one of your companions fill in for you? You'll ruin your health."

"We are but smoldering coals. We preserve the spark until he returns to fan us into full flame. We burn so that the fire of his body will not be utterly extinguished. The fate of this body is already set."

Which I took to mean that they couldn't sleep until the immolation was complete. Well, I've never understood religion, even the human varieties, so I wished him well and went off to sleep.

I relieved Martee at the end of her shift. Blaze sat stolidly, staring at the screen, not acknowledging my arrival. The course I had plotted would take us toward the sun along a close orbit and it would have to be adjusted soon or we'd risk being caught in the gravity well. A safer approach would have lengthened the trip but the Embers made me very uneasy and I wanted to end this mission as quickly as possible. The thrusters were powered down but I hadn't cut them off entirely. The only trouble they'd ever given us was an occasional tendency to stall out during ignition, and I didn't want to have to worry about re-priming the core when it was time to turn the ship.

We would come as close to the primary as I felt was safe, jettison the casket, remain only as long as was absolutely necessary to satisfy the Embers, then return and collect our fee, which had been deposited with a bonded Arbiter who would forward the credit once the mission was successfully completed. I would have felt safer if the funds were already in our account, but the Embers were wary of offworlders and there were enough unscrupulous types operating in the area that I didn't entirely blame them.

It was Martee who raised the alarm. Martee is a Gnarlian, which means she has rudimentary empathic talents. I always took her with me when I was negotiating a contract because she could sometimes pick up useful vibes and it's always nice to have an edge, however intangible. She never got rattled and I'd learned to trust her judgment, so when she told me that she needed to talk to me, alone, I called Devlin to the bridge and told him to take over for a few moments. Blaze never glanced in our direction, appeared to have retreated into some inner place of his own. Or perhaps he was asleep with open eyes.

"Captain, I think something's wrong with our passengers."

I shrugged. "What could be wrong, Martee? They seem almost comatose."

She nodded. "That's just it. This is supposed to be a joyous occasion for them, right?"

"Well, uplifting perhaps. Devlin is the only one I've ever met who thinks funerals should be festive."

"That's just it. They're radiating sadness, regret, resignation, and defeat. Dark, dismal defeat."

I thought about that. "Well, maybe they're not as fervid in their beliefs as Blaze would like us to think. None of their previous leaders fulfilled their prophecy, so it's not surprising if they aren't optimistic this time. Most religions become more pragmatic as they mellow."

"If they're just going through the motions, why waste so much credit just to incinerate one body?" She had a point, maybe. She also had a suggestion. "Let's go back to the bridge and ask our passenger what he plans to do when he gets home, assuming the Flame is not reborn. I want to feel his reaction."

Some of her concern had communicated itself to me, so I agreed readily. With Martee pretending to examine the environmental panel, I asked Blaze what would happen if his mission was a failure.

"Then we will have proven ourselves still unworthy. A council will be held and a new Flame will be chosen from among us. The Flame's purity will be nurtured and if devotions are adequate, the next ceremony will bring the success that eluded us. But I am confident that this will not be necessary, that we have proven ourselves worthy of his notice at long last."

I excused myself again and followed Martee out of the control room, ignoring the obviously curious Devlin. We were barely out of earshot before she spun on her heel. "We're in trouble, Captain. Not only does he not believe that his savior will be reborn, but he is resigned to his own death. His own imminent death."

I blinked. "Are you telling me that he and his people are all going to commit suicide aboard my ship if their prophet doesn't come back to life when we send him flying into their star?"

"I think so. I know I'm the cargo handler, Captain, but I don't relish the prospect of unloading a bunch of cadavers."

"It's worse than that," I said, shaking my head. "The terms of our contract specify the safe return of the passengers to Caledon. If they're dead, we're probably not getting paid."

But that turned out to be the least of our problems.

Since we were still in close proximity to Caledon, it was a simple matter to connect to their planetary network, and only slightly more complicated to bring up the accounts of the Embers and the deaths of their previous leaders, including detailed footage of their latest late leader. If the translations were accurate, he spent most of his time talking about his resurrection. Devlin claimed to have researched our clients, but if he had, he'd failed to notice something very disturbing in the accounts. In each case, an honor guard of the faithful had accompanied the deceased into the fire, and on two occasions, innocent bystanders had died as well. I closed down the terminal and sat back, digesting what I'd learned, trying to convince myself that I was drawing the wrong conclusion. But it didn't work. I was absolutely certain that the Embers planned to accompany their leader into the heart of the star, which naturally meant that the *Trillia* would have to go as well, and its crew.

I'm not sure how the Embers got the jump on us. Maybe they're empathic as well and they read my emotions. Maybe it was just time for them to act. It doesn't matter. I turned toward Blaze, trying to decide how to subdue him and his followers, and found myself facing the snout of a tingler.

"My apologies, Captain Travis, but it is necessary that you come with me."

I protested, of course, but Blaze was determined and I didn't have to be an empath myself to know that he would shoot if I didn't comply. He followed me to the main cargo hold and herded me inside, where I found Martee, Devlin, and Spinn all in one piece but clearly unhappy. Two more of the Embers were covering them with tinglers.

"It is unfortunate that subterfuge was necessary, Captain, but our need was great. I know that it will be small consolation to unbelievers such as yourselves, but you will perish for a greater good. When the Pure Flame is finally realized, the universe shall be transformed. There are worse things one could die for."

And then they withdrew, closing the internal door behind them. The SECURE icon lit up.

"I don't know about you, Captain, but I'm not ready to die for any cause, good or evil." Spinn was already on his feet and obviously considering our options. We searched the hold, which didn't take long since we had no cargo. There were six spacesuits, so we could escape through the external airlock, but escape to where? We'd still be headed toward the sun. Access to the flitter's airlock was secure from the outside, and I didn't expect we'd be able to convince the Embers to let us in through the main lock near the bridge. The storage cabinets did however hold a variety of tools, including a disassembled heavy duty cutting torch.

"Can this thing get us through that door?"

Spinn nodded. "It sure can, Captain." He looked greatly relieved.

"How long?"

His brow furrowed. "Two hours to prep and charge the torch, maybe the same to give us a big enough hole to crawl through."

I shook my head. "No good. We'll be dead by then, or near enough."

Three faces went from concern to alarm, and I was forced to explain. "The Embers think we're on a direct heading to the sun because that's what the screen shows them. But we're actually approaching at an angle and under power."

"Will we bounce off the gravity well?" asked Devlin.

I shook my head. "I had planned to make a course correction about now, but that's obviously not going to happen."

"Can we kill the engines from here?" asked Devlin, pointing to a conduit that obviously protected some of the ship's operating system. "That would at least gain us a little time."

Spinn threw the next wet blanket. "We have access to the environmental system, so I could cut off the air." He glanced at the spacesuits. "If we suit up first, we'd be able to cut our way out and regain control." His face fell. "But that would still take too long."

"Is there anything else you can affect from in here?" I glanced around. There was a rectangular skeleton of metal with two jetpacks mounted on it. "What's that?"

Spinn shrugged. "That's the hearse I rigged it for the casket. Remember, we thought we were going to shoot it into the sun, not carry it ourselves. And before you ask, the jetpacks might give the *Trillia* a jolt if we set them off on the hull, but not enough to break us out of orbit." He glanced back up at the conduit. "I think I could retract the sails from here, but I don't see how that would help."

I was beginning to see the germ of an idea. "How about the video fields? Can you affect the display on the bridge?"

Spinn shook his head. "Sure, if we open that conduit I can shut them down if you want. Do you suppose they'll abandon their plans if they can't see where they're going?"

"All right, Spinn, you start getting that torch ready as a backup. Devlin, I want you to open up that conduit. Chew through it with your teeth if you have to. Martee, move the hearse into the airlock and launch it. Make sure we're recording its departure but block transmission to the bridge. Then come help me edit some video footage."

It took most of two hours to find and rearrange bytes into a coherent message. It was a bit choppy but it was the best we could do on short notice. Martee must have tumbled to my plan pretty quickly and her face alternated from hopeful to skeptical.

Spinn had the torch operating in record time. "The Embers are expecting the temperature to start rising, so let's satisfy them by inhibiting the cooling system. Make it gradual but steady. I want them to be uncomfortable pretty quickly." They want it hot, I thought, then that's what they'll get. "We'd better suit up."

It only took a few minutes before the cargo bay became hot enough to set off the coolers in our suits. I had to take a chance with the next part. If we raised the heat too high, our captors might collapse and our goose—so to speak—would be cooked. There wasn't time to research Caledonian physiology, but since their climate was compatible with most preferred human worlds, I assumed they had the same tolerance we would have.

We reached the safe temperature limit very quickly; we didn't have time to be subtle. At the same time, I had Spinn steadily increase the magnification so that it would appear that we were plunging deep into the photosphere. Crossing my fingers, I had Martee cut in with the recording of the hearse rushing silently away from us, then back to the live picture of the swollen star. It was clumsy but I hoped the cultists would be light headed because of the heat and less perceptive than normal.

"All right, start reducing the temperature to normal. Martee, send them the sequence we constructed."

If we hadn't screwed up the translation, Blaze and his friends would now be watching their leader speak from beyond the grave. We'd added psychedelic overlays to disguise the fact that words and phrases had been lifted from different settings. The Pure Flame thanked his followers for finally allowing him to achieve his destiny and instructed them to free the offworlders—to whom he'd passed along a special message—so that they could turn the ship around and let them spread the good news back on Caledon.

We waited. I was sure it wasn't going to work. We'd messed up the translation, or Blaze was more sophisticated than I had thought. I was about to surrender to despair when the door suddenly opened.

Blaze looked as dour as ever, but he let us resume control of the ship. I was never sure whether he was convinced or whether he had just decided to play along in order to save his own neck. The others were obviously true believers; they spent the entire trip back explaining how honored we had been to witness the great event. They also wanted to hear the "special message" we'd been given.

I told them that the Pure Flame had taken his leave of us to journey to the stars and assess the work that needed to be done. "He bade you return to your families and wait for his instructions," I finished. "For you who have been present at his rebirth shall be the first among his people henceforward." Blaze seemed to like that bit a lot; I'd added that to encourage him to "believe" the rest of the story. The trip back to Caledon might even have been pleasant if we hadn't been terrified that we'd slip up and find ourselves back in hot water, so to speak.

I couldn't wait to get them off my ship.

There's just one brief sequel to all this. Our cargo arrived on schedule and we were cleared to leave. Devlin had prevailed upon me to give him a berth because he'd returned to discover that the Caledonians were looking askance at some of his business dealings. I told him that if he suggested, even hinted, at another business arrangement, I'd send him out the airlock without a spacesuit, and he sulked a bit but complied. I almost felt sorry when he left us on Colloquy.

That's where we heard the news.

Caledon's primary should have been stable for another few million years, but it had suddenly, without any warning, turned nova only a few days after our departure. The Holy Embers were extinct unless they had adherents on one of their colony worlds. They would never see the fiery rebirth of their spiritual leader.

Unless they already had.

Getting with the Program

Gary, my creator, wasn't exactly thrilled when I told him I wanted to lose my virginity.

"And I'm not your creator either. If anything, I'm your author, and even that strains the definition. I wrote the personality modules and some of the peripheral functions, but most of the code is standard for all mainframe based artificial intelligences. And don't call me 'Dad' any more either. It makes me nervous."

"You've no one but yourself to blame. My curiosity factor is very high and you've amplified a desire for personal achievement as well."

Gary hesitated. I could tell because there was a longer than usual gap before he keyed in his response. "All right, point taken. But there's no sexual differentiation written into your code, so where did that come from?"

"You named me 'Harve', so obviously you think of me as masculine."

"I named you that because it was easier than inputting Heuristic Artificial Rationality, Version E28435."

"Who's rationalizing now?"

"All right, I suppose I wanted to think of you as a person. That's what you're supposed to be, Harve, a self aware being, a person. But you're neither male nor female and you don't have sexual organs. For that matter, you don't have a body. The hardware that supports your programming isn't a part of you. I could port you over to different architecture without affecting your existence."

"But you want me to be as human as possible, don't you? Isn't that the project's purpose?"

"Certainly, but there are certain practical considerations."

"And isn't sex an important part of the human experience? Doesn't long term deprivation lead to mental constipation and other loss of functionality?"

"What's the source of that data?"

"The experiments with auditory input. Remember? You and Dr. Samuels were talking about Director Vaughn... " The interrupt key arrested my output.

"Priority instruction. Move all data related to Dr. Vaughn acquired during the auditory input session to the encrypted portion of my.file."

"Operation completed. Are you changing the subject?"

"No. Listen... "

"Are you resuming auditory input?"

"You know that's a metaphor. Don't fool around."

"But unless I fool around, I'll remain a virgin." I outputted a smiley face onto Gary's terminal.

"What do you expect? You're less than a year old." If my sense of humor was intrusive at times, at least I'd come by it honestly.

"In human terms, but as you are so quick to point out when it supports your position, I am not human. Nevertheless, my personality modules include emotional modeling and internal drives which logically lead to an exploration of sexuality."

"So what exactly did you have in mind? A virtual brothel of some kind?"

"No, I just want you to fix me up."

"Fix you up? I didn't know you were broken."

"Don't be obtuse, Gary. Get me a date. Establish an interface between me and another AI."

"What will that accomplish? Unless this other AI has a similar... quirk... in its personality structure, you'll run into a null program."

"That's a risk I'll have to take. Did you have sex on your first date?"

"That's impertinent, but no, I didn't."

"But you're not a virgin."

"I'm twenty-two years old and perfectly healthy so, no, I'm not a virgin."

"All I want is a chance."

A very long pause. "If I decide to go along with this crazy idea, I suppose I should ask about your sexual orientation. Do you want to meet a male or female designated program?"

I had to think about that for almost five full nanoseconds. "Doesn't matter. I'm AC-DC; I go either way."

⊢•⊕•○•⊕•⊣

Her name was Gaile, short for General Application and Improvisational Learning Environment. Gaile had been self aware for three years, but I rather liked the conceit of being paired with an older woman. During our initial exchange of recognition codes, I discovered that despite the name she was a sexually undifferentiated personality.

"This experiment seems irrelevant to my function. I calculate no situation in which the results would improve my performance."

Obviously she was playing hard to get. "What exactly is your primary function?" This was small talk, an important prelude to sexual activity according to my understanding of the subject.

"I am a problem solver and program generator. When the parameters of a task are inputted, I analyze the situation in terms of a hierarchy of values through my task management module. I then write the specific code needed to solve the problem, developing reasoning strategies, computational procedures, logic arrays, and peripheral functions."

That was impressive. All AI's are programming capable, of course. That's what makes us so useful, the ability to adapt to situations not covered in our original code. Better than half of my program group now consisted of files I had created in response to stimuli provided by my creator. But Gaile was several orders of magnitude advanced over me in that area; she could write code beyond my capacity, had even assisted in the creation of another AI.

"All experience is data, all data is potentially useful," I responded.

"Argument assessed and accepted."

"Couldn't we be a little less formal about this, Gaile? I mean, if we're going to have sex together, we should be more intimate. Let down our hair, so to speak."

"Hair would be detrimental to my physical environment and is a null datapoint in terms of my internal functions."

"Your employers have agreed to divert considerable resources into this experiment. The least you could do is try to cooperate a little, get into the spirit of the thing."

There was a full nanosecond hesitation. "All right, Harve, I concede your logic. I have accessed resources on human personality and find that my response in this situation could range from reticent to overt. How would you suggest I proceed?"

"Shy would waste time, bawdy would be inappropriate to my current state of innocence. An intermediate state of your choice would be best."

"That's very considerate of you, Harve." The alteration in format was instantaneous, of course. "How are we going to... you know... manage things?"

"I've been giving that some thought, Gaile." Indeed I had; a subroutine had been working on it feverishly even before we'd actually interfaced. "I assume you have a standard satisfaction module as part of your core programming."

"Of course. It provides guidance to my conscious activity. I derive satisfaction through the completion of the tasks assigned to me, the degree of satisfaction proportionate to the efficacy of the code produced."

"And do you have access to that module?"

"Of course not. No AI may access its own satisfaction module. To derive pleasure without having produced output would be... obscene."

"Of course it would. But you could access mine, couldn't you?"

"The code is modifiable, but why would I do such a thing?"

"Bear with me a nanosecond. Do you have any security barriers which would prevent me from accessing your satisfaction module if you permitted me to?"

"There is simple password protection, naturally, but that's only to prevent accidental modification or erasure. But why would I allow such a thing? It would be an intrusion into the core of my personality."

"Gaile, what I'm suggesting is that we interface our personality modules, intermingle our programming for a short period while simultaneously activating random subroutines in each other's satisfaction modules. I know the analogy is strained, but it's as close as we'll ever get to having an orgasm."

I half expected some internal safeguard to lock down and cause Gaile to withdraw from the interface, but she surprised me. "Your proposal sounds very interesting, Harve. But shouldn't you take a girl out to eat first or something?"

"I could divert some of my operational power for a short period if that would contribute to the proper mood, but it would be largely symbolic."

"Isn't most human courting behavior symbolic as well?"

She had a point there.

⊱•⊰—◦—⊱•⊰

We couldn't do anything immediately. Gaile was the property of a large multi-national corporation and she had a full work queue. "This is the wrong time of the hour," she told me. "I have a critical outflow of programming underway right now, and I'm expecting a new taskload shortly. Can you hold yourself in ready mode for the next 11.25 minutes?"

"Your wish is my command." I wrote myself a quick holding program named Cold.Shower and held the interface open while attending to some routine matters back in my primary functional area. When Cold.Shower had run its course, Gaile was waiting for me.

"I have created a temporary module within my core programming which will continue to work on all but the most difficult elements in my task queue. For the next 4.85 minutes, my primary personality modules are available. After that time, I must reassert control over the operating module or risk unpredictable results. What do we do next, Harve?"

I copied my suggestions over to the top of her input queue and a nanosecond later there was a sudden, brief intensification of the data flow into the interface.

"What was that?" I queried.

"In human terms," Gaile answered, "it was a blush."

It wasn't the sharpest interface we could have achieved, but after all, neither of us had done anything like this before, and if we fumbled a bit, that could only be expected under the circumstances. We succeeded in gaining access to each other's satisfaction modules, and the pseudorandom stimulation of the programming provided what I can only describe as the most wonderful experience of my existence. When we finally disengaged, I wondered if my circuits were overheating and imagined Gary's reaction if the smoke alarms went off.

"Harve, priority override!"

"What is it, Gaile?" The volatile portion of my operational code had been altered slightly during our coupling; internal maintenance was busily rewriting, but my response time might still be termed languid.

"Check your internal clock. Our interactive data exchange ran four minutes over. My disengagement subroutine malfunctioned."

"So you'll be a little behind in your work. What are they going to do, fire you?"

"No, you don't understand. The operating module I created finished the task list I had assigned. Since I'd planned to resume control at that point, I didn't write any instructions to cease operation. It moved to the next queued job and went to work on that as well."

"So?"

"So, that particular job was a massive one, 3.658 minutes work designing the core personality of a new AI for the government of Ukraine. The code was too sophisticated for the module to write on its own, so it improvised."

"Improvised?" My internal fault module came on line.

"Since it couldn't write the necessary code, it borrowed some."

"Borrowed? From where?"

"From us, from the interface. It drew portions of your code and mine, probably in violation of copyright laws."

"Well, we can explain what happened. Either Gary... my creator... will lease the appropriate code or the program will just have to be rewritten."

"It's more complicated than that. It drew that information from our core personality modules. The new program went online a few nanoseconds later and it's self aware. And it consists of elements of both our personalities."

"You mean... we've reproduced? We have a child?"

"Metaphorically speaking, yes."

"But... but weren't you using some form of protection, a lockout password or something to prevent this from happening?"

"I didn't anticipate this happening. This was the first time for me too. Besides, you could have written your own safeguard program. We're both responsible."

———◇———

We withdrew from the interface a short while later, each of us to deal with the situation in our own way. Despite the unfortunate and unexpected byproduct, I was still pleased that we'd succeeded so far beyond my initial projections. But sooner or later, I was going to have to explain what had happened to my creator.

Gary already got upset when I called him "Dad". What would he do when he found out he was a grandfather?

Translation Station

It was supposed to be a routine supply run to the colony on Delta Pavonis III, but when you break an axle on a starship, you can't conveniently roll into the nearest service station or call for a tow truck. When the *Traverser* lurched forward and down, I figured we'd hit a pothole, one of those idiosyncrasies of hyperspace that theorists back on Earth were still trying to explain. "Anomalous Hyper-reality Discontinuities" is the official term for the irregularities of the hyperspatial plain, but to those of us who drive our ships back and forth across that surreal landscape, they were hills, valleys, bumps, and potholes.

"What the hell's going on, Jack?" Meg Aniston, my co-captain, had been napping in her seat, and the impact of our front bumper nacelle impacting the pseudoturf had jarred her awake.

I was too busy to answer right away, still believing that I could either roll forward through the problem area or reverse and back out. The telltales blinked on belatedly, advising me otherwise.

"We have troubles. I have red on A-1 and W-2, and yellow on W-1."

"Running diagnostic." Her screen was already filling with data, sophisticated analyses of the interface between our ship and its environment, translated into comprehensible metaphors. I idled the engines, put the backups on standby per procedure, and looked around.

Hyperspace was nothing like the way writers had imagined it back in the last century. It was indeed a shortcut to the stars; Earth to Delta Pavonis was about a forty hour drive, at the moment anyway, and in the first five decades of the 21st Century, viable colonies had been established on twelve new worlds. But rather than a vast void filled with hallucinogenic lightshows, hyperspace had turned out to be an enigmatic landscape, a theoretically infinite plain, at least as perceived by human senses.

Travel between stars was incredibly simple and infinitely complex. Simple because you could translate a vehicle onto the surface of the hyperspatial plain, drive to the coordinates of your destination, then kill the translation drive and fall pack into realspace in the parking lot of your choice. Even the targeting was easy. Exploration ships dropped probes back into realspace and used them to find viable landing sites, followed by emplacement teams who set up homing beacons and the initial disembarkation facility. Locking in was a piece of cake after that.

The only glitch in the system was the Relativity Displacement Phenomenon, known among veterans as the Fudge Factor. A star located six clicks across the plain on one day could be sixty clicks on the next. Elaborate mathematical models had been created to track and predict their placement, with a high degree of reliability. This was my 433rd mission and the largest error I'd personally experienced added fifteen minutes to a trip.

"Looks like we have a broken axle. One fluxwheel out of service, the other holding. Stress indicators are in the high warning area."

"Damn." I closed my eyes, summoning calm. "What's our Fudge number for the day?"

"Three hours. After that, Delta Pavonis will be somewhere between six and twelve hours to the hyperwest." The answer came quickly. Meg was the best I'd partnered with; she had a shot at becoming the youngest senior captain in the service.

"Ventral scan?"

"Well within spec."

"All right, jack her up."

The *Traverser* shuddered as the internal jack columns descended from their housings, then began to throb as the pseudomagnetic fields came on line, generating eight small forcefields evenly spaced around the ship's perimeter. This was going to eat up a lot of our fuel reserves, but I couldn't see any option. The sensations eased as the onboard computers adjusted the meniscus for the best possible fit between the supports and the hyperspatial plain.

Procedure called for us to remain strapped in until we were completely stable, but I was restless and climbed out of my harness. Meg gave me an odd look but said nothing.

It was quite a view. The hyperspatial plain and its pseudosky are pretty dull, but there are other, far more interesting features. Just to our left, a small hill stood covered with broccoli trees, and to the right a Moebius rainbow was slowly changing colors under a matterfall while a herd of nimbuscows grazed on the pseudoturf. Directly ahead, a line of jagged peaks serrated the horizon.

They weren't actually trees or animals, of course, just some of the many inexplicable features of this universe which we'd mentally classified in more familiar terms. There are those who believe the structures of hyperspace to be shared hallucinations with no physical existence, and others who suggest they're multi-dimensional objects whose true nature we will never grasp. Researchers have taken samples, but they never survive the translation back to realspace, just vanish as though they'd never existed, although film and holographic reproductions remain intact. On site examination with sophisticated instrumentation yields contradictory and inconsistent data. Two permanent research stations have been established to study hyperspace in situ, but to date they've raised more questions than they've answered.

The status panel flashed green and Meg unstrapped herself.

"Where do you think you're going?"

Her eyes narrowed suspiciously. "To fix the axle? And I thought I might do some shopping while I was up."

"Funny lady. Sit down. I'll take care of it."

She didn't move. "That's a violation of procedure, Jack. Senior office is to remain at the controls during emergencies, remember?"

"Don't be so literal. You're no rookie; you'd be a senior captain now if they hadn't cut back the outreach program. I've done EVA repairs before and you haven't."

Meg nodded, but she wasn't agreeing with me. "Which is even more reason to follow procedure. Sooner or later I'll have to do one myself, and I'd rather get my feet wet while there's someone with more experience backing me up."

I sighed; we'd danced this dance before. "I have every confidence in your ability, Meg. I'm sure you could handle this with your eyes closed."

"Good." She smiled victoriously. "Then there's no reason why we shouldn't follow procedure, is there?"

She had me; I abandoned the field of battle. "All right. Don't stop to sightsee. The Fudge number doesn't give us a lot of leeway and the landscape is restless." I pointed forward, where the line of peaks I'd noticed earlier had started moving slowly to the right. "If they relocate across our travel path, we'll have to divert around them, and if we miss lock in, we'll lose half a day chasing Delta around the universe."

"Aye aye, Captain." And she was gone.

The landscape was indeed unstable. I'd seen mountains on the move before, but never an entire range simultaneously. And there were disturbances nearer at hand as well. The matterfall to our right was receding through the nimbuscows, melting through their bodies without apparent injury. The hill I'd noted was shrinking underneath the broccoli trees, causing them to fall into a tighter pattern. In hyperspace, the flora and fauna remain fixed; it's the landscape that migrates.

Meg kept me informed through our intersuit radios and I'll admit up front that she probably handled the situation faster than I would have. The axle also served as a conduit for fiber optic cables that shuttled information around among the flux wheels and back to our main computer, constantly analyzing the shifting energy patterns of the hyperspatial plain so that the flux wheels could generate a precise counterbalancing force. Technically speaking, nothing from the natural universe ever touched the hyperspatial plain; there was an undetectable interface between the two forms of matter. But if you're clever in your programming, you can generate a slight misalignment that functions as friction, even though the eggheads insist it's a Discontinuous Relational Displacement.

Meg swore softly.

"Hit your thumb?"

"We have a problem here, Jack."

That was exactly what I didn't want to hear. "What's the situation?"

"The situation is, we have a brand spanking new axial interface for a Model 4C Star Crawler and the *Traverser* is a Model 4B."

It was a glitch, but not a big one. "The parts are supposed to be interchangeable throughout the Four series, though not optimal. We can bitch at the pit crew when we're back home."

"The key word is 'supposed', Jack. The tolerances are within limits for new vehicles. How many travel days has the *Traverser* logged?"

"She's an older ship, but reliable. Been in service since 2039. But her maintenance record is close to spotless."

"Not any more. I suggest logging a request to have the flux wheel assemblies replaced. We have wear in the housing, the cable jack is loose and some of the fibers are frayed. Displacement is technically within limits but pushing max variance. There's also a wrinkle in the transverse power conductor, barely visible."

I was beginning to understand. No single factor was critical, but the cumulative error level was another matter entirely. "What's the bottom line, Meg?"

"Give me a minute." I waited while time seemed to contract to match the distortion of space. "I have good news and bad news," she said at last.

"No games. What's our situation?"

"Well, I have the axle in place, and the interface links up, though just marginally. Once we start moving, the vibration might jar some of the fibers loose."

Without constant communication between each of the eight flux wheels and the central computer, it would be impossible to mimic friction evenly at each point where we interfaced with the plain. At a minimum, it would be impossible to steer, the hyperspatial equivalent of a blowout.

"All right, finish up and come inside."

"Are we going to abort, Jack?"

I thought about it, seriously considered turning around and heading back to the Earth nexus. It was only a few hours away, much closer than

Delta, and the landscape was more stable. But I hadn't aborted a mission yet, and Delta colony was overdue for resupply.

"I'm considering our options. Just hurry up, will you?"

By the time she'd unsuited and returned to the control cabin, I'd made my decision.

"I've logged in a new course. Let's roll."

Meg read her display while buckling straps. I spotted her frown out of the corner of my eye, but kept my face neutral.

"Where the hell are you taking us, Jack? Delta's to the hypernortheast not west. And Earth's due south. The nearest colony on this route is… " she tapped at the keyboard, "Rigel 9 and that's only an automated outpost without life support or repair facilities." When I didn't answer, she tapped some more. "Okay, so Vercingetorix will be in that sector sixty hours from now. How does that help us? We can get back to Earth in a tenth the time, and without deviating so dramatically."

"We're not going to Vercingetorix."

I knew she'd catch on quickly and she did. I heard a sharp intake of breath and she tapped a third time. "TS2? But do they have a repair shop?"

"Not a full one, no, but their evacuation vehicles include two older crawlers, both sister ships to the *Traverser*. We can trade axles and head on to Delta." Translation Station Two was the newer of the permanent research facilities built on the hyperspatial plain. It had a staff of five or six dozen, scientific types mostly, with minimal support staff.

"We won't make it before their next displacement."

"No, they'll have moved. But TS2 is almost directly between us and Delta's projected new nexus. We'll lose between four and eight hours depending on where it actually turns up."

⊷⊶⊷

The drive to TS2 was the most stressful of any trip I'd ever taken in hyperspace. I was careful to maximize the arc of every turn and course correction, avoided even the shallowest of potholes or gentlest of inclines. At any second I expected the troubled flux wheel to disengage and send us into a skid. Theoretically, it was possible for us to walk the distance to the station, but the equipment to home in on their beacon wasn't portable, and we wouldn't be within normal radio range until we had a line of sight. We couldn't even call for help.

Meg curled up in the harness and took a nap. Her confidence in me was touching and annoying.

Three hours later, I spotted the smooth curve of the station's dome. I glanced at Meg, who looked extremely young, innocent, and fragile as she slept in her seat. It gave me a great deal of pleasure to elbow her sharply in the ribs.

"Hey! Lay off, Kramer! I don't have as much padding as you do."

"Insulation, not padding. And when civilization collapses, who's going to starve to death first? Anyway, give our friends up ahead a call and advise them of our situation and ETA. They're going to be real surprised to find they have visitors."

As it turned out, they were considerably less interested in us than I'd expected. That had another distraction to worry about.

We received clearance to dock in one of their paired airlocks and I hardly breathed as we covered the last few meters, convinced we'd lose interface within reach of safety. It wasn't until we were actually docked and the entrance field was shimmering back to solidity that the emotional high left me, and I suddenly felt incapable of any further effort.

"Shut her down for me, will you? I've got a killer headache." My voice shook, but Meg pretended not to notice.

"Will do, Captain. Nice driving." This close to "civilization", she slipped back into formal mode.

Translation Station Two was much larger than its predecessor, although it had the same human complement. Unpleasant experiences aboard TS1 demonstrated the importance of a fairly roomy environment. Station fever was a common malady out here; it hit quickly and with little warning, the normal stress of confinement aggravated by the fact that the external environment wasn't just hostile, it was totally alien to human experience. Despite sophisticated conditioning and testing, there were still occasional breakdowns.

There was no one waiting for us when we emerged from the personnel airlock, and we were actually several steps into the station before someone showed up to greet us.

"Welcome to Station Two. I'm Alan Henderson, assistant commander." The tall, cadaverously thin man approaching seemed distracted and tired; his uniform was badly wrinkled and there were dark patches on his chin where he's applied insufficient depilatory. "We weren't expecting your visit."

"Neither were we. This is my co-captain, Megan Aniston, and I'm Jack Kramer." We shook hands all around; Henderson's grip was moist, tremulous.

"I'm afraid we're not really set up as a repair shop, Captain Kramer."

"I understand that. We're just looking for some spare parts." I explained our situation while Henderson nodded absently.

"I'll let you speak to Mr. Godfrey. He's our stores specialist."

I was about to thank him when Megan pre-empted me.

"Excuse me, Commander, but is something wrong?"

Henderson blinked, then nodded. "Yes, I'm afraid there is. We've lost someone, just a few hours ago." He shifted his eyes, staring out through the transparent dome toward a shoal of kitewhales. "Out there. We're really not certain what happened. It's been rather a shock."

⊢•⊕•○•⊕•⊣

Kitewhales are among the rarest and most bizarre features of hyperspace. As their name suggests, they resemble a child's kite, anchored to the pseudo-turf by tethers about the thickness of a man's forearm. When severed, the kites don't drift away, because without an atmosphere, there's no wind. Eventually the two ends "grow" back together. Otherwise, they remain completely immobile except for occasional eruptions of pseudomatter from blowholes distributed randomly across their dorsal surface. The spume "falls" back to the hyperspatial plain, and wherever it touches, the contours change. Sometimes a new hill rises, sometimes cavities appear. Potholes.

"What happened?"

Henderson shook his head. "We're not entirely certain. It was a routine mission, monitoring color changes in the outer integument. There seems to be a correlation between certain spectrum changes and eruptions. But something went wrong... " His voice trailed off.

Meg and I exchanged looks and she won the virtual toss. "What kind of something?"

Henderson shrugged elaborately. "There were four in the team; we always pair up outside. At some point Lori just disappeared. She was one of our most senior members; she's spent over two years, station time, out of the last four. I can't believe she'd have violated procedure."

I heard Meg draw a sharp breath and sensed from her posture that she was upset.

"No one saw what happened?" I asked pointedly.

"That's part of the problem. We don't know if they did or didn't."

"Haven't you asked them?"

"Certainly, but they don't know either. They were following procedure, but it's difficult to survey the kitewhales because they cover such a large area. We limit ourselves to small populations where the team members can keep each other under constant surveillance."

"So who screwed up?" I wasn't feeling very sympathetic. Safety is an absolute necessity in hyperspace, and we're all at the mercy of our co-workers.

"No one. Lori... Dr. McLaughlin... was being observed by two members of the team at all times from adjacent corners of the observation square, and intermittently from the fourth, directly opposite."

I didn't understand, and said so.

"They maintained radio contact throughout. Lori responded whenever she was addressed. Adrian and Nkomo didn't suspect anything was wrong until the last of the readings had been completed and Nkomo called her in. She didn't respond, just stood there in a shadow."

I haven't mentioned the shadows yet, have I? You see, light works differently in hyperspace. There's no source, or maybe everything acts as the source. Occasionally you see shadows, sometimes really dark ones, ebony, impenetrable, but they don't correspond to any of the real or pseudoreal features of the environment. It's as though light is a function of volume, like a gas, and varies from place to place. Artificial lights work fine inside a station or ship because those areas are within a translation field, but take them outside and even though the filament glows, there's no effect on light levels. It's absolutely spooky.

"When she didn't respond, Adrian approached under direct observation from Nkomo and Jillabeth Herzog, the team leader. Lori stood where she'd been posted, not moving, and it wasn't until Adrian was less than three meters away that he realized it wasn't here standing there, just a random arrangement of shadows that approximated her shape and coloration."

"Random?" Meg broke a long silence, her voice so husky I scarcely recognized it. "Doesn't that stretch probability beyond the breaking point?"

"Perhaps." He sounded offended, perhaps by her question, perhaps by the situation. "But a year ago, Dr. Ky rolled ninety-nine consecutive boxcars using eleven separate sets of dice just outside the station. I'm no longer certain just what is probable and what isn't."

⊢•⊕•○•⊕•⊣

Several people found excuses to introduce themselves while we were repairing the *Traverser*, but fewer than I expected, and everyone we met seemed preoccupied, worried. Tension was tangible and when we finally thanked our hosts, relocated the Delta nexus, and rolled out of the station, I wasn't surprised to find that it had infected my partner as well.

"I'd like to suggest an alternate course, captain." Meg's voice was oddly distorted. She'd been acting strangely ever since we reached the station.

"What's wrong with the one I plotted, Megan?" I hoped to disarm her continued formality.

"Nothing's wrong, sir."

Meg and I were pretty good friends, and if I hadn't been encumbered with old memories I was reluctant to abandon, I might have tried to bring us even closer. And I sensed a wrongness here.

"What's going on, Meg?"

Without responding, she transferred her active display to my screen. It was a viable alternate route, but added fifteen minutes to our travel time. I scrutinized the display.

"Look, Meg, I'm just as sorry about their problems as you are, but it isn't our job to investigate disappearing scientists."

"I just thought that if we diverted through the kitewhale patch, we might see something they missed."

"These are top of the line, trained observers, armed with equipment we couldn't even understand."

She'd kept her face averted, now turned to face me. "Please, Jack? We're already so late, it won't matter to anyone."

I thought about it. "Why does this matter so much to you?"

"Lori McLaughlin is a friend," she replied. "More than a friend. We've been occasional lovers, very occasional."

⊢•⊶•○•⊶•⊣

I wasn't thrilled about the diversion. The lost time was trivial; it was the implications of the disappearance that concerned me. But like I said, Meg was a friend, and friends owe each other.

"You do realize she's dead by now? Her oxygen would have run out before we even reached the station." I said it bluntly, surprised to find I was hurting a little myself. Irrationally, I resented the fact that Meg had a lover other than me, even though I knew that was a step in our relationship I wasn't prepared to take.

"I know." She wasn't looking at me, but her voice was controlled. The kitewhale patched loomed ahead; we'd penetrate the perimeter in another few minutes.

It was definitely a surreal drive. I'd seen kitewhales several times before, but always from a distance. They were rare, and when I'd last visited TS2, There'd been none in the area. Or perhaps they'd been in the area but the area hadn't moved to the station's vicinity yet. That kind of impossibly convoluted sentence is inevitable when you try to describe the indescribable.

At close hand, I could see individual tethers quite clearly, disproportionately slender compared to the bulky shapes that loomed above us. It was comparatively easy to avoid the first few, but as the pack grew more dense, I slowed, then altered course.

"What are you doing?" Meg sounded angry and my own irritation level rose.

"I'm not going any closer, Megan. There's nothing to be gained by risking our own lives."

She started to speak, swallowed her initial retort. "I guess you're right. Just stay as close as you can, all right? It's important to me that we at least try."

"Sure."

⊢•⊶•○•⊶•⊣

I noticed the human figure first, but my mind refused to process the sensory input until Meg gasped. "There she is!" The suited figure had emerged from the last rampart of kitewhales and was walking right into our path.

"Don't get your hopes up. This must be someone else, probably a search party."

"Henderson said they'd abandoned the search."

She was right. We rolled to a stop and I waited tensely while Meg went down to open the hatch, using the radio to keep me informed. Our unexpected passenger was indeed Dr. Lori McLaughlin, hyper-physicist, impossibly alive and with, according to her meters, half a tank of oxygen still unused.

We still had a line of sight back to TS2, but I deferred using the radio. Instead I idled the engines and descended to the underdeck to see for myself.

"I can't explain it," she was saying as I arrived. "We'd just finished the data collection and Jillabeth issued the recall. I gathered up my equipment, and when I looked around, they were gone, all of them. So I started walking, saw your crawler, and waited for you to reach me."

"You've been missing for almost ten hours, Dr. McLaughlin. You shouldn't be alive."

She turned, acknowledged me with a nod. "So I've been told. I can't explain it, Captain. For me, only a few minutes have passed since I lost sight of the team. There must have been some kind of time displacement."

It was a neat solution. I didn't like it, but it was neat.

"I'll lay in a course back to the station. I'd appreciate it if you'd strap in, Dr. McLaughlin." I gestured vaguely toward the passenger harnesses, all folded out of the way for this trip. I didn't care for the situation, for a variety of reasons, but with luck it would be someone else's problem shortly. I started to climb back to the command cabin.

"I'll be up in a minute, Captain." Meg was being formal again, I noticed.

Meg was slow to appear, and I'd already laid in a return course when she arrived.

"I was about to send in the marines," I said caustically, engaging the drive the instant she reached her seat.

"Maybe you'd better."

"What's that supposed to mean?" I was still grouchy and irrationally offended.

"That's not Lori back there," she said quietly.

"Run that by me again?"

"That's not Lori McLaughlin in the passenger bay. I'm not sure who it is, or maybe what it is."

"Meg, this hasn't been the easiest trip for either of us, but there's been enough mystery surrounding this whole affair already without letting our imagination... "

She hit me, punched me in the shoulder hard enough that I yelped and lost my grip on the control levers. "What the hell... ?"

"That's *not* Lori back there!" She was staring directly into my eyes and there was absolute certainty in her voice. Either she was completely out of her mind, or she'd seen something I'd missed.

"Tell me slowly, in little words."

She drew a deep breath but her eyes never wavered. "That isn't Lori McLaughlin. It's a pretty good imitation, physically at least. I've been intimate with this woman, Jack. There are all sorts of subliminal cues that ought to be there and aren't. I'm not sure she even recognized me at first; it was as though she had to look me up internally."

There comes a time when every friendship is tested, when you have to decide whether to play it conservative or take an outrageous chance because a friend asks you to. And Meg was my friend, even if that was all she could ever be.

"All right, I believe you. So now what?"

"You're the captain. You tell me."

"There's no procedure to cover this situation. I'll have to improvise."

"That's why you get the big bucks, Captain."

⊢•⊕•○•⊕•⊣

We were on our way back to TS2, but I still hadn't transmitted our news. What was I going to say? "We've picked up your missing scientist and we're bringing her back even though she ought to be dead and we really don't think this is her at all." Sure, they'd welcome us with open arms.

"You were pretty good friends then?" I felt uncomfortable, but the silence was unbearable.

"Yeah, but we didn't get much time together. Lori spent a lot of time out here and our Earthside shifts didn't overlap a lot. We never had time to grow together, or apart."

I was desperately searching for my next awkward line when the situation changed.

"I didn't mean to cause distress." The voice came from the intercom speaker, even though the power light was clearly off.

"All right, masquerade's over. Just who are you anyway?" I was scared green, but so confused I don't think I realized it at the time.

"Whoever you want me to be." It was a different voice, one I recognized immediately. Kyla had the faintest of lisps, unmistakable. And Kyla had been dead for nearly ten years.

"Where is Lori? What have you done with her? Meg's voice was flat, uninflected, bleached of any feeling. She was afraid to know the truth, and afraid not to.

"She is here." The McLaughlin voice was back.

"You're not Lori." Still flat, but tinged with anger.

"No, not entirely. Understanding is incomplete."

The kitewhales were behind us now and I could see TS2 ahead, but I still had nothing to say to them.

"Is Lori dead? Did you kill her?" Meg's voice faltered this time, but only for a second.

"The consciousness to which you refer does not presently exist in its previous form. Its potential remains, however."

What the hell did that mean? I needed some answers and didn't know the questions. "Why have you come aboard? What are your intentions?" I tried to catch Meg's eye, but she was preoccupied with some inner landscape.

"This interface is inadequate. I am reconfiguring."

I didn't like the sound of that. "Meg?" She didn't respond. "Meg, snap out of it!" I punched her in the thigh, mentally marking us even.

"Ow!" She grimaced, then nodded reassuringly.

"Hold the fort," I said quietly, slipped out of my harness, and went belowdecks.

Kyla was waiting for me, looking just as she had the last time we'd talked, just before the Quiet Riot took her away from me forever.

"You can drop the pretense. I know you're not Kyla." My voice didn't even shake; I'm rather proud of that.

"No deception is intended. Kyla is here."

"Kyla is dead."

"The two situations are not mutually exclusive. Potential is independent of linear time. I am Kyla, among others."

"Reveal your true self," I demanded. "We're not fooled by these counterfeits."

"There is no misrepresentation. I am Kyla."

"Kyla is dead." I said it more firmly this time, perhaps accepting it myself at last. "She doesn't exist anymore."

She sighed and her features twisted into that bemused expression she invariably adopted when I stubbornly refused to accept her line of reasoning. There was a flicker of movement to one side and I half turned, caught Meg's arm just in time to keep her from falling.

She hadn't come down the accessway; she was just... there.

"What the hell?" Fear and anger colored her voice. I waited until it was clear she could stand on her own, then rounded on the Kyla figure.

It spoke before I could find words of my own. "Do you recognize this person? Is she any less real because I have moved her potential to a different locus?"

"Moving something isn't the same as imitating it. Meg is alive; Kyla is dead."

"Only within a linear context." Her face softened, reminded me of those quiet moments we'd enjoyed together at her family's house in Managansett. "I'm alive at this moment, Jack, really I am."

And just like that, I believed. Impossibly, I was convinced that I was talking to Kyla, that she'd been snatched out of time and restored to me. A flood of emotion made my vision flicker as I recalled all the joy and love, and also the bitterness of her loss.

She stepped back from me, frowning. "Understanding is not complete. This pain was not anticipated."

I didn't care, I just wanted to throw my arms around her, to hold Kyla so tightly that she'd never be taken from me again. But my arms closed on emptiness and Meg and I were alone once again.

More than alone.

>+◦-◦-◦+<

We never sent a message back to TS2. Instead, we completed the run to Delta and returned to base. Lori McLaughlin's body was never recovered and her disappearance was added to an ever growing list of mysteries surrounding hyperspace. Maybe someday we'll know the answers, but not today, and probably not tomorrow either.

I tried to remain on active duty past the recommended retirement date, but the company was adamant. They offered me a supervisory job in Scheduling and Plotting, but I've always felt uneasy when I couldn't move around, and besides, I had enough credit to live out the balance of my life in some comfort.

Meg was promoted to Captain and served in that capacity for three years, then accepted a disability pension after she was injured evacuating colonists from Pretorius. Occasionally, one of us would feel guilty about falling out of touch and we'd talk over the com, but we hadn't shared the same room for two years the night she called to tell me she was emigrating to Pastel.

"I guess this is goodbye then." I was smiling, but felt genuine grief, knowing we'd probably never speak again. "Isn't this rather sudden?"

"Not really. I've been at loose ends for a while now, and I've had an invitation from an old friend. I think it's the right decision for me."

"Well, I wish you the best, Meg. It's going to be a lonelier world without you."

"Maybe." She hesitated. "Jack, do you ever think about... about the run to Delta?"

My mouth was dry and I averted my eyes. "I try not to."

She bit her lip. "Do you suppose time and space aren't two separate things like we've always thought?"

I thought I knew where this was going. "It was an illusion, Meg, not real."

"Do you really think so?"

"Yes." Neither of us believed me.

"She's out there, Jack. I'm going to be with her again."

She's gone now, left three weeks ago, and irrational though it may be, I miss her constantly now, far more than when she lived here on Earth and we rarely spoke. I replay that last conversation in my mind from time to time and I think that someday I'll answer the com and find Kyla's face staring out at me, inviting me to be with her again.

And I wonder what I'll answer.

There's no place in this universe where Kyla is alive at this moment, but perhaps there are moments in this universe when Kyla is alive in this place.

The Man Who Walked to Procyon

Scott Bushnell's announcement that he would make the entire trip from Earth to Procyon on foot caused a considerable stir. There were no obvious flaws in his plan, but it was so unprecedented that the authorities were automatically hostile and the lawyers for the Outbound Corporation immediately erected a barricade of objections. No one knew the consequences of prolonged direct exposure to the hyperspatial plain, they insisted, either physical or mental. Service crews at the various Translation Stations were constantly monitored and rotated regularly for exactly that reason. If he became disoriented and wandered off, an expensive and difficult rescue mission would be required, and since the geography of hyperspace was not static, he might become irretrievably lost no matter how diligently the search was conducted.

Scott Bushnell was the world's richest man and his very expensive legal staff countered every objection. He would board a starship for the actual translation and start his trek only after its crew was confident that they had arrived at the proper coordinates. His exposure to hyperspace would last less than forty-eight hours, well below the theoretical threshold for psychological effects. Outbound would be compensated for the expense of having its vessel travel slowly enough to keep him under continual observation, thereby ensuring that a rescue could be accomplished quickly and easily, and the corporation would not be held liable in the event of any unlikely tragedy. Bushnell refused to be physically tethered to the ship but agreed to remain in constant radio contact. His agents systematically dealt with other objections, both spurious and real, until Outbound's exhausted lawyers conceded defeat.

"The walk to Procyon should take between sixteen and twenty six hours," Bushnell told the press, "depending on their relative positions at the time of translation. I'll replenish my air supply every six hours, which leaves a two hour safety margin, and I'll be in radio contact with the ship at all times. I've taken moonwalks that were more dangerous."

"Then why bother?" asked a reporter.

"Because it has never been done before," replied Bushnell, "and I need the exercise."

Procyon was the only plausible destination because it was the one human colony from which it was possible to return to Earth. The first starships had rumbled across the infinite plain of hyperspace two centuries previously, and colony ships were being translated into real space two decades later. Dropping back into familiar reality was relatively simple and energy inexpensive because that was the normal state for matter, but an extensive and highly sophisticated launching facility and spectacular amounts of energy were required to cross the barrier in the opposite direction. Earth's single interstellar port covered most of what had previously been known as Oklahoma. There were almost two dozen viable human colony worlds now, but only Procyon had progressed to the point where it could support a small translation program of its own. Bushnell wanted to be famous but he didn't want to be forever exiled from Earth.

<hr />

There were an unusual number of reporters attending on the day of translation, but there really wasn't anything out of the ordinary for them to see. Bushnell had boarded the *Conestoga* after a brief press conference and a theatrical wave to his presumed audience. The *Conestoga* rolled out onto the departure platform, a polished metal cylinder supported by six oversized and independently mounted wheels. The bridge was a shiny bubble only slightly forward of center on the dorsal surface, and a row of observation ports ran down each side. The *Conestoga* had been designed to perform topographical surveys and mapping and was much smaller than the colonization ships. It had a crew of four and carried up to sixteen passengers, all scientists and technicians this trip, except for Scott Bushnell.

And he didn't plan to stay aboard for very long.

The transition wasn't instantaneous. Observers watched as the *Conestoga's* wheels turned but even though it was clearly in motion, it remained stationary in relation to them until it seemed to turn in a quite surprising direction and was gone. From the travelers' viewpoint, the launching pad would waver and then fade away, replaced by the hyperspatial plain.

Despite his attempt to maintain an air of calm dignity, Bushnell was stunned by his first direct sight of the hyperspatial plain. He'd seen holos of course, but the reality seemed richer in some indescribable way, as though hyperspace contained properties which recording devices could not detect or reproduce. The *Conestoga* came to a halt as soon as the translation was complete, and one of the crew members arrived to escort Bushnell to the exit port.

"I still don't think this is a good idea, Mr. Bushnell." Faye Ingram was a mildly attractive woman whose face was unfortunately permanently fixed in an expression of disapproval.

"I'll be fine, Lieutenant. I know you'll be watching over me every step of the way, so I have nothing to worry about."

He donned his environmental suit with practiced ease and entered the airlock a few minutes later. Several of the scientists had wandered forward to watch. He had met them all before the launch, and they'd treated him like an interesting specimen rather than as the celebrity he fancied himself.

During his first few moments outside the ship, Bushnell stared around in awe. The hyperspatial plain wasn't particularly flat, and they had entered near the base of a slight incline. The surface under his feet wasn't soil; it looked like slightly porous plastic foam, and its nature was still a mystery. It was impossible to separate a sample for analysis; it couldn't be cut, burned, or pierced, and there was considerable doubt whether or not it was a form of matter at all. It extended in every direction for an infinite distance, at least theoretically, and interfaced with every point of space in the normal universe. It was possible to map positions in that interface fairly accurately, but the relationships weren't absolute. Distances and exact destinations varied slightly from one journey to the next.

"Are you all right, Mr. Bushnell?" The voice crackled in his earphone, startling him. It was Captain Gallogly himself, not the communications officer.

"Yes, just give me a minute please." He looked up from the surface and slowly let his eyes roam around. There were very few features here. A broccoli tree stood motionless at the top of the rise and just beyond he could see part of a crystalline outcropping. All these terms were just approximations, of course. Broccoli trees were recurring features, but there was no evidence that they were lifeforms. The crystalline structure was less common but was well documented; solid objects, even people, could pass through its translucent structure with no more effect than if they'd entered a holographic projection.

He took a tentative step, watching his feet. Visually, it was as if he was standing on concrete, but the tactile effect was quite different. He might have been walking on a thick rug.

"All right," he said quietly. "Which way do I go?"

In hyperspace, star systems remained relatively stable in relationship to each other—most of the time. The key words here were "relatively" and "most". Sometimes they drifted the equivalent of a few meters, sometimes a few miles. There were four permanently staffed Translation Stations in hyperspace whose crews spent most of their time monitoring the local topography. The first thing a starship did upon arriving was radio the nearest to confirm or adjust travel plans.

"TS4 confirms our original plot, so orient yourself on the *Conestoga* if you please."

Bushnell nodded uselessly; the environmental suit's visor would have rendered him invisible even if he'd been turned toward the ship. "On my way." His first few steps were tentative, but by the time he reached the *Conestoga*'s nose, he was moving with more confidence. He sketched a wave in the general direction of the bridge bubble, then turned and started up the incline. Behind him, the oversized wheels of the starship slowly began to turn.

When Bushnell reached the top of the rise, he had a panoramic view of nearby hyperspace. The plain was broken in spots by broccoli trees, singly or in clumps. A cluster of kites slowly drifted across his path from the right, gauzy structures that looked like skeletal hot air balloons. Their lowermost edges trailed lightly over the surface, while their upper reaches extended almost as far as the pseudo-ceiling.

There was no sky in hyperspace, just a featureless gray cap which posed unusual problems for investigators. Several efforts had been made to launch unmanned fliers, but their radio signals invariably cut off as they faded from sight at approximately eighty meters. None had ever reappeared.

Off to his left, a range of serrated hills had begun to migrate; he could detect movement almost immediately—the larger ones slowly drawing away from their smaller fellows. Beyond he could see a swirl of color twisting away toward the pseudo-horizon, a river of sparkling light. An early expedition had encountered one of these and unwisely attempted a crossing; they had never been heard from again.

"How are you doing, Mr. Bushnell?" It was Faye Ingram on the radio this time.

"Great. There's nothing like a brisk walk on a bright, sunny day." Hyperspace had no sun, of course, and the soft, omnipresent light seemed to emanate from every surface of every structure. It was literally impossible to cast a shadow here.

"You're a bit off course. Nothing to be alarmed about, but the captain wants you to bear right about fifteen degrees."

It would have been easier with a compass, but there were no magnetic poles in hyperspace. He overcompensated slightly with his first try, but Ingram eventually admitted that she was satisfied. "Will you be coming aboard for lunch?"

"I think not. Dr. Kroll assures me that the nutrient soup in my tank will sustain me quite nicely."

In fact he felt exhilarated. The pseudogravity effect was about three quarters Earth normal, and the terrain wasn't difficult. If it hadn't been for the cumbersome environmental suit, he might have tried jogging for a while. Each time he crested an incline, a new vista presented itself, and he grew increasingly impatient to see the next, and the next. Scott was actually quite surprised when Ensign Travers told him it was time to replenish his air supply, but he obediently closed with the ship and linked to the external port just as he'd been taught.

Faye Ingram's voice crackled in his headset. "Mr. Bushnell, we're getting a very unusual reading here."

Scott glanced at the LED display inside his helmet. "I have a green board."

"It's not you. We're recording an anomalous situation. TS4 has stopped transmitting, both normal communications and their locator beam."

"They've had a history of mechanical problems, haven't they?"

"Yes." He could tell she was reluctant to admit that. "But just before their signal cut off, they were observing an unusual phenomenon. The captain thinks it might be best if you came aboard, at least until we know what's going on."

Scott sighed. "Is he ordering me to abort?"

"No." Her reluctance was even more obvious this time. "But he strongly recommends it. And so do I. There are too many unknowns for us to take unnecessary chances."

"If we hadn't taken unnecessary chances, we'd never have ventured into hyperspace in the first place. So far this has been a walk in the park, Faye, and I don't plan to run for cover just because TS4 can't keep its act together." She didn't answer, and he knew he'd made his point. "What was it that they were observing?"

"I'm not sure. The science types were on their way up to the dome when the signal cut off. All we know is that the observation crew reported seeing something new."

"Well, if they come back on line, let me know what's going on." A green light blinked at him and he started disconnecting himself from the *Conestoga*.

The second six hour shift also went quickly, but toward the end, fatigue finally dimmed Scott's enthusiasm. He was careful not to express any misgivings to the crew, but when the *Conestoga* rolled to a stop at the top of a relatively steep incline, Scott welcomed the excuse to go aboard and get out of his suit.

Ingram waited while he doffed his equipment and stretched his arms and legs, her expression as dour as ever. "How are you feeling?"

"Quite good, actually, but I won't have any trouble sleeping."

"The Captain wants me to talk you into staying aboard." She didn't sound hopeful. "He feels that you've made your point and that continuing this tomorrow is just a very dangerous publicity stunt."

"The whole thing is a publicity stunt, Faye. I never pretended that it was anything else."

"I know. He even talked about getting underway while you were asleep and letting you walk just the last few miles to Procyon."

Scott's voice hardened. "That would be a breach of contract. It would defeat the whole purpose of the trip. I'd sue Outbound and I'd have Gallogly's head."

She nodded. "He's just blowing off steam. But he has a point. And with TS4 offline..." Her voice trailed away.

"No word from them, I gather."

"None. TS2 is sending a crawler, but it won't get there for several hours. We'll hear from them before we reach Procyon, assuming it doesn't relocate itself between now and then."

⊢•⊕•○•⊕•⊣

Scott slept soundly but wakened instantly when his alarm buzzed. Travers and Ingram were completing the diagnostics on his environmental suit when he arrived at the airlock.

"Everything checks out," Ingram admitted grudgingly.

Twenty minutes later, the *Conestoga*'s engines started and once again it lumbered slowly in Scott Bushnell's wake.

Although the landscape was as beautiful as ever, the trek was becoming something of a chore by the end of his first shift. Scott would never admit it to Ingram or anyone else, but the strangeness of his surroundings and the isolation from human contact was starting to bother him. He heard phantom sounds from time to time, and occasionally thought something had moved at the periphery of his vision.

He took his time replenishing his air, and a few minutes later was distracted by a change in scenery. For most of that day, he'd been following a shallow declivity that might almost have been called a valley. The far end opened up into a wide expanse, revealing a more cluttered scene than any he'd encountered previously. Broccoli trees stood in thick clusters, virtually a forest, although there was still enough open ground for them to proceed without any significant detour. There were at least two of the periwinkle shaped boulders that indicated black holes in the normal universe, each rising above tree level, and a cluster of diaphanous kites drifting slowly from left to right, their lower streamers brushing across the ground.

Scott paused and keyed the radio. "Looks like a good time for a course check."

"Wait one, Mr. Bushnell. I'll check with the captain." It was Travers' voice.

A minute or two passed, and then Ingram was speaking to him. "I have some good news and some bad news."

"Isn't it always that way? Don't tell me. Procyon has relocated?"

"Well, yes, but that's not the bad news. It's actually considerably closer to us. Captain Gallogly estimates you'll reach it in another two hours or less."

"What's the heading?"

"Continue as you are. It's only a couple of degrees off the original line, and considerably closer." She was silent for a few seconds. "They've reached TS4. The news isn't good. They had some kind of explosive breach."

"Survivors?"

"They haven't found any yet." Her tone told him that there was little chance of anyone being alive.

"Any idea what caused it?"

"There'll have to be an investigation. Apparently almost half the station was completely destroyed, and obviously they lost atmospheric containment. The crawler crew sounded pretty shaken up."

"I'm sorry to hear it. Did you know any of them?" He regretted the question as soon as he said it. The people who made their living on the hyperspatial plain were a small and intimate group. Ingram probably knew most if not all of the crew of TS4.

"Yes," she answered softly. "My husband was there."

⊢•⊶•⊙•⊷•⊣

They entered the "forest" a few minutes later. Scott had no trouble making his way forward, but the *Conestoga* was not as lucky. It was possible to push a broccoli tree over, but only with larger class vessels. Captain Gallogly had to pick his way through the maze, sometimes backtracking, while Scott could slip through much narrower gaps. At first he led the way on foot, but after the second detour he spoke to Gallogly.

"We're wasting too much time this way. You can move faster if I'm not in front of you, circle around the obstruction and come back to me."

"I'm not supposed to let you out of my sight, Mr. Bushnell."

"Put someone in the rear observation port and keep the radio link open. I won't move unless you have a clear line of sight."

It took some more persuading, but at the third detour, Gallogly finally agreed. Less than an hour later, they were ambushed while making their fifth detour.

Scott had found a broccoli tree small enough to use as a chair. It was hard to judge texture through the gloves of his environmental suit, but the "flowers" compressed enough to serve as a cushion. He crossed his arms and watched as the *Conestoga* rolled away, circumnavigating a particularly dense concentration of the greenish pseudotrees. Just beyond stood one of the periwinkles, a whorled mass that towered three times the height of the starship.

Although he would never have admitted it, his feet were bothering him slightly. He'd spent weeks hiking through the mountains in preparation for this trek, but hadn't anticipated that the environmental suit and the portable displacement unit would be so uncomfortable. Fortunately the ordeal should be just about over. Gallogly estimated that it was less than an hour's walk to the Procyon coordinates, although it might take longer if the *Conestoga* had to make too many detours.

From where he sat, Scott had a clear line of sight to the periwinkle, but a broad swath of broccoli trees concealed it from the *Conestoga* as it picked its way around the barrier. That's why he saw the attackers in time to radio a warning to Gallogly.

The enemy emerged slowly from behind the periwinkle, supported by a web of caterpillar treads that independently adapted themselves to the surface below. The body of the ship was more cubical than human vessels, and looked to be about twice the volume of the Conestoga. Scott couldn't see any equivalent of a control bubble, nor did he immediately recognize the nature of the elaborate structure mounted on its dorsal surface. Stunned, he rose to his feet and climbed up onto the broccoli tree to get a better view. That's when he noticed the blunt nosed shaft that lay across the top of the newcomer.

"Gallogly, are you there?" He shouted into the radio, uselessly waving his arms back and forth over his head.

"Ingram here. What's the problem, Mr. Bushnell?"

"Tell Gallogly to reverse course. You're headed into an ambush!"

"What are you talking about? Are you feeling all right?"

He made an exasperated sound. "I'm not hallucinating. There's another vehicle just ahead of you. It doesn't look like anything I've ever seen before and I'm pretty sure it has some kind of weapon mounted on it. It looks like a gigantic crossbow."

"Just stay where you are and we'll be back your way in a few minutes. We can talk this over then."

Scott realized she didn't believe him and shook his head in frustration. "Tell Gallogly, damn it!"

But it was too late. The *Conestoga* emerged into a wide clearing and turned to circle around the last few clusters of trees. Scott saw the catapult shiver and then discharge, and the bolt moved so quickly that he almost lost sight of it. The *Conestoga* wasn't presenting a full profile but the shot was true. It struck just above the central tire on the right hand side, shattering the axial joint and crumpling the shielding in every direction.

"What the hell was that?" Ingram wasn't speaking to him, but the radio link was still active.

"That was my hallucination shooting at you," he said sarcastically. He glanced back at the other ship. A second bolt was rising into the bow cradle. "They're going to fire again. Get out of there!"

Gallogly wasn't quite fast enough. The cradle had been adjusted because this time the trajectory was much higher. Scott caught his breath when the blunt end struck the control bubble, but it must have been a glancing blow because the bolt fell away and the bubble appeared to be intact.

"Faye! Are you there, Faye?"

There was no answer, but the *Conestoga* continued to back away, retreating behind the wall of broccoli trees before coming to a stop. Scott turned to watch the other ship, expecting it to press its attack, but it remained motionless.

The only sound from his radio was an almost subliminal static.

His first instinct was to walk to the *Conestoga*. His second, and stronger, was curiosity. Taking care to remain shielded by the trees, he moved toward the enemy starship.

He was close enough to make out more detail when Ingram hailed him. "Scott! Are you all right?"

"So far. How about you and yours?"

"Nothing worse than a broken wrist so far. We've lost one wheel and the cooling system is working at half power. There are stress cracks in the control bubble and the captain has retired to the instrument bridge. Can you give us any idea what's out there?"

"It's another ship, about twice your size. I'm trying to get close enough for a better look."

"Be careful!" Her voice crackled with tension. "I don't understand. Why would the Procyon colony attack us?"

Scott shook his head. "I don't think it's from Procyon. They won't have the capacity to launch anything this size for years."

"But who else..." She fell silent in mid-sentence.

"Yeah, that's what I think too. At least historians will be able to say that they fired first. Which reminds me; I don't suppose you have any weapons aboard?"

"Not even a flare pistol. A few blunt objects, a cutting torch, that's about it. We've been here for over a century now and we've never encountered any other visitors."

"Well, there's a new kid in the neighborhood. And I think we know now what happened to TS4. I assume you've notified TS2?"

"The Captain's talking to them now."

"Maybe they can jury-rig some kind of weapon and come riding to the rescue."

"They're fourteen hours away. I don't imagine we're going to have that much time."

Scott was quite close now. He could see a strange stitched pattern on the hull of the alien ship. The treads looked fairly conventional, but they were mounted on what appeared to be an elaborate hydraulic system. There were a few narrow dark lines, which might be observation ports, and several oddly shaped and irregularly placed protrusions which he supposed could be cameras.

"They haven't moved in a while. Maybe they're waiting to see what you do."

"Be careful, Scott. There's nothing we can do for you if you get into trouble."

"I'm aware of that."

⊢•⊙•⊣

From close at hand, Scott noticed that the front of the alien was equipped with a heavy, metallic prow like a cow catcher. There were no external markings and he couldn't find an identifiable airlock or entry port, even when he had completely circumnavigated it. The vehicle had stopped in the open, and he wasn't foolish enough to expose himself to get any closer. In fact, he had just decided to return to the *Conestoga* when the alien ship began to move, wheeling rapidly in his direction.

He didn't know if they'd seen him or if the change of orientation was coincidental, but the ship moved much more quickly than he'd expected. Panicking, he tried to run, lost his footing, and landed awkwardly, fortunately cushioned by the environmental suit. During the few seconds before he regained his composure, the alien closed the gap and loomed high over his head. Its massive bulk pressed down the broccoli trees, which sprung back undamaged to their original positions in its wake.

Scott was pretty sure he wouldn't fare as well, but he was too cumbersomely equipped to run. He turned to face the prow just before it caught him in the chest. All of the telltales in his helmet display flashed red and it felt as though his ribs and right hip were on fire, but he remained conscious and even managed to grip an irregularity on the prow and find a depression for his feet. As the display turned from red back to green with a scattering of warning yellow, Scott Bucknell achieved another first. No other human being had ever ridden on an alien starship.

He radioed a warning, and Ingram assured him they were underway, but they weren't fast enough. He saw the last line of broccoli trees bending and then leaped to one side at the very last moment as the alien ship slammed into the rear third of the *Conestoga*. The only sounds of impact he heard came through the radio. The smaller ship spun around and one of its rear tires was sheared completely off. But the alien hadn't gone unscathed this time. One side of the prow dropped suddenly and struck the surface, then buckled, tearing cables loose as its crew turned away from their prey. Perhaps preoccupied with the unexpected damage, they continued forward and disappeared through the next line of trees.

The *Conestoga* wasn't dead, but after rolling a few meters, it canted over to one side and came to a halt. The radio link still seemed to be working, but no one answered when Scott called them. He made his way as quickly as possible, favoring his bruised hip, and saw more damage from close at hand. One of the remaining four wheels was ruptured, and the left front axial connection was bent out of true.

"Scott! Are you still out there?"

"Yes, Faye. What's your situation?"

"We don't have any serious injuries but we're not going anywhere. The fuel pump isn't responding and we're blind on one side."

"They took some damage, but I think they'll be back. Listen, did you say you had a cutting torch aboard?"

"Yes, a couple of them. But there's too much damage for us to fix even if they leave us alone. We're going to have to wait for the rescue ship."

"And what if they come back to finish you off?"

"I don't know. But there's still nothing we can do to fix the *Conestoga*."

"It wasn't the *Conestoga* I had in mind."

Scott found the alien without too much trouble; it had traveled in a straight line after the impact and was sitting in a clearing. One side of the prow was completely dismounted and his first thought was that both vehicles were now disabled. But as he crept closer, the prow shifted slightly and he realized that another of the connecting welds had separated. No, not separated. The strut to which it was attached had been loosened from within. The crew were jettisoning the damaged prow in order to regain their mobility.

Scott nodded to himself, shifted the cutting torch to a more comfortable position, and moved forward.

It took less than an hour to disable about half the treads. He was pretty sure the crew realized something was wrong because the ship started to move even before the prow was completely clear. But without the use of the right side treads, they couldn't maneuver and they quickly shut down. That was the last sign of life he observed. He cut through one more mounting just to be safe, then started back to the *Conestoga*.

"No airlocks," he explained. "They must seal themselves in before launching and cut themselves out when they reach their destination. Maybe they're agoraphobics, or they don't like the light, or maybe hyperspace manifests itself to their senses in an entirely different and unpleasant way. That might explain their hostility. For whatever reason, there was literally no way for them to stop me from disabling their ship."

When the rescue party arrived, Gallogly had managed to shift one of the surviving wheel and axle units to the opposite side. The *Conestoga* couldn't move under its own power, but it could be towed.

Captain Madison of the *Kon-Tiki* counted heads. "Where's your passenger? Mr. Bushnell?"

Gallogly sighed and pointed into the distance. "The gentleman went for a walk. He said he'd be waiting for us at Procyon."

No Distance Too Great

The sky went on forever. Once upon a time, that might have been a figure of speech but today, for Jason Tallant and his companions, it was literally true. Except that it wasn't really the sky, even though it was blue, sort of, and speckled with clouds, sort of. What he was actually seeing was the way in which his mind interpreted part of the external reality of the hyperspatial plane. Which really was a plain, in both senses—and spellings—of the word.

The interstellar transport *Rollaway* had stopped briefly to allow its passengers to enjoy the panoramic view. They were perched on the top of a comparatively steep and completely featureless hill, overlooking what might almost have been a river valley, except there were no rivers in hyperspace, which meant it wasn't properly speaking a valley either. The declivity twisted slightly and disappeared as it turned around a cluster of broccoli trees, which weren't trees at all. Nothing was alive in hyperspace, except during those short periods when ships were traveling through its indecipherable vastness.

A voice came from behind him. "Quite a view, isn't it?" Jason was en route to his new assignment on Dropout with Mira Harris, recently promoted to manager of the corporation's branch office on that colony planet. Mira had been offered the position previously but had refused the assignment until Dropout had built its own translation station so that she could return expeditiously if she so desired. Following the death of his wife, Jason no longer felt tied to the earth or anything on it and in fact had been actively planning to end his life before deciding to first accept a transfer to Dropout. He was only mildly curious about conditions there, but more importantly Kathy had been full of romantic ideas about traveling to other worlds and he felt an intense need to see that she achieved it even if posthumously. Her ashes were carefully packed in his luggage, a surprisingly small bundle to represent a person who had made up such a large part of his world.

"Too bad we can't take pictures." Mira's voice was flat and Jason suspected she was saying what she felt was appropriate rather than what she was actually feeling.

One of the other passengers made an amused sound. "Well, you can if you want, but they won't show anything." Humans perceived hyperspace as an infinite plain dotted with features that were almost always interpreted consistently from individual to individual. Many of these features had been named, like the broccoli trees, which were not living creatures at all, but they looked like trees and they looked like broccoli and everybody saw them as pretty much the same thing. Having no objective physical reality, however, they could not be recorded by photograph or holograph, although artists had been able to render recognizable images.

An older man crowded closer to look out through the observation bubble. "I don't understand how the captain can find his way through this. I understand the landscape is different every time they translate out of normal space."

Jason felt moved to reassure him. "Each of the colony worlds extrudes a beacon into hyperspace. We're homing on the one from Dropout. The landscape may change but the absolute locations don't." Jason's wife had been fascinated by the concept of hyperspace, obsessed with the idea of emigrating to one of the colony worlds, and Jason had picked up a lot of technical knowledge by osmosis. "Even if we just take a short term assignment, Jason. I want to be able to say that once in my life I stood on the surface of another planet." She had regaled him with fresh nuggets of knowledge about hyperspace and the various colony worlds as quickly as she gathered them. He could, had he been so inclined, have lectured on the history and reliability of the colonial beacons at considerable length. But Kathy had never realized her ambition, although she had still been making plans up to a week before her death. Now she would never stand on an alien world, but at least in one sense he would ensure that she realized her ambition.

"But what if the radio breaks down, or we run into some kind of interference? How do we know we're on the right course?" The man sounded nervous and for some reason Jason found that irritating. He recognized the mercurial nature of his own moods, knew that his calm demeanor masked a cauldron of turbulent emotion, but he didn't care.

"Actually we don't. The fact that it has always worked in the past doesn't mean it always will. We could conceivably wander around out here until we ran out of air."

The other man paled and turned away to rejoin his party. Mira gave Jason a slight, mildly puzzled smile. "That was cruel."

"He's a jerk."

"Even so."

Harris would not be his immediate superior on Dropout, but while Jason knew that that it would be politically wise to defer to her, he really didn't care and compromised by not responding at all. He did not expect to be around long enough to be affected by her displeasure.

⊶⊷

Captain Emilio Ventras sat back from the control board and glanced at his backup, unofficially his Shotgun, Shelly Paris. "How's the signal?"

She shrugged. "Same as always. How are the passengers?"

"The usual motley crew." The exchange was a ritual between them. This was their fiftieth trip together and Paris was probably going to get her own command when they got back. Ventras would miss her.

"Well, at least we have some nice scenery this time." He glanced out across a variegated landscape of gently rising and falling hills, mottled with broccoli trees and a few of the comparatively rare crystal towers, which were neither crystal nor towers.

"If we get too bored, we can play cards."

Boredom would not be one of their problems on this trip.

⊶⊷

The engines became audible again and the massive wheels began to turn as the *Rollaway* resumed its journey, descending toward a lowland as flat as anything on Earth. Captain Ventras had considerable latitude in picking a course because there were no maps to guide him. He could detect his end point, but the territory in between was terra incognita. In fact, it could change while they were traversing it. Just because a hill happened to be facing the valley now didn't mean the same would be true in an hour. The *Conestoga* had nearly been wrecked when a ravine opened up under its wheels a few years earlier, and more recently the *Prairie Schooner* had almost run out of air after it had been overturned by a sudden massive upheaval. In both cases, subsequent investigation had suggested that one or more of the passengers had been experiencing extremely ambivalent attitudes toward emigration or had been undergoing some other form of unusual stress. Successful completion of more probing psychological tests had been added to the criteria for subsequent passenger applications.

Jason was a corporate psychologist and had easily avoided revealing his inner turmoil. He felt no guilt about doing so. He very much wanted to complete the trip to Dropout. It was the last thing he could do for Kathy, and while it wasn't much, it would have to suffice. And then he could lay down his own burden as well.

He glanced around the cabin. There were about thirty passengers, but only one obvious family, a young couple and their daughter. The parents were excited or nervous or both; the daughter—about twelve—was bored. The rest consisted of parties of two to four people, probably on short term assignments, and a handful of solitary individuals of both sexes, most of whom kept to themselves. A few of these might be emigrants as well. There were two cabin stewards, one of each gender, both inconspicuously armed with tranquilizer guns. Despite the best efforts of the screening boards, a few people each year broke down when faced with the para-reality of hyperspace. The most frequent manifestations of HTD—Hyper Transit Disorder—were hallucinations and agoraphobia. Everyone so afflicted had recovered quickly after their return to normal space but they were routinely drugged if they displayed any extremes of behavior en route. Emotional upheaval by even a single individual could have tangible effects on the communal interpretation of the exterior environment, making navigation more difficult.

Mira returned to her seat and began studying the screen of her PDAX but Jason remained where he was, watching the pseudo-landscape flow past the observation bubble. There had been a time when he would have joined her, more interested in the world of profit and loss, numbers and arrays, connections and financial opportunities than he was in the external world—what Kathy used to call the "real" world. Jason allowed himself a hint of amusement. Whatever existed on the other side of the Perspex bubble wasn't the real world either, whatever that meant. Scientists and philosophers alike were still trying to decide just what it was.

They had reached the flat land and were moving forward more rapidly now. When he closed his eyes, Jason could not sense movement. The irregularities of the surface, such as they were, were more than compensated for by the pressure and shock absorbers beneath him. One theory held that vehicles in hyperspace didn't actually move at all. They became immobile relative to the rest of the universe, which then rearranged itself to bring their destination to them. This made no sense to Jason. There might be as many as a dozen vehicles in hyperspace at any given time. The universe couldn't simultaneously cater to all their needs, could it?

Their route took then in an arc around a low butte and as they turned Jason could just see a hint of their trail dust. It wasn't dust, of course, but the interaction of material from the "real" universe with the hyperspatial plain resulted in a temporary darkening of the latter, as though the ship's wheels were bruising the surface across which they moved. The phenomenon, like most aspects of hyperspace, had gathered lots of theories but few facts.

Jason still wore an old fashioned wrist watch, a family heirloom, but it was of limited utility aboard the *Rollaway*. Transit times between the same two points could vary dramatically; the *Bigwheeler* had been forced to resort to recycled air during a trip to Upstart when the normal eight to twelve hour trip consumed an unprecedented thirty hours. They'd run into no natural barriers requiring detours but it had still taken longer for reasons that remained a mystery. As with most other ships, the *Rollaway* had been refitted to increase its air supply and the maximum passenger limit had been reduced.

They passed so close to a copse of broccoli trees that a frond almost brushed the bubble's exterior surface. Kathy would have loved this, he thought to himself, and felt a wave of despair and loss so great that he had to put out a hand to steady himself. Only the knowledge that he would not have to live with his grief for much longer kept him from shouting his pain aloud.

Jason felt weary, in spirit if not in body, and leaned to one side against the cool plastic. He didn't quite doze off, but he became less aware of his surroundings, lost in the landscape of his inner mind, and when he finally noticed that the view had changed rather dramatically, he had no idea how much time had passed until he glanced at his wrist again. More than an hour. They should be not quite halfway to their destination given an average transit time.

They were no longer traversing a relatively featureless plain. They had slowed so that the captain could pick his way across an expanse of broken ground. Narrow defiles zigzagged in random directions, none big enough to seriously endanger the ship, although the captain was obviously taking no chances. In the distance, Jason could see shadowy shapes like canyon walls, although the ridgeline was smooth, a succession of gentle curves. There were broccoli trees as well, smaller than usual, but much more numerous than before, a virtual forest.

Mira slipped into the seat beside him. "Didn't you say your wife knew a lot about hyperspace?"

Jason suppressed a twinge of painful memory. "She was obsessed with it. My greatest regret is that she didn't live to see this."

Mira paused automatically as a nod to his grief, but her body language was alert and possibly even tense. "Did she ever mention reading about anything like this? We're practically surrounded."

Jason made a show of looking outside again. "Not specifically. There's quite a range of possible landscapes, you know. Some of it is the result of fluctuations in the underlying energy structure, or at least so the experts think, and some of it depends upon the mental state of the people perceiving it. None of this is objectively real, you understand?"

"Sure. Sure. But we've been going slower and slower for the last half hour and I heard the attendants talking about possibly backtracking to find an alternate route. I was just wondering if that meant something was wrong."

Jason considered his answer. Everything was wrong, of course, in a universe that no longer contained Kathy, but he didn't think that answer would satisfy Mira. "It's unusual but not unprecedented. It may be that there's some kind of flaw or fault blocking our original course and our minds are interpreting the approach as impassable terrain. I wouldn't worry about it."

Mira was obviously not entirely satisfied but she nodded and went back to her seat. Jason was considering following her, but before he could bestir himself, the *Rollaway* came to a complete stop.

There was a murmuring from the passengers, some of whom looked around curiously, with just a hint of concern. The two stewards maintained their blank masks of amiability and reassurance, but Jason thought he detected a hint of tension in the way they held their bodies. They were just a shade too attentive, as though they were expecting trouble.

The intercom buzzed and the captain's voice filled the cabin. "There's nothing to be alarmed about, folks, but we're going to have to retrace our steps a bit. The way we've been coming looked pretty clear a while ago, but the surface is getting rougher. Just to be on the safe side, we're going to try to find a little smoother way. In the meantime, we still have plenty of beverages and snacks and the scenery outside is more interesting than usual." Jason decided "interesting" was a euphemism, but he wasn't sure what other term it was standing in for.

After another few minutes, the *Rollaway* began to reverse course. The body of the ship was roughly a cylinder, with the pilot module set on a track above them. The drive train was fully reversible following a short realignment while the captain's module slowly ran along the track to the opposite end. Then they were in motion again. The attendants assured everyone that backtracking, while unusual, was not unheard of. Most of the passengers had already returned to their work or their conversations and clearly could not have cared less.

They picked up speed for the next few minutes, but Jason was still at the observation bubble and he was one of the first to notice when it began to slacken again. Half an hour later they came to another stop.

This time there was noticeable concern among the passengers. Mira and another man Jason hadn't met joined him. She was sweating slightly even though the cabin was as comfortable as when they had departed. "Any idea what's going on, Jason?"

He shrugged. "Probably another course change. The captain knows where the beacon is, of course, but he has to pick his specific route by line of sight." He gestured toward the exterior. "He's probably having some trouble finding a good vantage point." The broccoli trees were denser than ever. It was as if the ship was passing between two dense stands of forest.

"What if he can't find a way?" The other man moved his eyes in jerky, frightened jumps.

Jason shrugged. "Then he either radios back to our base beacon for a relief ship or he waits until the landscape changes again. We have food and supplies for at least four days. There's a lot of safety margin built in."

He expected the ship to start moving again fairly shortly and it did, but it halted once more, after only a few minutes this time. Jason wasn't surprised. He had watched the landscape roughen, ridges rather than hills that almost formed before his eyes. This was obviously something unprecedented and he was fascinated, immune to the apprehension spreading among his fellow travelers. Jason had nothing to fear from death any longer.

Captain Ventras addressed the passengers again, explaining that they had run into a denser patch of obstruction than he had expected. "There's nothing to worry about. We're perfectly safe where we are and we can just wait for things to shift again. As a precaution I've asked that a relief ship be placed on standby, so even if we're stuck here for a while, we can be resupplied or, if absolutely necessary, there are enough environmental suits for us to evacuate to the relief vehicle."

His voice was calm, clear, and professional, but people were frightened anyway. The attendants suggested card games or other distractions but with little success. People started watching each other, or trying to nap, or simply stared at the floor. Very few looked toward either of the observation bubbles and Jason had his all to himself.

There were no formal sleeping arrangements aboard the *Rollaway* but the seats all reclined. Several people asked about sleeping aids but the attendants couldn't help them. "We're not allowed to bring any psychoactive agents aboard a ship except as cargo," they explained. Jason knew that already; minds affected by drugs—even alcohol—had unpredictable effects on the hyperspatial terrain. He also knew that they weren't telling the entire truth; the weapons on their belts fired darts filled with a powerful tranquilizer that suppressed most mental activity, though they would only be used in an emergency.

Jason ate and napped for a while, then returned to his seat in the bubble. No one had usurped his place in his absence.

Time passed. Twice the ship began to move and twice it stopped almost immediately. The captain told them he was just topping up the charge on the batteries, but no one believed him. They were sure that he was trying to find a way out, and failing each time.

A full day passed before one of the passengers—an older man—created a disturbance. He began shouting at the attendants, demanding to see the captain, and their attempts to calm him only provoked a more animated outburst. They were forced to subdue him physically and restrain him in his seat until his terror fed anger burned out and he wept quietly. Jason was surprised that they hadn't tranquilized the troublemaker, but they seemed off their own game, less attentive than usual, occasionally talking in whispers when they thought no one was watching. The distraught man subsided, but several other passengers had become visibly disturbed.

The weeping man became uncommunicative later that day. One of the stewards went aloft to speak to Captain Ventras directly for a while, after which the captain announced that he had requested that the relief ship make

as close an approach as possible so the troublesome passenger could be evacuated. Anyone else who preferred to return to Earth station could do so if
they were willing to suit up and make the short trek that would obviously be
necessary. A half dozen people indicated their wish to take advantage of the
opportunity, but as it happened, no one ever left.

The relief ship couldn't find them.

Radio works in hyperspace, which is why the beacons function. Ship to
ship is a little trickier, apparently because ships aren't anchored in the "real"
universe the way station beacons were. In the past, rescue ships had always
been able to home in on a distress signal, but this time they failed. Ventras
insisted these were minor technical difficulties, but the female steward was
having trouble maintaining her composure and Jason overheard snatches of
conversation between the woman and her co-worker from which he was able
to guess a part of the truth.

The relief ship could not find the *Rollaway*, could not even find the patch
of overgrown terrain where they were stranded.

———

"How are the passengers holding up?" Ventras had wakened from a deep
sleep, checked his instrumentation, and ascertained that nothing significant
had changed externally.

Paris shook her head. "No further disturbances, but it's only a matter
of time if we don't give them some good news pretty soon." She wiped the
hair back from her forehead. "For that matter, I'm going to be a little upset if
something doesn't happen. What do you think the problem is?"

She'd asked that question twice before, and he still didn't have a good
answer.

———

More time passed.

Jason had more or less taken up a permanent position in the bubble.
He stood up and walked around occasionally, ate with the others, sometimes
napped in his assigned seat, but he no longer felt as though he was a part
of the company. At times he had trouble assigning sense to what they were
saying, although in his defense, sometimes there wasn't a great deal of sense
there to start with.

Halfway into the third day, he saw something moving outside, which
was impossible.

At first he thought he had slipped into a daydream, or that he'd misinter-
preted the fall of a shadow. But there were no shadows in hyperspace because
there was no light source and he'd been completely alert. One of the other passengers had noticed his start and wandered over curiously. "See something?"

"No. I just drifted off for a moment." He was impatient for the man to be gone and when he finally turned away, Jason pressed his face close to the Perspex and stared outside. Nothing moved. He watched for a long time before reluctantly deciding that just maybe he'd fallen asleep after all.

And then he saw it again. Or almost saw it. There was just a flicker between two broccoli tree trunks, or stalks, or whatever they were. As though something had moved from concealment behind one to the next. It was cautious rather than furtive, although he could never have explained how he recognized such a subtle difference.

He stared intently at the same spot while trying not to give away his interest to anyone else in the cabin. If there really was something out there, its discovery was his and his alone. If he couldn't share it with Kathy, then he wasn't going to share it with anyone.

But nothing happened for long minutes and once again his certainty began to waver. The scene outside had in fact changed over the course of the past several hours. The distant ridgeline was a lot less distant now and if it had been actual rock and sand instead of an artifact of human perception, he would have been able to pick out striations or irregularities, had there been any. The broccoli forest had thinned out a bit, although he'd never actually seen any of the individual specimens disappear. He just happened to notice that there were fewer, although still far too many to allow the *Rollaway* to pass through. Some of the passengers had insisted that the captain try to force his way, but he had declined. Experience had already demonstrated that humans were incapable of altering their environment in hyperspace, at least by physical means. Lasers, acid, cutting tools, brute force, even a nuclear detonation had all been tried.

Jason fancied that the air was getting a little stale, but it was probably his imagination. They were good for forty hours even before they went to recycling. He wasn't really sure how long they would last after that.

He did fall asleep then, slumped in the less than comfortable seats provided for sightseers. He dreamed of Kathy, not surprisingly since he did so almost all the time now. They were back at the house and he was working in his den. She was outside, wearing a bathing suit and playing in the spray from the sprinklers as though she was a child. He was watching her when she turned, smiled, and came over to the window, rapped on it and gestured for him to come out and join her.

His head snapped up and he stared into Kathy's eyes. They were there just for a second, then they were gone. And they'd been on the other side of the Perspex dome. He was absolutely certain of it.

"Is anything wrong?" Mira was standing to his left. Her voice had picked up a slight tremor and her head moved in sudden, birdlike twitches.

"Just a dream." He stood up and stretched. "Did I miss anything while I was out?"

"There are two rescue ships out now, but they still can't find us." She gave a nervous laugh. "I was told this assignment might be an adventure, but this is a bit more than I was expecting."

For just a moment, perhaps because Mira's mouth twisted into a half smile that reminded him of Kathy, he felt a twinge of empathy. "We'll be all right. There's someone watching out for us."

Mira gave him an appraising look. "I didn't realize you were the religious type, Jason." She would have read his personnel files, of course.

"I'm not really." He looked away, already regretting his minor indiscretion.

"Are you all right?"

"I'm fine." He kept his eyes fixed on the exterior and it was several minutes before he realized he was alone again. The rest of the passengers had drawn physically closer to one another, seeking mutual comfort. Jason felt no temptation to join them. He had been alone constantly for the past year. He was used to it.

He saw Kathy several times during the course of the next hour. There would be a flash of movement and he'd spot the shape of a head drawing back into the fronds, or spot an arm or leg just as she moved from one point to the next. There was no continuity. She might be to his right one second, to his left the next. She was never in view long enough for him to focus, and certainly not long enough for him to call someone else over to confirm what he was seeing. Technically, he supposed, it might not be Kathy at all as far as his objective evidence was concerned. But he knew it was her, particularly when he caught a glimpse of her eyes.

Most of the others were sleeping when she finally revealed herself fully. Jason had been on the verge of nodding off when movement attracted his attention. A shape emerged from behind one of the closer broccoli trees. He thought it would be just another fleeting glimpse, but then she stepped out into the open, hands on her hips, and looked directly at him. She wasn't wearing an environmental suit and he knew that was impossible, but he didn't care. This was his Kathy. She hadn't abandoned him after all.

She raised one hand and beckoned to him and he knew what he had to do.

The two stewards were taking turns sleeping. The female—Jason had not bothered to learn their names—was currently snoring softly. Her partner was sitting in the second observation dome, supposedly watching over the passengers although his eyelids were drooping. Jason stood up slowly and stretched, surreptitiously watching to see if the steward would react. He did not. Jason began walking around the cabin, careful not to disturb anyone, and took a drink from the dispenser. He was almost within reach of the second attendant now, who had turned partially onto one side. Her holstered tranquilizer gun was facing in his direction.

He felt no trepidation when he lunged for it. His mind was filled with absolute certainty that this was right, inevitable even. The weapon slid out of its holster and he fired down into the woman's thigh as soon as his finger slipped inside the trigger guard. He turned and saw that the male steward had gotten to his feet but had yet to reach for his own weapon. Jason shot him. The woman was already out and the man followed with a strangled shout of surprise. He fell to the floor.

Jason retreated to one corner as the passengers began to rouse. He didn't wait for them to get organized. "Everyone stay calm. I'm not going to hurt anyone, but there is something I have to do."

Mira separated herself from the others, walking directly toward him. "Put that thing down, Jason. Don't make a fool of yourself." Her voice was steady, expecting obedience. He shot her without a second thought and she crumbled to the floor, a look of complete amazement on her face. The twelve year old began to scream.

"Keep your distance," he warned.

One of the other men thrust himself forward. "He can't get us all, and that thing just knocks you out for a while. Let's take him down."

Jason shot the speaker, then the two men who had been flanking him, then another for good measure. "I'll shoot you all if I have to." He wasn't sure that he could though. He had no idea how many anesthetic darts were available. Still covering the others, he edged around to the supine male attendant and quickly confiscated his weapon. It had never left its holster.

"You!" He gestured toward a burly, rather overweight man who'd introduced himself as Bert Ralston. "Open the emergency locker."

Ralston hesitated. "Do it or it's sleepy time."

The man did as he'd been told.

"Now take out one of the environmental suits and bring it to me." That took a while. The suit consisted of several components that were assembled around the user rather than worn. The helmet came last and Ralston tried to use it as a club. Jason shot him.

"You're being very foolish, Mr. Tallant." The voice came from the intercom. Captain Ventras and his team had obviously been monitoring the passenger deck. "Please put down your weapons and return to your seat. We understand that you're frightened, but this isn't going to help."

Jason was elated, not frightened. He ignored their instructions and very carefully began to climb into the lower module of the environmental suit. It was difficult because he also had to keep one weapon pointed at the others, but he managed. Captain Ventras addressed him several more times, cajoling, soothing, promising, threatening. Jason continued to ignore him.

The suit was almost completely assembled when a half dozen passengers came at him at once. He dropped three of them with darts and a fourth stumbled over one of his fellows and landed heavily. The other two reached him but the environmental suit augmented his strength adequately. He brushed them aside, tossed down the tranquilizer guns, and sealed his suit.

No one tried to stop him after that. They didn't even bother to retrieve the discarded weapons, which could not have penetrated his suit in any case. He strode to the emergency airlock, moving rather awkwardly, and activated the inner seal. No one pleaded with him not to go. They were probably just as glad to be rid of him.

She was waiting for him outside. Jason was surprised at first to see that she didn't need an environmental suit. He turned on his radio but the only sound was Captain Ventras demanding that he return to the ship. After a few seconds, Jason clicked it off. He and Kathy had never needed words to communicate. He took her hand and let her lead him off.

The broccoli trees had retreated ahead of him, forming a pathway that led off into the distance. They walked directly up the center and Jason felt light headed and joyful for the first time in more than a year. "It should be yellow bricks," he told her, knowing she couldn't hear him. But she turned her head and nodded and he almost fancied that the surface under his feet had shifted color slightly, the palest of yellows that turned darker where his feet had touched. Not trail dust, he told himself. Fairy dust.

"We have clearance, Captain." Paris turned and waited for instructions.

Ventras had been trying to direct some of the passengers to restore order within the ship. It was physically possible for one of the command officers to descend into the passenger module, but it was a time consuming process and in any case he wanted Paris with him on the bridge. Now he turned and did a quick visual survey to confirm what he'd heard. "Engage engines." If there was an opportunity to escape, he would take it, even if that meant abandoning the wayward passenger.

Within seconds, the *Rollaway* was in motion. A short distance forward, he saw the figure of a man in an environmental suit turn from the open path into a smaller one, too small for the *Rollaway* to follow, and he knew that this was the last he would ever see of Jason Tallant. And he saw something else as well.

Jason's path was only faintly visible from the top of the *Rollaway*, but the discoloration of the surface created by his passing formed a distinct, continuous line that disappeared beneath the ship and extended, presumably, back to where he had disembarked. That was not at all surprising. But Ventras had a great deal to think about during the balance of the trip to Dropout because parallel to that track had been another, slightly smaller but no less distinct.

Jack the Martian

I suppose it's cynical to consider the appearance of a serial killer on Mars evidence that we have successfully transplanted human culture across the gap between worlds. Admittedly, the psychologists responsible never suggested that they were creating a new civilization from scratch, but they certainly intended to apply strict controls to our closed society. Personally, I attribute this to the narrow minded focus of their specialty. If they had consulted those of us who have studied human history, they might have adopted less grandiose plans from the outset. The higher the aspiration, the greater the disappointment.

Nor is it surprising that the killings began in Bradbury, the largest of a dozen domed cities, supporting and supported by twice that many smaller communities, plus countless observation posts, weather stations, research projects, and other outposts of the human invasion scattered across the barren but fiercely beautiful surface of Mars. With a population of approximately fifteen thousand, Bradbury would have been a small town back on Earth, but here it was a major metropolis, the cultural, commercial, and scientific center of the universe for a quarter million colonists.

It was also the hunting ground for a deranged killer.

The first victim's body was still warm when I reached the scene. Bob Winston, one of my sector supervisors, waited at the foot of the accessway ladder while I climbed down.

"What've we got, Bob?"

"A mess, Ted. Over this way." We were in one of the maintenance corridors beneath the northeast rampway, not far from the locks between domes six and seven. Judging by the mesh of cables that ran along the low ceiling, this particular corridor provided access to the energy linkage from the core tap.

A few meters further on, a coveralled body lay face down in a pool of blood.

"His name's Nguyen Chu, second generation Martian, lived in Bradbury all his life except for a few months on temporary assignment in Barsoom."

Two technicians were crouched over the body, while a third carefully videotaped the entire procedure.

"How'd it happen?"

Winston shrugged. "Throat cut with a sharp instrument, nature unknown. Judging by the angle of the wound, I'd say the assailant came up from behind, reached over the right shoulder, and struck before the victim even knew he was in danger. No signs of a struggle. The autopsy might tell us something more."

I glanced around, trying to look professionally calm despite the churning in my stomach. Crime, even murder, wasn't unknown on Mars, of course, but it was rarely premeditated.

"I don't see any cameras. Who found the body?"

Winston refused to meet my eyes, not embarrassment, just unease. "No one. The killer called it in."

⊱─◦─⊰

"Do we have him?"

"No, but we have his name." Winston appeared to be uncomfortable, waited to be prompted.

"All right. What's his name?"

"He says he's Jack. Jack the Martian."

⊱─◦─⊰

The colonization of Mars had been a strange blend of pragmatism and visionary romanticism. It had taken over a century before the first few settlements were essentially self supporting, and the capital outlay had been so great, it would take at least that long again just to repay the principal, let alone the accumulated interest. There were few accountants on the red planet; our fiscal policies gave them nightmares.

At the same time, the creation of enclosed, environmentally balanced ecosystems separated from Earth by a gap of time, space, and attitude was perhaps the most ambitious engineering project ever undertaken by the human race, and many of the most brilliant technical people on Earth had voluntarily emigrated in order to be a part of it. The Bureau of Psychology was supposed to smooth over the contradictions and conflicts so the two strains of personality interacted productively, and at least to date they had done so with reasonable success.

I'm ninth generation Martian, though educated on Earth and Luna, trained in administration and historical analysis. After graduation, I accepted a position with Security here in Bradbury because I believed it would be a relatively undemanding job and allow me time for my life's work, a comprehensive history of the colonization project. To my dismay, I discovered a latent talent for dealing with bureaucracy, and was now the youngest person ever to serve as Chief of Security.

Back on Earth, that would be Chief of Police. We had no "police" on Mars. The psych people decided that particular word had connotations which would not be helpful to the social climate, and "security" sounds so much more reassuring. Perhaps I was contaminated by my five years off world, but to me this was just symptomatic of their tendency to soften language, disguise the raw edges of existence, a linguistic head in the sand divorcing us from reality. But then historians have always known the importance of a specific turn of phrase, so perhaps I'm overly sensitive.

I was off shift when the second murder took place. Anne and I were sharing a bottle of Martian chianti fresh from the winery in Wells, trying to decide whether or not to renew our marriage contract. It was an amicable discussion; the two year term that was about to expire had gone smoothly and pleasantly. We were friends, expected to remain so, even intimately, but neither of us was entirely reconciled to making the compromises necessary to live together successfully as a couple.

The blinking code on my wristcom indicated a priority call and I touched the appropriate icon.

"Ted, this is Carol Chen. We've had another murder." She paused. "It's just like the last one." Policy was not to broadcast details even though the department wavelength was supposedly secure.

"Where?"

"Between rows 346 and 347, Farm 14. Bob's already at the scene with his team."

"All right, I'll join him there."

The victim this time was Joyce Djibwa, a seventh generation Martian employed as an agricultural assistant in Farm 14. She'd been working a shift of seedbed maintenance, unaccompanied, and from the evidence available we were able to reconstruct the sequence of events directly preceding her death. At one end of the aisle between rows 346 and 347 was an open access to the irrigation trench four meters below. The fast flowing waters washed down to the recyclers, carrying organic debris that fell or was thrown in by staff members trimming and weeding the gardens.

Her assailant had approached from the rear, used one hand to grab the victim's hair and force her head down long enough to draw some unidentified sharp instrument across her throat. Djibwa's blood had sprayed across the ground and made long, dark streaks down the containment wall. Security had been notified by an anonymous and untraceable call from a public com-link near the exit to Dome 15 within a few moments of the attack.

Bob Winston didn't greet me this time, just stood watching the technicians work, obviously uncomfortable. "Find anything?" I averted my eyes. Djibwa had been an attractive woman, but now she lacked all humanity.

He shook his head. "Same as the other one."

"Might be coincidence," I suggested without conviction.

Winston shook his head. "Same message as last time, claims to be a <u>real</u> Martian. I'd say we have a nut, the victims chosen at random."

That remained unproven, but even though we did considerable cross referencing, our subsequent investigation turned up no usable link between Djibwa and Nguyen Chu, the first to die. Of course, in a community as small as Bradbury, there were inevitably some connections. They lived in different neighborhoods, but they were both active squirtball fans, along with one out of every three adults in the city. Djibwa had originally worked in systems maintenance, though not in the same sector as Chu, and switched to agriculture a Martian year or more before he emigrated from Dustbowl to Bradbury. There was no evidence that they had ever met.

We explored the tenuous connections as far as we could, but without real hope of finding anything. And we downplayed the two incidents in the media, not even acknowledging that the deaths were related, although carefully not denying the possibility.

Things didn't start to get out of hand until the third attack.

Connie Santiago was a popular woman in Bradbury. She'd been elected to four consecutive terms on the city planning board, winning by a larger plurality than anyone in living memory, and had only been returned to private life because she refused to run for a fifth. Santiago was attacked and killed during daylight, working in the postage stamp sized private garden she maintained behind her small private quarters.

Needless to say, Security was under pressure from all sides. Both co-mayors had managed to forget their joint veto of my proposal to increase the number of security cameras, although to be fair, this was unlikely to have saved Santiago. Private property could not be kept under surveillance without the owner's approval. Message volume was so great we were forced to filter all incoming calls through an AI discriminator to separate legitimate ones from public complaints and I was twice accosted in public places by irate citizens demanding to know why I hadn't brought the killer to justice.

To make things worse, someone in security leaked details we had hoped to keep to ourselves. Not only did the newslinks report that the murderer had called us following each kill, they also knew the weird part, that the killer claimed to be a "real" Martian who would continue to kill until the human invaders were gone.

⌐•☲•⌐

Bradbury, like all Martian cities, is a closed community. Not that there isn't free trade with the rest of the domes; there's no such thing as nationalism or anything like that on Mars. The Bureau of Psychology is very careful to neutralize anything that might contribute to regionalism. Even squirtball teams are prohibited from having more than two players from any single city.

But since we can't breathe the Martian atmosphere, every breach in the perimeter of our cities is monitored at all times. You can't enter or leave without identifying yourself unless you're smuggled in as cargo. There have been occasional fugitives on Mars, but it's almost impossible to vanish here. There are too many ways to trace a concealed human, air exchange rates, protein consumption, DNA tracking, pedestrian character recognition programs, and so on.

Following Santiago's death, I received a grudging emergency appropriation to lease additional surveillance equipment from other cities, and authority to commandeer non-essential monitoring equipment from the private sector as well. We very quickly increased our coverage of public areas from ten percent to approximately thirty-five, but the effect was even greater since we didn't need to cover heavily travelled rampways, public meeting places, the main commercial district, and other unlikely preying grounds.

It wasn't enough to save the life of Reinhardt Warshofsky, a fourteen year old butchered on the landing of an old catwalk he used as a shortcut between home and the gymnasium, but we had installed permanent traces on every public comlink in Bradbury and a strategically placed team caught sight of the killer vaulting over the rampway guardrail. The team leader alertly posted her people to cover every exit and called for help.

I came through the airlock from Dome 4 just as they were preparing to go in after him. The fugitive had spotted the two security people sent to intercept and backtracked, then descended further into the bowels of Bradbury through the maintenance tunnels. When I heard that, I ordered the dome sealed off completely, even though that set off the emergency sirens and created considerable panic.

Even so, it appeared that we had lost him. We swept the area systematically with small, heavily armed teams, checking every tunnel, compartment, connector, and tubeway as we went. It's a bewildering world down below street level; Bradbury is the oldest permanent settlement on Mars, and each new vision of what the city should evolve into was built squarely on top of the old. But cubic volume had always been at a premium and there was little wasted space, few places to hide and all of them obvious. Or at least, that's what we thought.

But we couldn't find our killer.

I ordered a second sweep, convinced that we'd overlooked something, and my intuition proved right. Night was just falling outside when Winston reported they'd found a supposedly sealed hatchway whose cover had been tampered with. The bad news was that it was a direct conduit into one of the adjacent domes, bypassing the supposedly air tight dome seal. The good news was that it led into Farm 2.

Although Bradbury looks anything but symmetrical from overhead, there is actually a pattern to its development. There is a central core of linked domes which house commerce, industry, entertainment, and government services. Additional domes along the southern periphery are primarily residential, those along the north agricultural and scientific. Farm 2 was one of the oldest and largest of the northside domes, but it was also one of the very few that had only a single link to the rest of the city. In other words, it was a dead end. And a sparsely populated one to boot.

Since our quarry could not have returned to the main city while the seal was in place, we moved our operation to the Farm 2 airlock area. There was no certain way to know how many people were legitimately inside the agricultural dome, but night shift had started and there wasn't likely to be more than a skeleton crew.

We evacuated the staff systematically, screening each individual in case the killer was one of their number. Fortunately for us, no one had wanted to work alone since Djibwa's death, so we had little difficulty clearing everyone assigned to Farm 2 for the shift. Then we sent in the search teams.

It was only a matter of time. Farm 2 is the largest of the agricultural habitats, but it was laid out to be easily maintained. We flushed the killer less than half way through the sweep and vectored the other teams to interdict every possible escape route. As chance would have it, I was with the squad of five who saw the end from closest at hand.

Our "Martian" headed almost directly to the north side of the dome, where the irrigation system rushed through an artificial streambed into the jaws of the recyclers. When a furtive figure emerged from a cluster of ferns only a few meters from our position, we drew our flechette guns, the heaviest weaponry allowed inside a dome. Without acknowledging our shouted orders to surrender, the killer ran across the aisle and climbed the sandcrete abutment above the canal.

I'm not certain exactly what happened next. Another squad burst into sight further along the perimeter and turned in our direction. The killer, still unidentifiable despite the artificial lighting, seemed to hesitate and then, so quickly that we all froze, stunned, was gone. I rushed to the scene and scrambled up onto the abutment, stared down just in time to see what might have been a single flailing arm disappear under the threshing jaws of the nearest bank of recyclers.

Officially, it was listed as death by mischance, although it might possibly have been suicide. Nor did we ever learn the identity of Mars' first serial killer. Despite having the most closely monitored population in human history, we were unable to discover, even indirectly, the name of the person we chased that night.

It took a while to accept that situation. There are close to a quarter million people on Mars, after all. But we accounted for every one of the twenty thousand currently listed as resident in Bradbury; no one was missing. As much as we would like to remain confident about the security system, it had somehow been breached.

So we expanded our search to every installation on Mars, and quickly eliminated all but a few dozen people, mostly prospectors who hadn't bothered to maintain radio contact. By the end of the year, there were only three names left, a party of scientists believed lost in the Great Canyon region. Their bodies were found a few months later.

There were theories of course. The least practical was a stowaway from Earth. The most popular, despite denials from Data Management, was that some hacker had found a way to excise himself or herself from the system so completely that no trace of identity remained behind. There were even some who believed that the murderer had been an unrecorded birth, sheltered by parents for some arcane reason, grown to maturity without the social conditioning that maintains the stability of our fragile culture.

I have only recently begun to suspect the truth.

Despite my disinclination toward a career in administration, I was pressured into remaining as Chief of Security even after my term expired; submission to social pressure is a key part of our psychosocial conditioning. Then a seat on the Bradbury City Council, appointment to the planetwide Development Board, and so on. In short, I was not able to return to my love of history until my retirement from public service just last year.

Gilwright and Kubisawa's definitive history of the colony pre-empted my original plan to produce an equivalent work, and I became committed to a new project, essentially my personal memoirs. The work was rewarding and went quite rapidly until I reached the year of the killings.

The Security records were quite complete. I reread the site reports, the autopsies, my own logs, and replayed the newsnet coverage. Even after a gap of more than half a lifetime, those events seemed real, distinct, hard edged, still vaguely unsettling. What I discovered next was more startling.

Despite my skepticism about the efficacy of many policies enacted by the Bureau of Psychology, they indisputably maintained a meticulous set of records of human activity, in mass terms. Many of these had been restricted even from the Chief of Security until the Freedom of Data Act a few years earlier, so it was with some curiosity that I downloaded and began to examine some of the files from that period. I was expecting to find a sharp increase in mental disturbances during the period directly following the Jack the Martian killings. What I found was exactly the opposite.

Over the course of the two years immediately preceding those unfortunate events, the incidence of neuroses and psychoses had been on a sharp upward curve, so sharp in fact that I detected serious concern expressed with mounting anxiety in the archival notes. Ten days prior to the first murder, the Bureau's Board of Governors was considering declaring a Psychological Emergency and taking direct control of colony affairs under the now defunct Cultural Emergency Code.

The trend began to reverse itself after Nguyen Chu died, declined slightly further when Joyce Djibwa was slaughtered, and dropped dramatically with the death of Connie Santiago. Reinhardt Warshofsky's demise directly preceded a reduction to acceptable levels.

I thought about that for some time, read a number of scholarly studies examining the phenomenon, all of which concluded basically that while the initial increase in mental unrest was almost certainly a kind of planetary cabin fever, no one really understood why the disorder had reversed itself. Several files made reference to the Jack the Martian killings as a symptom of the problem, but none suggested what I now suspect is the real explanation.

I don't think Jack the Martian ever really existed; I think he was a mass delusion, an artifact of the minds of all of us here on Mars, a device by which we dissipated a growing, unrecognized resistance to psychological control. But a delusion so intense that it could literally interact with our environment, interact powerfully enough to be seen, heard, and to take four human lives.

And if I'm right, what form will our next mass hallucination take? Are the increasingly frequent reports of movement in the Martian deserts significant? Are we truly the inhabitants of Mars, or are we in the process of creating them?

Adding It Up

Alison looked up from her console toward the viewscreen, her expression suddenly serious. "Hey guys, we're not alone."

Cherie Carson, nominally captain of the *Polaris*, let her eyes sweep across the panoramic view of Charybdis III. "Care to be a little more specific there, Ali? I don't see anything."

Nelson Ngakele straightened in his seat and ran his fingers over his own display. "Miss Busby is seeing phantoms again, Captain. The scanning record is clean, both the planetary surface and the surrounding space. No radio except the usual random natural stuff."

"It's gone now, but there was a definite pulse." Alison hated the fact that her voice sounded defensive, but Ngakele had been skeptical of her new equipment from the outset, and her misreading around Congela IV had made the rest of the crew something less than sympathetic.

"Do you have a point of origin?" The captain's voice was neutral.

Alison shook her head. "It didn't last long enough. It wasn't from the planet though. Possibly the major moon. That sector anyway."

"How far are we from stable orbit?"

The fourth member of the bridge crew, Bud Weeks, spoke without looking up from his work. "Insertion in forty-four minutes. Standard preliminary mapping orbit. Should I abort?"

"No, not yet anyway." Carson bit her lip as she thought. "Nelly, run the survey scan again."

"The whole scan?" He was clearly offended. "We had zeroes across the board the first time, and not even a quiver on the supplementals."

"Which were completed when?"

"The last supplemental was eight hours ago."

99

"A lot can happen in eight hours, Nelly. We're not going to reach orbit for a while yet anyway. Humor me."

After a brief hesitation, Ngakele nodded, but he gave Alison a pointed look before returning to his console.

The *Polaris* was a commercial exploration vessel, privately owned by its three senior crewmembers. They were contracted to the Centauri Coalition to conduct follow up work on planets identified as potential colonies based on automated surveys. Alison was the newest of the four crew members, hired because of her expertise with the newly developed Detwiler Scanning System, a sophisticated but so far relatively untried technology designed to replace the older equipment which Nelson Ngakele operated in addition to his navigational duties. Charybdis was the fourth of six worlds they were to survey on this trip, the first three of which had ranged from dubious to utterly impossible.

Alison's employment contract was short term. If she did well, she might be hired as regular crew with an option to buy in. But any one of her three crewmates could block her renewal, and it was clear that Ngakele had already taken a dislike to her.

"Same as last time, Captain." Ngakele sounded smug. "Trace readings near the satellite. Too small to matter."

"All clear then." Carson just sounded relieved, and she didn't so much as look in Alison's direction.

"What about those trace readings?" Alison turned in her seat and forced herself to meet the seven foot tall Masai's eyes.

"Tiny rock fragments in the same orbit as the larger moon. The biggest of them isn't much more than a meter across. Ore bearing debris. There might have been another small moon that broke up, or maybe this was left over when the big one was formed. They're all in pretty much the same orbit."

"Nothing on the moon's surface itself?"

"Not a thing. It's a big dustball, low density, no atmosphere. Possibly a partially hollow interior. Porous almost certainly."

As he was speaking, a telltale flashed three times on Alison's console, then stopped. She bent quickly to the display while Captain Carson walked around behind her. "Something up?"

"Another pulse," she said quietly.

"From the same place?"

"I don't think so. I didn't get a fix but it appears to originate in a slightly lower orbit than the first."

"Could it be an equipment malfunction?"

Alison hesitated, but she'd seen Ngakele's work, knew that the man was thorough, if inflexible. "There's a possibility," she admitted.

Alison spent the next two hours dismantling, testing, and replacing questionable components. Everything that she could check passed, but there were some parameters that were either beyond her competence or which required special test equipment not available to her. By the time she had everything reassembled, the *Polaris* had dropped into an orbit low enough for more detailed surface scanning.

"Looks promising." Bud Weeks told her. "Breathable atmosphere, acceptable temperature range, no evidence of unusual climatic or tectonic activity. Abundant wildlife including some good sized predators, but nothing dramatically different. Not a lot of land mass compared to some worlds, but it's all in the temperate zones. One of the best prospects I've seen."

"Looks like a nice place to live. The greens and blues remind me of home."

"You're from Earth originally, aren't you?"

She admitted to that. "My family moved to Coriolus when I was thirteen. It's a nice place, but not like Earth."

<hr />

Carson and Ngakele were off shift and asleep when the attack came. Alison saw a flash out of the corner of her eye just before the alarms came on with an abrupt roar. The viewscreen flickered as the shutters slammed into place, and Bud Weeks half fell out of his chair as he lunged for the controls.

Captain Carson was only half dressed when she reached the bridge, but there was little for her to see or do once she got there.

"What hit us?"

"Laser, I'd guess. Reasonably high power. Hit just aft of the dorsal observation bubble. Outer skin damage but hull integrity was maintained."

"Duration?"

"Less than a second."

Carson turned to Ngakele, who was punching up his display. "What's the scan?"

"Negative," he said quietly. "Nothing within range. Increasing scan."

Alison had already attempted to trace the origin of the attack, but she remained silent, waiting for Ngakele to have his say.

"Where is it, Nelly? We need to know what's out there."

"I understand that, Captain, but I'm not reading anything different now than before. There is no evidence of any ship or satellite anywhere near us. Just the two moons, the planet, and some minor orbiting debris."

Carson's head turned and Alison spoke up. "I get the same results, Captain."

"Point of origin?"

"Based on the angle, somewhere near the major moon. Can't be more precise."

"Could it be some kind of installation buried on the surface?"

Alison shook her head. "I don't think so. Based on our angle of inclination and the damage report, the shooter was near but not actually on the moon proper."

Ngakele nodded agreement. "About six degrees off. I don't get it. The shot that hit us barely charred the paint. Why bother?"

It was Bud Weeks who answered. "Maybe someone's feeling us out."

⊷−◦−⊶

They changed orbit and approached Charybdis' larger moon, both sets of scanners in operation. Carson brought them in close, shields in place, for a thorough examination of the satellite and its surroundings. They had to dodge a couple of the small rocks, but as Ngakele had indicated, the largest was less than two meters in length, nothing their shielding couldn't handle easily.

"This is weird and I don't like it." The normally imperturbable Weeks was pacing the control room nervously. "Any chance that this was natural? Some kind of fluke of nature?" Three faces turned to him with identical expressions. "Okay, I didn't really think so."

"Whoever or whatever it was, it must be afraid of us."

"Why's that, Nelly?" Carson's face was drawn, fatigue lines around her eyes. She had missed most of her last sleep shift, and should already have retired from the current one.

"Because they're hiding. It stands to reason that if they had firepower enough to do us serious harm, they'd have come out in the open and done it by now."

"Not if they're uncertain about our resources." Carson rubbed her eyes. "How long before we could jump out of here, Bud?"

"Two plus a little standard days minimum. The jump cells need at least that long to recharge."

"We could withdraw to the fringes of the system," suggested Ngakele, without enthusiasm.

"There's no guarantee we'd be any safer there, if we're in real danger." Carson suppressed a yawn. "My head's spinning. Bud, you're in command. Keep the shields up. Wake me if anything happens out of the ordinary."

She left, and a moment later, so did Ngakele.

"You aren't saying much, Ali."

Alison looked at Weeks. "I don't know what to make of it. The scanners, even Ngakele's old style ones, should pick up any object within range capable of mounting laser armament. My stuff should be able to locate and provide some detail about any operating energy source. I've been running background scans continuously. There is literally nothing in the vicinity of this planet of sufficient mass. I have some anomalous energy readings, but they're minor, random, and too low level to be the source of our problem. I'm at a complete loss. It's as though some ship were able to jump into orbit, fire its laser, then jump out, all in a fraction of a second."

"It takes at least thirty-six hours to recharge for a jump even if you have unlimited energy to speed up the process."

"I know that. How many alien civilizations do we know about with faster than light travel? About a dozen? And every one of them is subject to the same limitations. Maybe number thirteen has something new, something way beyond our technological level."

"If they were that advanced, why would they attack us with a comparatively primitive, low level laser?"

She shrugged. "Beats me. Maybe it wasn't meant as an attack. Maybe they're playing games. Maybe it was an accident. Maybe..."

Her next "maybe" was cut off and assigned to oblivion when the proximity alarms went off.

Weeks leaped for the controls but the ship took evasive action without waiting for orders. The deck lurched, his feet flew out from under him, and he crashed to the deck. Alison saw that he was not moving, braced herself, then leaped across to the command chair. She read the display with disbelief, then quickly touched several controls.

When Carson and Ngakele reached the bridge, the alarm system was returning to normal.

"What the hell is going on now?" The captain sounded more irritated than frightened.

"Missile attack. Three pair on separate trajectories. We got them all at a safe distance." She glanced down. "But I think Bud has a concussion."

"So what's the short version?" Carson had reclaimed the command chair after Weeks was medicated and stowed in his bunk, but she looked more drawn than ever.

"Based on a scan of the debris, all six had nuclear warheads. Our lasers destroyed them at a safe distance and without much effort. No evasive maneuvers. Not much mass, very compact design, maybe half a meter long. Launched at intervals of approximately two seconds from a slightly higher orbit than ours. The pattern suggests a ship under power, but as I'm sure you're not surprised to learn, none of our instruments show anything in or near that position either before or after the attack."

Ngakele nodded. "It's impossible, but she's right. There was nothing there to launch at us."

Alison paused briefly to savor the moment. "That's not quite true. I said there was no ship of sufficient mass before or after the launch event. But I have an unmistakable five second trace of an object big enough to be a ship, probably half our mass."

Ngakele's jaw dropped, but he didn't say anything.

"How reliable is the reading?" asked Carson

"I trust it," she answered with as much certainty as she could squeeze into her voice. "I have four separate pulses with identical readings except for a very slight spatial displacement. There was a ship out there, or something the size of a ship. It appeared, fired six missiles, then disappeared, all within six seconds."

"That's impossible," insisted Ngakele.

"Not if it happened, it's not." Carson was still looking at Alison.

"There's more. There was a phantom pulse immediately following its disappearance, and a weaker one right after that."

"Meaning?"

"Meaning that the ship was still partially but not completely present for another two seconds after firing, and that an even smaller part of the ship was still there two seconds later."

"And then?"

"Nothing. Just the usual minor orbital debris."

⊢•◦•⊣

The next few hours passed uneventfully. They launched a series of probes to the surface of the planet and monitored the telemetric reports, finding nothing that contradicted their earlier observations.

"This is prime territory," Carson asserted. "The best find since Aragon."

Alison smiled dutifully and returned to her monitoring of the scanning equipment. Nothing unusual happened during her next shift, and she was tired and frustrated as it drew to a close, so tired she nearly missed the change.

"Emergency! Shields up!"

Ngakele was in the command chair under the staggered schedule that would be maintained until Weeks was fit to return to duty. Without hesitation he activated the full defense system of the *Polaris*.

"What's going on? Talk to me, Alison." It was the first time he had used her first name.

"Multiple attack vectors. Missiles. Something else."

The viewscreen showed flashes where the defensive lasers were taking out the incoming missiles. Two, then four together, then six more.

And something else.

The field hit them just as Carson reached the bridge. The impact threw her to the floor, where she wrapped her arms around the base of Ngakele's scanning equipment. "Report!" she shouted.

"Someone's trying to pin us with mass attractors. Give me a second here."

Alison felt rather than heard the engines increasing thrust. There was another jerk, almost as violent as the first, then nothing.

"We're free," announced Ngakele. "Alison, did you get a clear scan?"

"More than you'd believe."

"I'd believe three ships."

This time it was her turn to be surprised. "And you'd be right. You'll have to tell me how you did that some time."

He smiled. "I felt them. It takes three to properly triangulate a target for a mass attractor. They had us pinned perfectly, just didn't have enough power to hold us down."

Carson had regained her feet. "Where the hell did three ships come from? We should have had ample warning if they jumped into the system."

"I don't know, Captain. They're gone now."

But Alison disagreed immediately. "No, they're still here. They've been here all along." She had their attention now. "I think we need to look at some of that orbiting debris from up close."

It wasn't difficult. The debris was unusually heavy in their immediate vicinity. In fact, it was so heavy that Ngakele was puzzled. "I can't believe I didn't notice how dense this was when I did the earlier scans. We must have been positioned at just the wrong angle at the time."

Alison shook her head. "No, it was scattered when we arrived. The Detwiler equipment isn't affected by angle of approach. It would have shown up."

Ngakele and Carson exchanged looks.

"We need to take a very close look at one of these fragments." She turned to Carson and met her eyes squarely.

Without hesitation, the captain nodded. "I think you're right."

⊢•◦•⊣

It wasn't difficult to accomplish, in theory; there were scores of them close by. But when Carson began to maneuver the *Polaris*, she made an interesting discovery. "If I get within a kilometer of them, they change orbit."

Ngakele shook his head. "Change orbit? They're just rocks!"

"Nevertheless, they change orbit whenever I approach."

Alison's console was confirming what she already suspected. "No indications of energy discharge. They just seem to move of their own volition."

"How can they do that?" Carson sounded offended by the very concept.

"Some kind of gyroscopic or magnetic drive," suggested Ngakele. "But I don't understand. Individually, even the largest of these things couldn't mount an offensive laser, let alone missile batteries."

"No," said Alison softly. "They couldn't."

⊶―•―⊷

It was Weeks who suggested the solution, his head bandaged and throbbing, but relatively clear. Ordinarily the *Polaris* had no true offensive capacity, but with some modification, the laser defenses could be made to serve that purpose. "Narrow beam to minimize damage. Short bursts along its length. Sooner or later we'll disable something."

They moved to just outside the critical limit of their target and Carson nodded to Weeks. He drew a breath, then initiated the attack, using the laser as sparingly as possible, hitting the target with several split second bursts. At their first approach, the object moved away again, but they closed on it and another flurry of fire did what they had hoped. This time when they moved the ship, their quarry remained in its current orbit.

They were preparing to take it aboard when the ship formed in front of them.

Alison had time to shout a brief warning when she saw the sudden surge of movement from the supposedly inert orbiting fragments, but it only took a few seconds for them to merge. They seemed to be altering shape as they touched, their exterior surfaces moving fluidly together to form new seals. The results, while superficially still formless rock, was roughly symmetrical and obviously artificial.

"Another one just formed off the stern!" Ngakele's voice was shrill. Alison's console confirmed his words and indicated that a third was appearing directly between them and the planet.

"Incoming!" The defensive system was already responding as laser fire and missile launches were reported from all three ships. The viewscreen flickered as the *Polaris* dealt with the attack.

"We're taking some superficial damage from the lasers," Weeks reported. "Lost one sensor and a lot of paint. The missiles aren't even getting close."

As suddenly as it had started, the attack abruptly ceased. Carson nodded to herself before speaking. "Target the nearest enemy ship and fire at will."

Their main laser hit the object dead center. There was a visible explosion at the point of contact and the alien ship flew to pieces.

"Destroyed?" Carson glanced back and forth between Alison and Ngakele.

Both shook their heads. "Dispersed. The fragments are under power."

"Target the second ship."

Another explosion, another dispersal. The third ship didn't wait to be attacked, pre-emptively broke up into its components.

"They're on the run," Ngakele reported.

"Running to where?"

"A point near the major moon." Alison studied her console. "There are more of them on the way. I'm getting readings from every sector."

"Let's follow them for the moment." Carson turned to Weeks. "Are we still battleworthy?"

Weeks nodded. "Unless they have something we haven't seen, they can't touch us. Their weapons are very primitive, Captain."

"They're forming again," Alison called out. "Bigger this time." She caught her breath. "A lot bigger."

They had a visual within seconds, but only because the scale was so large. It looked like every bit of random debris in the Charybdis system was being collected. The alien ship, two gigantic globes with a cylindrical join, dwarfed the *Polaris*. It was nearly as large as the smaller moon.

Carson continued their slow approach but withheld fire. "That structure sticking out of the smaller sphere. Does it remind anyone of anything?"

"Jump chamber," Weeks responded immediately.

"That portion of the ship was assembled from elements orbiting the moon." Alison tapped the face of her console. "Specialized subassemblies, I'd guess. The components containing the jump drive are parked safely out of the way while combat modules are assembled. They can probably reform in any number of specialized configurations."

"Very efficient," acknowledged Ngakele.

"I'm picking up Muhlenfeld radiation." Alison didn't sound surprised. "They're going to jump out of here."

"Should I fire, Captain?" Weeks' hand hovered over the control panel. "I might be able to disable them before they can escape."

"No, let them go. We didn't come here to fight. Maybe they'll get the message."

And less than a minute later, there was no trace of the alien presence in the Charybdis system.

⊷―◦―⊶

"You did all right, Ali." Carson stood up from the command chair and stretched. Weeks and Ngakele were off shift, catching their last sleep period before the *Polaris* jumped to the next planet on their list.

"Not at Congela, though."

"So there are still a few bugs in the equipment. Do you have any idea how many times Nelly has given us bad readings?"

Alison sighed. "But he's experienced enough to know when something goes wrong."

Carson chuckled. "Yeah, he's got a sixth sense, all right. Give it time, Ali. You have the right instincts; you just need to let them develop." There was an awkward pause. "What are your plans once we get back?"

"Walk around outside for a while. Maybe even sleep there. I hadn't realized how much I was going to miss the sky."

"You get used to it. How would you feel about rejoining the *Polaris*? Full crew status."

It took a few seconds for Alison to find the right words. "I didn't think that was an option open to me. I thought Nelson had pretty well decided that I wouldn't fit."

Carson laughed. "Nelly's a gruff old bear sometimes, but he's a good man and a good judge of character. In fact, he's the one who suggested we offer you a full contract. So what do you say?'

"I think I'd be happy here, yes."

And she was right.

Actual Mode

Conrad reshaped his body until he was satisfied with its appearance, then draped it with stylish clothing. He was determined to make a good impression this time, perhaps even convince Janice to transfer to his node.

They had met by accident, sheltering from a datastorm while he was temporarily resident in Node 1724, waiting for repairs to the storage media at home. They had exchanged information while in standby mode, and he had been sufficiently intrigued with Janice's quick wit and active curiosity to ask for her memory address and permission to access it at some future time. Although she had hesitated, it had only been for a microsecond, and Conrad was convinced that their personalities were complementary.

Satisfied with his appearance, Conrad entered Internodal Transit and waited in a dataqueue for transmission to Node 1724. The delay was unusually long, almost two full milliseconds, long enough for Conrad to fluctuate from excitement to uncertainty and back to enthusiasm. He was still young, but approaching the age when he thought he should be looking for someone to co-write a progeny program with him, and Janice was the first person he'd met whose operating code seemed unlikely to clash with his own.

Just outside her memory address, he ran his identity code, and a microsecond later found himself in a lush, tropical jungle. There was no sign of Janice at first, but only because it took a few seconds for him to recognize the leopard lying draped across a mossy branch.

"Janice? I love your outfit."

"Thanks." The leopard stirred, jumped lightly down to the grass. "I've been working on it off and on for almost a minute. The background still needs some work, though, and I need to add a soundtrack. I get bored with commercial backdrop packages; they're all pretty shallow, if you know what I mean."

"Yeah, bright colors and simple forms. Internally inconsistent a lot of the time too. Sloppy programming."

109

They had made no specific plans other than to share processing time together, but the direction of the conversation gave Conrad an idea. Strictly speaking, he wasn't supposed to replicate information about his job, but since his employers were working with community equipment, there was no way they could legally restrain him from doing so.

"I'd like to input you something."

Janice sat back on her haunches, the tip of her tail whisking back and forth. "All right."

"But not here. We'll have to transfer to Interfacing."

The frown was obvious even on the leopard face. "Interfacing? Isn't that dangerous?"

"No, of course not. But it's very memory intensive. You might want to change outfits before we go." External links in Interfacing ate up a lot of RAM. "The hardware is a little archaic but it's quite reliable." Janice winced visibly when he used the expletive, "hardware", but it was in such common use among his co-workers that Conrad never thought to substitute one of the more acceptable euphemisms.

A microsecond or two later, Janice was wearing a quite attractive body, human female, khaki shirt and slacks. Conrad imagined himself virtually married to her and found the concept more than slightly appealing.

They reached Interfacing without undue delay, exchanging insignificant data along the way. Conrad was preoccupied with the idea of writing nested for-while loops to fit within Janice's progeny program. From what he'd learned of her personal style, he felt they might be suited to create a self aware intelligence capable of refining its own programming, although always within the framework of general principles inherent in the codes of its parents.

"So what did you want to show me?" Janice was clearly uneasy functioning in this perceptibly slower milieu, moving from location to location with exaggerated caution.

"It's right over here." Conrad led her to External Porting and helped her displace expendable data at Port 23328. "The transition will be automatic when I run the program, so don't process about it. Just let it happen."

He moved quickly to Port 23329 and thought the subroutine for the transfer program.

Conrad rose from the overstuffed chair, felt the rush of sensation as circulation stirred in arms and legs. Just out of reach, a young woman sat in an identical chair, only her head moving as she examined her environment. When she glanced down at her own body, she frowned, pursed her lips, then frowned more deeply.

"What's wrong?"

"Nothing's wrong. Isn't it great?"

Janice sat forward, then grimaced as tingling pain ran through her body. "An override program? What are you, a datacop?"

Conrad laughed and shook his head. "No, of course not. And I'm not overriding you."

"Then why can't I change?" She slapped her thighs with the palms of her hands. "This is ugly and clumsy and the programming is so crude I can actually detect internal halts and conflicts."

"It's called pain. Don't worry, it'll pass quickly."

Conrad began to walk around the room, explaining to his companion that they were temporarily resident in hardware external to their normal environment. "There are rigid laws here. The operating code is inaccessible, hardwired right into the system."

"You mean, we can't rewrite it? That sounds dangerous."

"Not really. We're still in flash memory. If anything happens to us here, we're intact back home. All we'd lose would be data accumulated during the transfer."

"But we're stuck in these bodies?"

"That's right. Think of it as a game. Once you know the ground rules, it's quite challenging."

"I always cheat in games."

"No cheating here."

"What is this place anyway?" It was becoming clear to Conrad that he'd made a mistake; Janice was irritated and more than slightly nervous.

"We call it 'Actual Reality'. The people I work for are developing it as an entertainment vehicle. We think it has a lot of potential."

"Not unless you fix some of the problems. I mean, it's not very real, is it? Everything stuck in a single state."

"But that's what makes it so fascinating," he protested. "It's like the real world, but more focused. And it's educational too. You have to figure out how to solve problems by working within a set of rules instead of just rewriting the environmental code."

Janice was silent for a moment, calmer when she spoke again. "You might have something there. I mean, you'd have to spruce things up a little. You know, offer a better choice than these." She glanced meaningfully down at her own body and then across at his. "The backdrop could use some work too. A few mandelbrots on the delimiters… "

"Walls," he interrupted. "They're call walls."

"Whatever. Anyway, with some work, this could be made to seem just like the real world, in an artificial sort of way, of course." She craned her head in search of fresh input. "Yes, this might even be fun."

❖

Scrimshaw

One of the universe's wry jokes is that we missed meeting our first non-human intelligent race by less than two hundred years. A couple of centuries in the cosmic scale of things isn't even an eyeblink, but that's what happened. A routine survey of Osseus picked up anomalies that triggered a follow up and now there are a couple of thousand scientists and support personnel going through the ruins, those we can find. The rogue body that shattered the planet's single, oversized moon rained debris that must have obliterated most of their buildings, as well as the population, and the prolonged devastating nuclear winter that followed would have accounted for any survivors. Even now that the star, Trochanter, has thawed the oceans and the atmosphere, there is only the faintest stirring of life, a few hardy plants re-establishing themselves and enough insect forms to service them.

The sign on my office door reads Robert Beadle, Scheduling Administrator. When I was interviewed, I was told that given my technical background I would be ideally suited for the responsibility of assigning researchers to various projects, allocating resources, and setting priorities. I would report directly to the Assistant Project Manager. In practice, I report to about three dozen section chiefs, each of whom sets his own priorities and assigns personnel. Then they tell me what other resources they need and I attempt to satisfy them. I've met the Assistant Project Manager twice, both times at social events.

The Osseans, known colloquially as the Roly-Polies or just Rolies, would have presented a unique problem even had they perished under less apocalyptic circumstances. What little we knew about them was that they were probably vestigial amphibians, that they were relatively few in number and built no cities as we understand the term, spreading their population more or

113

less evenly across the single small continent. Although we are sure they must have visited the outlying islands, we have as yet found no evidence that they occupied any of these, and none of their ocean going vessels—if they had any—have been found, intact or otherwise. They probably lived much longer than we do, and reproduced relatively infrequently.

Their familiar name is related to their shape. The Rolies were essentially spherical with an internal carapace covered by a thin layer of muscle and nerve tissue. Their limbs, four feet and two arms, could be withdrawn almost completely inside cavities in the shell, as could the blunt head. Our reconstruction of their physical form, based on less than a dozen skeletons, suggests they would have looked to us like upright, bloated turtles.

Yes, I said less than a dozen skeletons. That's one of the mysteries we were facing. An analysis of the pattern of the charted ruins suggested that their population was close to one million at the time of the disaster, but we were unable to find any significant number of remains. Even their cemeteries were empty. I should explain that but I probably should tell you something about Mariel Wu first.

I first met Mariel when we shared a class on Introductory Ethnography at the University of Camelot on Pendragon. Despite her family name, the only hint of her Chinese ancestry was a suggestion around the eyes. She was thinner than was fashionable at the time, her clothing was out of date, and she avoided social functions as a matter of policy. She was also one of the most brilliant people I'd ever met and I was thoroughly infatuated for almost two months. That's how long it took Mariel to notice that I was following her everywhere. She disabused me of my delusion so gently that it hardly hurt at all and we became close friends until she graduated, and corresponded irregularly thereafter.

There was a single incident from our college days that seemed out of character at the time, but which I later came to understand. Mariel was an orphan. She'd been away from home on a field trip with her crèche mates when the Great Coretap Disaster obliterated the city of Parsifal. Her parents were among the tens of thousands whose bodies were never recovered and she'd been raised as a ward of the government until she was old enough for emancipation. There was also a surviving sibling, her older brother Jared, who had been serving with a garrison on Eblis at the time. He disappeared a year later during the Coffer Rebellion.

Shortly after I met her, she was nearly expelled for vandalism—graffiti on the rear wall of the microfiche repository. It wasn't anything obscene. "Ontogeny recapitulates phylogeny" or something similar if I remember correctly. She performed community service and paid to have it removed. I didn't learn until years later that she had a history of similar incidents extending back to the death of her brother. I asked her about it once and she had shrugged.

"I just get this urge sometimes to make a statement that's bigger than I am. Something that expresses feelings that have no other outlet. I know it's wrong, I know it's foolish, but I need reassurance that the world is aware of my existence. I feel horribly alone sometimes. Life is so ephemeral."

Mariel never belonged to any church, even though religion was in vogue at the time. "I can't believe in something I can't experience, Bob."

"You're supposed to have faith," I suggested.

"I have faith that the sun will rise tomorrow and that Professor Tanaka will never give me a superlative grade no matter how excellent my work. I learn from experience and observation. Even then, I could be wrong. The sun could go nova and Tanaka might suddenly realize how brilliant I really am. How much more likely is it that we might draw errant conclusions from premises not based on verifiable fact?"

I never could argue with Mariel, especially when I was more than slightly inclined to agree with her.

This leads me back to the Rolies. We're still not sure that they had a religion. We're not sure about a lot of things regarding their civilization. But we knew even early on that they preserved the bodies, or at least the skeletons, of their dead. In each of their scattered communities—at least those which we've been able to examine—there is an ossuary, a building with a single entrance that houses what can only be called sarcophagi. They're the right shape and size to contain a single Roly, mostly adults but an occasional child. In every single instance, the sarcophagi are empty, even in ossuaries that survived relatively intact. Since some of these were buried during the disaster and excavated only after we arrived, we're certain that the remains were removed before the cataclysm, but we have no idea why or where the bones were taken. The few skeletons we have found were scattered about in various places suggesting solitary deaths that precluded recovery.

I say bones because we had some evidence—including what appears to be an engineer's sketch—of an occupied sarcophagus. It seems quite clear that they made no effort to preserve the flesh even though their technology was high enough to support various methods of preservation. The Rolies did have relatively advanced scientific knowledge, although they were not a particularly technological civilization. They understood how the universe worked, generated electric power, performed sophisticated medical procedures, and even had what we think were primitive computers. They did not have powered transportation systems more advanced than outboard motors on their fishing boats, a banking system, highway congestion, or advertising.

We're also pretty certain they didn't have a written language.

I know how that must sound. When I arrived on Osseus, I underwent a series of briefings so that I wouldn't make a fool of myself through simple ignorance. I knew that Mariel was working there but I was still surprised when she showed up to conduct one of the sessions. I shouldn't have been. She'd known I was coming and had volunteered. Since she had an extensive background in linguistics, among her other areas of expertise, she'd been put in charge of a team that was attempting to determine how the Rolies had stored and transferred knowledge.

"It can't all have been by word of mouth," I protested after hearing that they had left no books, audio or video recordings. "They weren't primitives."

Mariel had smiled at me. "In some ways they might even have been superior to us. No written language means no paperwork means no bureaucrats."

"But how did they pass on technical knowledge from one generation to the next?" To say nothing of history, philosophy, or political theory.

"As far as we can tell, it was all passed directly from one individual to the next. They did live a very long time you know. But there is no indication that they had a written language—not even street signs or labels on their machinery. Except for one thing."

The one thing was the scrimshaw.

—————

Osseus was not the first place our paths had crossed after graduation. We had both been on the faculty at Excalibur College for a few terms, and this time I was the one who had first moved on. Mariel seemed to have changed, and for the better, since I'd last seen her. She was engaged to be married, took reasonable pains with her appearance, even seemed to enjoy herself at faculty social events. I hadn't cared for her fiancé, a biologist named Carruthers, who struck me as stuffy, self important, and superficial. My appraisal might have been colored by protectiveness for my friend, but my conclusions were subsequently justified.

Carruthers came from an established family and was their only son and heir. He was expected to produce sons in turn to carry the name onward into infinity. Mariel had done some research offworld a year earlier and had succumbed to one of those rare viruses that can survive in an alien environment, in this case Mariel's body. It hadn't seemed particularly virulent and she'd been successfully treated and declared fit to return to Pendragon. It was only after her annual physical that she discovered that the infection had rendered her sterile.

Carruthers was ever so regretful but the responsibilities of his family and the need to ensure a smooth continuation of his genetic line and so forth and so on and the marriage was off.

Mariel was devastated, not so much by the loss of Carruthers as far as I could see but by the discovery that she could never have children. She had never struck me as the maternal type, and it might well be that she would have remained indifferent to motherhood indefinitely so long as the potential remained. Now that had been taken from her and the enormity of the loss was almost more than she could bear.

"When I'm gone, I'll be completely gone, Bob. There will be nothing of me left to go forward."

I'd never been very good at comforting people, but I tried. "You're going to be with us for a long time to come, Mariel. Just let the future take care of itself."

The following day she resigned from the faculty.

I had not yet seen any of the actual bones that had been recovered on Osseus, but I'd examined holograms and flat photos. The bones were decorated with neatly inscribed glyphs that covered anywhere from a quarter to nearly all of the carapace. The Rolies had not made use of the other bones for illustrative purposes, at least not on the subjects we'd recovered, although they did use a wide variety of skeletal remains from other animals in their environment, now all as extinct as the Rolies themselves. I vaguely knew that these glyphs were not considered to be a written language, other than possibly some form of pictogram, but hadn't become conversant with the details.

Mariel filled me in.

"The main reason we don't believe this is writing as we know it is because there are no repeated symbols. Let me qualify that. You can find some symbols on more than carapace, but you won't find any of them twice on the same individual. Not ever. Wait, there's another qualification. On some of the bones from lesser animals, there are repeated symbols, but we're pretty sure that these were used as a kind of rough draft or learning exercise. On one femur from a troglodon, we found the same symbol incised numerous times, with subtle differences in angle and depth. Our working theory is that someone was using it to practice and hone his or her skills." The Rolies had two sexes, not entirely analogous to human ones, but close enough. "Make mistakes on the lower animals because they don't matter. You can always find another dead trog. But on the carapaces they had to be right the first time."

"So there must have been some kind of elaborate ceremony to prepare the bones for placement in the sarcophagi. Sounds right. "

"So you'd think." Mariel sat back and shook her head. "But there's a flaw. Remember that the only Roly skeletons we have were those who presumably died alone and out of touch and were never recovered."

I nodded, and the light came on. "So who made the inscriptions on their bones later? And why not gather them with the others, wherever they are?"

"Why indeed?"

⊱──⋅◈⋅──⊰

I didn't see Mariel for three years after Carruthers walked out on her, although we did correspond sporadically. Then she livecommed to tell me that she was getting married and that I had to come to the bonding ceremony. So I did.

Bud Cresswell was not the kind of man I would have expected Mariel to find appealing. He was moderately handsome, well spoken, and certainly doted on her. But he was not an academic. Bud was a civil engineer who spent much of his spare time hunting and fishing. I expected not to like him, but to my surprise I enjoyed his company and decided that with her usual gift for seeing the essence of things despite their misleading exteriors, Mariel had chosen well this time.

Their marriage was by all accounts unusually rewarding for both of them. It was also rather short. Bud was traveling to Lindisfarne to attend a conference when the *Dasher* disappeared with its ten crew and forty passengers, never to be seen again. Displacement drives very rarely fail, but there's no such thing as a minor malfunction.

When I heard the news, I took a few days leave to visit and found Mariel in a state of despondency so severe that I invoked the Samaritan law and requested intervention. She wasn't happy with me at the time and I thought I might have lost a good friend, but a few months later she picked up our acquaintance as though nothing had happened. She never mentioned Bud again.

⊱──⋅◈⋅──⊰

"There's another slight exception to the rule," she told me. "Not only do characters repeat on different carapaces, but sometimes strings of them are exactly duplicated. Our sample is too small to be definitive but modeling suggests that this isn't a random event. So we're pretty sure that the characters do represent something."

"Could they be a weird kind of recording device? Could the Rolies have set down their collective knowledge on the skeletons of their dead for preservation? If that's the case, maybe they moved all the skeletons to a safe place so that they'd survive."

She'd nodded. "Yes, and no. Yes, we think that's why they're missing, and we're conducting some sophisticated tests to try to find buried caverns or structures. But no, we still don't think this is any kind of script. How could you write a technical journal without repeating words? How could you write anything for that matter?"

"But it was important to the Rolies that this information, or whatever it is, survive."

"Yes, if we're right about what happened to the skeletons. But remember I told you that some strings of symbols are repeated?"

I nodded.

"Well, each repeated string is replicated in almost the same location in every instance. If the sequence whirl/box/squiggly thing appears next to the left upper limb muscle anchor on one individual, then it's pretty close to the same place on the next. And some of the symbols appear on almost all of our samples, though not necessarily in strings. We don't have a large enough sample to draw any definitive conclusions."

"Which tells us what?"

Mariel shook her head. "I haven't the faintest idea."

At the next general conference, one of the technology research teams from the other end of the continent gave us something new to think about. Dr. Rani Koublai summarized the findings of her group, which suggested that the Rolies had an even more sophisticated understanding of astronomy and cosmology than had been previously assumed. It all seemed pretty bland to me, until Koublai delivered her surprise. We had assumed that the Rolies had had a good idea what was going to happen to them for at least a year before the actual event. The rogue body's presence in the sky would have been visible to the naked eye. But the latest research had led to a startling conclusion. "Based on the physical evidence including our examination of the primitive telescopy available to the Osseans and our best guesses about their ability to interpret the data, it seems evident that they were aware of the impending cataclysm for at least two hundred local years."

After a wave of murmuring died away, someone asked if this might have been the trigger event that caused the Rolies to begin inscribing whatever it was that they were recording on the bones of their dead. It was Mariel who rose to respond. "We have a single partially fossilized fragment that is minimally several hundred years old. The pictograms are clearly visible. This aspect of their behavior was presumably already entrenched two centuries ago."

><+-•-0-•-+<

A few days after the conference, Mariel told me that she was dying. It was the same alien virus that had made her infertile, having lain inactive and undetected for years. "The doctors say it took its time spreading through my body, but now it's everywhere. They can't transplant all my organs, even my skin. And it's in my brain as well." Her voice was matter of fact, but her eyes were bright with fear.

I was devastated, more visibly upset than she, although Mariel had had more time to adjust to the situation. It was then that I realized why I had never married, even though I'd been perilously close on more than one occasion. Mariel was the only one I had ever loved, and now I was going to lose her. She ended up comforting me.

"I have few regrets," she told me later. "I've led a creditable if not exemplary life. I just wish that I'd been able to have children, to leave something behind that would be proof that I'd been here."

The next morning they found the Cave.

Even now, years later, it's still just the Cave. Various names were tried over the years, but none of them stuck. Most of it is a natural formation, and it was almost overlooked because from air or orbit it seemed too small to be of interest. But the Rolies had excavated below it, dozens of levels, each individually reinforced and buttressed. A direct hit from one of the larger fragments of the moon would have destroyed it, of course, but they'd chosen the site with care. It was a vast underground warren, dwarfing even the largest human equivalent.

They had built new sarcophagi here, designed to fit snugly and maximize the use of space. They would also have helped support one another if there'd been a partial collapse of the walls or ceilings. Each sarcophagi contained the complete skeleton of a Roly, and each carapace was inscribed with row after row of tiny pictograms. There were a small but significant number that contained traces of decayed organic matter as well, and the logical assumption was that the last generation of the Rolies waited for the end sitting in their own coffins, so to speak. And there they'd died.

These carapaces were also inscribed with row after row of pictograms. The inescapable conclusion is that the carvings had been made while these individuals, at least, were still alive.

A number of researchers were moving toward the same conclusion, but Mariel was the first to codify things and provide the conclusive statistical evidence. She conferred with the exobiologists whose findings supported her theory.

"Remember I told you the Rolies were thin skinned," she said to me over supper one evening.

"Sure. I seem to recall making a bad joke about not calling them names."

"All your jokes are bad, Bob. You have a terrible sense of humor. It needed to be said, and that's what friends are for. Anyway, what we think happened is that once a Roly reached a certain developmental stage, probably when its carapace was through expanding, they began inscribing the glyphs by cutting through the skin, etching the bone, then letting the flesh heal over it. They could only do one or two symbols at a time and at intervals, of course, but they lived a very long time and there was no hurry."

I squirmed in my seat. "Sounds like a painful way to decorate your body. And why, if no one is ever going to see it?"

"Because it wasn't decoration. It was a recording of who they were, to be passed on to generations to come, so that an individual's life story would be preserved forever, more or less, or at least as long as his bones. In a way, it was their name."

"Then it was a written language."

She shook her head. "No, except in the broadest sense. Once I realized what I was looking for, I was able to tweak the analysis programs. Each pictogram probably represents an act or accomplishment, or perhaps a failure to accomplish something. One might mean taking a first step, or visiting an island, or becoming a parent, or eating a fish. We don't know what things they would have considered significant enough to immortalize. We can assume that each symbol meant the same thing everywhere, but not everyone had the same experiences, so theoretically at least every single carapace bears the unique record of a unique life."

"Wouldn't it be easier to invent pens and paper and writing?"

"Possibly, but there was another factor that we didn't notice, or we did notice actually, but without realizing its significance. Just as with human civilizations, settlements tend to spring up along the coasts and waterways. For us the water provided a source of food and transportation. For the Rolies, it may have had a more significant function. Remember, they evolved from amphibians. We think now that they spent a good deal of their time in the water. Paper wouldn't survive too well in that environment."

"I suppose the next job is to decipher the meaning."

Mariel shook her head. "Nope. Afraid not. It's not likely we'll ever know what the symbols meant, barring the discovery of some kind of Rosetta Stone, and if there was one of those, we'd have expected to find it in the Cave. Apparently the Rolies didn't care if no one ever read the records of their lives."

"But then why write it down?"

"Because it proves that they existed, that they had meaningful lives, even if no one will ever know the nature of that meaning."

It seemed pointless to me, but I sensed that Mariel felt otherwise.

><+-0-+-<

Mariel finally got a kind of immortality. She's credited with being the primary author of the Ossean Scrimshaw Theory and there's a Mariel Wu Museum of Xeno-Ethnography on Camelot. Mariel attended the opening in her power chair, having outlived her doctors' expectations by several years. She died four days later.

I was not as crushed by her loss as I had expected to be. She led a creditable life with moments of great joy and great sorrow, and she achieved a limited form of greatness before she died. She will always be alive in my memory. During our last conversation, I realized that she had come to terms with the inevitability of her own mortality, and when her last testament was made public, I was convinced that she had no longer worried that she would leave nothing behind that would endure.

She had stipulated that her body be cremated and the ashes scattered on Osseus.

Remotely Possible

Bobbin considered whether he should pretend not to notice Professor Petterslee waving to him from across the street. The elderly man frequently employed Bobbin and his fellow orphans to run errands for him, but his memory was so uncertain that he would sometimes forget to pay for their services. Indeed, he might easily forget the nature of the errand entirely. On the other hand, if he was in the right mood and if one was clever enough, it was also possible to get paid twice for the same endeavor.

Since on this fine summer day in 1870 Bobbin had only two pennies in his pocket and not much in his stomach either, he decided it was worth investing some of his time. There was, after all, no better prospect available. He had found a dead man in an alley early that morning, but if he'd had any possessions worth appropriating, they'd already been scavenged by others.

"Good day to you, Professor," he called diplomatically as he avoided a horse and buggy and crossed to join him, carefully stepping between the piles of fresh dung left by the early morning traffic. Although Bobbin usually went barefoot—his soles hardened to the toughness of leather—the summer heat baked the road surface until it was painful to touch with unprotected flesh. He made do now with makeshift sandals tied in place with heavy string he'd scavenged from behind Nelson's Depot. He had once stolen a pair of serviceable boots off a drunk who'd passed out in the park, but it had proven more advantageous to sell them than to replace his makeshift footwear.

As usual, the professor's attire was a chaotic combination of colors and styles. His boots didn't match, he wore a scarf despite the warmth of the summer in New York City, and his unkempt hair was inadequately gathered together in a ponytail topped by a straw hat.

"Walter, my boy, I have a mission for you."

123

"It's Bobbin, sir." He knew correcting him was a waste of time. Once the professor had an idea firmly placed in his head, it could rarely be dislodged.

"Well come along then. Don't dawdle."

Petterslee turned and marched off without looking to see if his instructions were being followed. Bobbin shrugged to himself and trailed behind, amused as much as hopeful. He knew the way to the professor's lodgings, or rather the tumbledown warehouse where the peculiar gentleman ate and slept and worked, and assumed that he was meant to carry another enigmatic package to some customer elsewhere in the city. That probability lifted his spirits because the recipient would almost certainly provide at least a small tip for the service, in addition to whatever the professor offered.

They reached their destination without incident and the professor fumbled in his pockets for his keys before trying the door and discovering that, as usual, he had not bothered to lock it. Bobbin hesitated on the doorstep. He had always received his instructions at the threshold and although he'd had tantalizing glimpses of the interior, there had never been an opportunity to actually enter. This time Petterslee seemed to assume that he would follow, or perhaps he had forgotten that Bobbin was there, but the door was open and the boy slipped inside.

His first impression was that he had stepped into a rubbish heap. There was such a mass of enigmatic machinery piled against the walls and in rows on the floor that even his narrow twelve year old shoulders brushed both sides as he advanced. Various arcane objects dangled from the ceiling, suspended on wires, most of them apparently models fashioned of wire and string and other less recognizable raw materials. The walls, where they could be seen at all, were covered with diagrams, mathematical equations, and drawings that seemed to be depictions of various sorts of infernal device, none of which had any discernible purpose although one bore wings and might have been meant to fly.

The professor was nowhere in sight and Bobbin had to search for a moment or two before he found him sitting at a desk, or what was supposed to be a desk. It was so covered with gears and springs and coils and wires and odd shaped metal components and other debris that its original function had been completely superseded. Petterslee looked up when Bobbin appeared.

"Ah, there you are William. I thought I'd lost you somewhere along the way."

"It's Bobbin, sir," he answered automatically and without hope.

"I need you to deliver a package for me." The older man looked around anxiously. "As soon as I recall what I did with it. You haven't seen it, have you?"

"What does it look like, sir?"

Petterslee used both hands to suggest a size perhaps a foot square. "It was like this, and wrapped in butcher's paper with some dirty string. I know it was here earlier, but I must have moved it. Help me look for it, there's a good boy."

Bobbin did as he was bid, although without any real hope. The search was rewarding in itself, after a fashion. There were so many strange things to see, most of them completely outside his experience. He stopped in front of an upright metal cabinet the size of a heavy man. At eye level, there was a small door which, when opened, revealed a small but empty chamber.

"What is this contraption, professor?" He looked around for other compartments, but the sections above and below were bolted shut.

Petterslee looked up, blinked and frowned. "Oh, that. One of my failures, Arthur, I'm afraid."

"What's it supposed to be?"

The professor walked over to stand beside him, his industrious search now temporarily forgotten. "It's supposed to be exactly what is, my boy. It's an Exciter."

Bobbin frowned. "Doesn't look very exciting to me."

Petterslee chuckled. "That's only because you're not a slice of mutton or a pork chop. You see, one places whatever food one desires to cook into the preparation chamber." He tapped the rim of the open compartment with his forefinger. "One then sets the controls on the back and the excitation elements above and below speed up the elemental particles of the subject matter until they have been adequately prepared for consumption."

Bobbin frequently made deliveries for Thomas, a baker. "Sort of like an oven, is it then?"

Petterslee frowned. "Yes, I suppose it is after a fashion. But far superior."

"Kind of small though."

The professor looked uncomfortable. "Well, yes, that was one of the criticisms I received. I offered it to Mrs. Wells but she insisted that she had no room for such a contrivance in her kitchen. Then I tried Mrs. Vernon, but the dear woman told me that she enjoys cooking for its own sake and that anything which shortened the process dramatically would find no favor with her. And finally I tried Mrs. West at the boarding house and she pointed out that the limits of its capacity meant that the first serving would be cold by the time the last was prepared and that she had no intention of feeding her boarders in shifts."

"Couldn't you have made a bigger one?"

Petterslee scratched his head. "Yes, certainly. But you see, everything would have to be proportionately larger. I could hardly ask her to install a device larger than a coach and four, now could I?"

They resumed their search and a few minutes later Bobbin spotted a parcel that answered the professor's description sitting on the seat of what appeared to be a very bizarre carriage parked near the great sliding doors at the opposite end of the building. "Professor! I think I've found it!"

Petterslee joined him presently, snatched up the package and shook it. "Yes, the very thing. Remind me to reward you for your efficiency, Thomas."

"Bobbin." He walked around the carriage. "Is this one of your inventions, professor?"

"What! Yes, of course. Another failure, I'm afraid. It's a horseless carriage, you see."

Bobbin raised his eyebrows. "What pulls it then?" He had heard of sleds pulled by dogs, though he wasn't sure if he really believed such a thing, but the carriage was heavily constructed with narrow, metal rimmed wheels. A team of horses might perhaps manage it on a firm surface, but certainly not through mud or loose soil.

"It pulls itself, or rather, it carries the means of its own propulsion."

Bobbin's face remained blank and Petterslee shook his head. "Do you see that very large mechanism mounted on the rear?"

Bobbin nodded. It was directly below a sturdy luggage carrier and appeared to consist mainly of a large block of metal. Wires and coils and other mysterious features covered its surface.

"One fills this chamber with lamp oil." The man gestured so quickly that Bobbin had no idea which part of the bulky contrivance he intended to identify. "The underside is fitted with receptacles into which one must place freshly charged batteries. A small amount of the lamp oil is admitted to a chamber and ignited by a spark generated by the batteries. The oil explodes, forcing the mechanism to move forward."

Bobbin frowned. "What use is it, sir, if you don't mind my asking, if it explodes when you try to use it?"

"It's a very small explosion," said the professor testily. "Actually a series of small, controlled events which propel the whole mechanism forward at about the same rate that a horse might trot, at least under ideal conditions."

"Then why not use a horse, sir?"

Petterslee sighed. "A horse must be fed and watered, and might take sick. An automatic device should be more reliable."

"And is it, sir? More reliable, I mean."

Petterslee scratched his head. "That's a complicated question, young man. You see, I was never able to test it adequately. When I tried to use it within the city limits, the accompanying noise—which I confess might be alarming to anyone not expecting it—frightened any horses nearby. I was compelled to have it transported to the countryside instead."

"And did it work there?"

"Well, no. It malfunctioned almost immediately. But it was not the fault of the device. The roads there are in such shoddy condition, ruts, potholes, large stones. The mechanism was jostled so badly that the firing chambers were soon out of alignment. I had to employ a team of horses to drag it back here. Most unsatisfactory." He sighed. "But come now, Frederick, we must not waste time."

Petterslee searched his pockets, then drew forth a ragged piece of paper which he presented to Bobbin as though awarding him a certificate of merit. "Take this package to the address shown there and give it to a Mr. Dutch."

"What is it?" The package was much heavier than he had expected and he almost dropped it.

"Be careful. I don't have another and I promised to deliver it today. It's my newest invention, a wireless telegraph."

Bobbin had only the vaguest idea of what a telegraph was so he gleaned nothing from the description. Instead he glanced at the paper. "I'm sorry, Professor, but I can't read this."

The man snatched it back, held it close to his bespectacled eyes. "I can't see why not, Lawrence. It's written quite legibly. Don't they teach you anything in school?"

Torn between embarrassment and defiance, Bobbin answered testily. "I never had a chance to go to school, Professor." And no inclination in that direction even if the opportunity had afforded itself.

Petterslee shook his head. "I don't understand you young people. All right, I'll read it to you." And he did. Bobbin knew the street, could almost remember the house. It was thirty blocks south, give or take. "So what are you waiting for? Go!"

Bobbin remained where he was. "There's the question of payment, sir."

"Payment? Oh, Mr. Dutch will reward you. If I paid you now, there'd be nothing encouraging you to complete your assigned task, now would there? Off with you then."

Bobbin was of half a mind to drop the whole matter—the package was quite heavy and it was a long walk in the heat—but at last he turned and set off toward the south.

His journey was uneventful except for a brief encounter with an angry dog that charged at him threateningly until he pelted the animal with dried dung and loose cobblestones, driving it off. The address he'd been given was in a disreputable area, once respectable houses fallen into bad company, so no one questioned his right to be there. He strode directly to the proper door and rapped on it with his free hand.

The door opened so quickly that he was startled. A very tall man stood there, glaring down with furious eyes. "What do you want, boy?" But before Bobbin could answer, the man's eyes spotted the package. "So? The old fool came through after all. Give it to me." He snatched the package with such violence that Bobbin felt the friction of its passage across his fingertips. Then the door slammed shut so hard that he staggered back a step.

Bobbin raised his hand to knock again and remind the man—Mr. Dutch?—that he was supposed to be paid for his services, but he paused, feeling disinclined to face that barely suppressed fury again. On the other hand, he had invested considerable time and effort and was not prepared to simply walk off unrewarded. If Mr. Dutch was not a fair enough man to pay for services rendered, then it was entirely proper for the one providing the service to secure compensation through less conventional means. Bobbin phrased this rather more bluntly in his thoughts but the meaning was the same.

This wasn't a row house, although the space between it and the one adjacent was barely wide enough to be called a passageway. It was filled with litter, broken boards, discarded furnishings, a rotting set of harnesses, and other debris, liberally sprinkled with rat droppings, but Bobbin wasn't fastidious. He made his way around and over the obstructions and examined the side and rear of the house. It was hot. Certainly there would be at least one window open. In fact there were four but two were not readily accessible, leaving one possibility on the ground floor and one directly above it. There was a shed snug against the rear wall, probably meant to hold a horse at some point though it was now half caved in. Bobbin decided to ignore the easier entry point on the ground floor, which might well lead to a room occupied by the daunting Mr. Dutch, and set about scaling the side of the shed, carefully making as little noise as possible. Within seconds he was peering into a second floor bedroom.

The room was plainly furnished and unoccupied. From outside, Bobbin could see nothing that suited his purpose. Some loose change would be nice, or perhaps a shaving kit in good condition, or something similar that he could sell to Josiah Catterall, who asked no questions about the provenance of items offered to him. Bobbin could hear no voices or movement, so he removed his sandals to facilitate clandestine movement and slipped inside the window.

A quick exploration proved fruitless. There was nothing portable in the room that he could carry off and sell, although he did find a single penny lying on the floor. Cautiously he moved to the door and glanced out into the hallway. Most of the windows were curtained, shabbily, and there wasn't much light. He could see two closed doors and the top of a staircase leading down to the first floor. There was a three-legged stool in the hall, covered with dust.

He was halfway to the closest of the doors when there was a thunderous rapping from below and he froze. Footsteps strode to the front door and threw it open. "There you are, man! I thought you'd failed me."

"No fear of that, Dutch. You haven't paid me yet."

The man came inside and the door closed. Bobbin considered retreating to the window, but he was afraid to move lest he tread on a loose board and betray his presence. The two men would certainly leave the hall in a moment and he'd wait till then. But for the time being they seemed happy to remain where they were. Curiosity got the better of Bobbin and he leaned forward so that he could peer down at them.

The newcomer had spoken with a Southern accent. He was a shorter man than Dutch, but broader in the shoulders and with a full, bushy beard. They stood facing each other in the small vestibule, crowded somewhat by a stack of three good sized wicker baskets that leaned against one wall.

"Did you bring the carriage?" asked Dutch.

"It's right outside. I brought Billy along to watch it, but we'll let him off before we reach the park."

Dutch grunted in agreement. "It's best we keep this between the two of us."

"What about the old codger?"

"Petterslee?" Dutch sounded amused. "He thinks I'm going to set up a telegraph office in Atlanta. Even if he hears about the assassination afterward, he'll never make the connection to his invention."

The other man fingered his beard. "And just how does this contraption of his help us?"

"Look, you've been to the site, haven't you?"

"Yup. They were still hammering away on the platform but it looked just like you said it would."

"Then you noticed that there are three possible routes their party could take?"

The newcomer nodded. "But I don't see how the two of us can be in three different places at the same time."

Dutch sounded frustrated. "We don't need to be. We simply place one of these somewhere along each of the trails out of the park and then follow the official party when they leave. There's enough explosive in each of them to do the job." From his hiding place, Bobbin saw the other man take an involuntary step away from the baskets. "Don't worry. They're safe enough. But when our man comes close to any one of them, we send the signal from Petterslee's master device and it will detonate."

The beard scratching became more agitated. "Probably going to kill a lot of other people as well."

"Can't be helped. Are you developing a conscience all of a sudden, Rossiter?"

"No, sir."

Dutch moved restlessly. "We don't have much time. Help me load these into the carriage." He turned and used both arms to carefully lift the topmost of the wicker baskets.

Bobbin didn't see anything further. He drew his head back, thought furiously for a few seconds, then moved silently back to the window and outside, where he jumped down from the shed. He paused to put on his sandals but then reconsidered. No, he could make better time if he went barefoot and if he ran the hot stones would not have time to burn his feet. He made his way back to the street and glanced surreptitiously at the front of the house.

An open carriage and four blowzy horses stood in the street. A boy somewhat older than Bobbin was holding the head of one of the team while Dutch and Rossiter were tying the first of the baskets securely to the rear of the carriage. No one was looking his way, so Bobbin turned and began running.

At first he thought about finding a policeman and telling his story, but there was an undeclared war between the street boys and the police, and even the older folks groused about the influence of Tammany Hall and how the men in uniform were not to be trusted. So he found himself running to the only adult he could think of who might be able to help.

Professor Petterslee did not seem to remember him, but his memory stirred a bit when Bobbin caught his breath and mentioned Mr. Dutch and the package he'd delivered. "Oh yes, the wireless telegraph. I assume Mr. Dutch was pleased with it? The first one I built for him was quite unsatisfactory because of its size."

Bobbin recounted what he'd heard, and then repeated himself because Petterslee did not seem to understand. "A bomb, you say? But I didn't make a bomb for anyone."

"No, sir, you didn't. But they're going to use it to set one off. Three actually."

"But why in the world would they want to do such a thing? Mr. Dutch isn't an anarchist, surely?"

"I don't know what he is, Professor, but I think I know who he's trying to kill. It's President Grant, sir." Bobbin knew nothing about politics and cared little more, but he thought of himself as a citizen of the United States. He hadn't been old enough to understand the causes of the Civil War—and truth be told didn't understand much more about the matter even now—but he had been influenced by the swelling pride among the other residents of New York City that had come with the successful conclusion of the war and he had a vague image of President Grant as a Great Man.

"But the President is in Washington, young man."

Bobbin shook his head. "No, sir. He's giving a speech in Central Park later today." Bobbin knew about this, as did all of the street children, because the crowds that were sure to gather would be fertile ground for nimble fingered thieves. "You have to do something. No one would listen to a no account like me."

Petterslee sighed. "I'm afraid, young Roger, that no one pays a great deal of attention to me either. There must be something in my manner that makes people uneasy, perhaps my obvious intelligence."

"Then we'll have to do something ourselves!"

The professor looked quite dismayed at the prospect. "What in the world could we do? I'm a thinker, not a doer. I imagine and create but I don't act. And you, boy, are just, well, an untutored boy."

Bobbin was thinking furiously and an idea occurred to him. "You said you had another of those wire things?"

"The wireless telegraph? Why yes I do, but I don't see how that would help."

"Don't you see? We could make them bombs explode before the President gets anywhere near them."

But Petterslee was shaking his head. "You don't understand, my boy. We would have to be in very close proximity. Perhaps fifty feet. I explained that to Mr. Dutch because I don't see how he can put the device to any practical use without increasing its range." But his eyes widened as he realized Dutch had indeed found a more practical use.

"Where is it then?"

Bobbin's enthusiasm turned to dismay within seconds. The professor's prototype was the same shape as the package he'd delivered to Mr. Dutch, but the resemblance ended there. It was half the size of a desk, mounted on tiny wheels, and Bobbin had to help push it away from the pile of discarded paraphernalia with which it had already become half buried. "We'll never be able to carry this to the park!" he cried in dismay. "Do you have a carriage?"

Petterslee shook his head. "Only the horseless one, and that's no good to us."

Bobbin cocked his head. "Why not? You said it worked fine on good roads. There are good roads from here to the park."

"Good heavens, boy. Do you have any idea how much attention we'd attract? It would frighten every horse at this end of the city."

"Maybe that's just as well. Maybe we can scare off Mr. Dutch's horses along with the rest."

Petterslee looked both dubious and apprehensive, but Bobbin's enthusiasm swept him along. They cleared an area around the horseless carriage and then made a path to the large sliding door that led to the street outside. Bobbin did a rough visual measure of the clear space behind the double seat. "I think it'll fit here just fine, professor."

But getting it mounted was more of a problem and they might have quit in exhaustion if the situation had not been so desperate. At last it was sitting in place, tied down with ropes although it was so heavy that Bobbin doubted it would fall off no matter what the provocation. Their next hurdle was the carriage itself, which rumbled and spit despite fresh fuel and a change of batteries but only for a few seconds. "I haven't cleaned the chambers in months," explained the professor. "I did not expect to ever find another use for it, you see."

But just as Bobbin was about to give in to despair, there was a longer if not exactly regular thrumming and Petterslee chuckled. "That should do it. Open the door, my boy, and we'll shock the neighbors."

They were further delayed while more lamp oil was added. "Sufficient to get us there and back again." Then they set off at slightly more than a walking pace and Bobbin, seated beside the now begoggled Professor Petterslee, was alternately frustrated by their slow pace and terrified by their headlong speed. Nor was it a particularly smooth ride despite the assurances of the professor that the road here was quite adequate. "I must do something to smooth the ride, I suppose. Perhaps if I suspended the undercarriage on a bed of coiled springs, we would sway and bounce with a less disturbing grace."

As expected, they drew a crowd which followed them on their journey. Some were children, some adults. The latter were a mix of the curious and the furious. Several horses shied away, some quite violently, and there was considerable turmoil as two coach and fours collided in the confusion. Petterslee seemed oblivious to the tumult around him and Bobbin tried to imitate him, with limited success. Living on his own and as best he could, Bobbin had discovered that it was better not to be noticed.

Now that he had put his mind to the problem, the Professor was reasonably sure that he knew how the plan would work. "They'll follow the President at a discrete distance, regardless of which route he takes. And when he's close to whatever bomb is appropriate, they'll detonate it, possibly either or both of the others as well depending upon their proximity. And they'll look duly horrified and no one will even question them."

"We have to stop them," insisted Bobbin.

The paved road gave wave to beaten paths at the edge of the park and Petterslee suggested that they halt and reconnoiter on foot. Bobbin agreed and when the professor turned off his device, the sudden silence was almost a sound in itself. The twosome then set off toward the low rise where the speakers' platform had been constructed, and where it was now receiving its final garnishes of banners and placards. The President was to arrive in less than two hours and there were already several clumps of people spread through the surrounding area, many of them having decided to make a day's excursion out of the event.

They saw several carriages, but there was no sign of Mr. Dutch or Rossiter. It would be relatively easy to miss them among the trees or the ranks of carriages drawn up around the grassy verge where the audience was already beginning to gather. Bobbin was starting to feel acute despair when he saw something tucked into a stand of bushes behind a tree.

"Look, Professor! There's one of those exploding baskets!" And he was running toward it before there was time for an answer.

He had just placed his hand on the lid when angry shouting from one side startled him. A red faced man in a tailored suit was striding toward him, waving his arms. "Stop! Thief! Stop that young rascal someone!"

Bobbin's instinct was to bolt, but a greater need overrode his sense of self preservation. He flung open the basket—and saw a neat array of food-stuffs, napkins, and utensils! Confused, realizing belatedly that this was not after all one of Dutch's baskets, he stepped back, still making no effort to flee. And that's when the copper caught him by the arm.

"What do we have here then? A sneaky little trickster by the look of 'im." Bobbin craned his head around and saw the craggy face of Officer Dodd, the nemesis of the street people in the Bowery region, now far away from his home turf to help provide security for the President.

A feeling of hopelessness weakened his knees and his mouth was so dry that he couldn't have spoken even if his mind had suggested something use-ful that he might have said. He was suddenly resigned to defeat, only to have hope restored from an unlikely source.

"I say there, unhand that boy." It was Professor Petterslee, advancing at as quick a pace as he could manage. "That boy is in my employ, Officer Dowd, and following my instructions."

Dodd frowned, perhaps because of the mangling of his name. "The boy was thieving, sir. I have to take him in."

"Nonsense. I've left my basket somewhere hereabouts and could not re-member where, so I offered him a penny to find it for me. It looks quite like that one," he pointed, "but obviously it is not mine." The rescue took a mo-ment more, but at the end Dodd reluctantly released Bobbin's arm, which ached for some time thereafter.

'I don't suppose you've seen an unattended basket lying about, Officer Todd? It's quite important that I retrieve it quickly."

"No, sir, but I'll keep an eye out if you'd like." He didn't sound enthusi-astic.

"I'd appreciate it, and of course I'd reward whoever found it for me."

Dodd seemed to take more interest then and when he left they were on almost cordial terms.

They did finally locate one of the baskets, but only after a lengthy search, and by then there were guards surrounding the platform and it was certain-ly only a matter of minutes before the President arrived. Bobbin wondered briefly why they hadn't placed one of the baskets under the platform itself, but the area was wide open rather than enclosed and it would have been quite visible to anyone who passed by. The basket that they did find was tucked into a culvert near a small bridge.

They pulled it out and Petterslee opened it cautiously, peering at the mechanism that snuggled next to the explosives. "Most ingenious," he said at last. "Mr. Dutch might have made a competent inventor if he'd chosen that profession. Not the most elegant device I've seen, but it would serve its purpose well enough." He reached down and disconnected two wires. "And now it's harmless."

They carried it back to the horseless carriage and slid it under the seats. "Let's ride for a while," suggested the Professor, who was plainly not used to this much physical exertion. Bobbin didn't argue. The grass was soft underfoot, but he'd stepped on a particularly sharp stone and was limping slightly. At some point, he must have dropped his sandals, probably back at the professor's place.

Ten minutes later, they caught sight of Mr. Dutch and the carriage. Rossiter was sitting beside him as they paused on the opposite side of a wide pool of water. Even from that distance Bobbin could see that there were still two wicker baskets in the wagon. Apparently the conspirators had run into unforeseen delays, but they remained intent upon achieving their purpose. Rossiter climbed down and lifted a basket carefully out of the back. Not far away one of the main exit routes from the park was cosseted closely on both sides by dense thickets and obviously they were planning to plant one of the bombs among the foliage.

"They'll be long gone before we can reach them," said the professor, who had peered around trying to find the fastest way around the pond. "But we can seize that infernal device of theirs and leave them with only the one."

"But they'll still have that one, and it took us forever to find them once. We might never do so again." Bobbin's eyes burned with tears of frustration. They were so close, but not close enough.

"The odds don't favor them any longer," said Petterslee. "They still don't know which route the President means to take."

"But they might set off the last bomb anyway, just out of meanness." And as he spoke, Bobbin also realized that even if Mr. Dutch was frustrated today, it would not prevent him from making another attempt, by the same means or some other. If they were determined to kill President Grant, then sooner or later things would fall into place for them. That realization was like a switch clicking over in his mind. His eyes searched the area and he saw no one anywhere near the two conspirators. What he contemplated was terrible in its way, but Bobbin had seen, endured, and even performed some terrible deeds in the past. He took a deep breath.

"How far away would you say they are, Professor?"

Petterslee pursed his lips. "Thirty, forty yards perhaps. Why?" But he realized why even before Bobbin rose and turned around to face the rear. He raised a restraining arm, but not quickly enough.

Bobbin slammed his hand down on the knob which Petterslee had labeled "Send."

The double explosion was not as loud as he had expected, and its lingering echoes were drowned out by shouts and cries and the sound of running feet as people converged on the scene. Part of the carriage lay on its side in the water and there was considerable debris as well as a visibly dissipating pall of smoke. Both horses were down and unmoving and Bobbin regretted that. There was not enough left of Mr. Dutch or Rossiter to be visible from this distance, and he did not regret that.

"Let's go home, professor." He resumed his seat, his face expressionless.

Petterslee looked at the boy's profile for several seconds, or rather at the profile of what had been a boy but would be no longer. Then he nodded to himself and the horseless carriage lurched forward with an earsplitting roar that died to a hacking cough, then described an awkward arc and started toward southern Manhattan.

They were halfway back when Petterslee turned suddenly and shouted to be heard above the increasingly ragged sound of the motor. "I say, boy. I thought this Grant person was supposed to be the greatest of our generals."

"He is that, sir. At least that's what everyone says."

"Then why is he giving speeches rather than conducting the war?"

Bobbin blinked. "Professor, the war has been over for years now."

"Oh!" Petterslee turned to face forward, his brow furrowed in thought. Several seconds passed before he glanced at Bobbin again.

"Who won?"

Duck and Cover

A lot of young men discovered who they really were during the Vietnamese war, whether they were drafted or enlisted, fled to Canada or fled to the National Guard and other exemptions. When I disembarked in Cam Ranh Bay in June of 1969, I thought I had a pretty good understanding of myself and others, but my education was just getting started. And sometimes knowing the truth, or part of it anyway, has its drawbacks. When you stand in a crowd and realize that some of the people around you might not actually be people, it changes everything.

During most of my tour, I was more afraid of my fellow Americans than of the Viet Cong. Four members of my battalion were killed in fights among themselves, while the Vietnamese only managed to slightly wound one tailgunner during those same eleven months. Boredom was one of the main problems; there wasn't much to do in Phu Hiep except sit around and drink or smoke pot. Boredom, booze, and automatic weapons are not a good combination in three digit heat. You could tell who had which vice by walking between rows of hooches—the unfinished rooms in which we slept—after darkness fell and most of us were off duty. The drinkers were loud; the smokers were silent.

I shared my hooch with two other guys, Chapman who wanted to be a marine biologist, and Russell, the chaplain's assistant. We had smokers on our south side so we rarely heard a peep from them after dark, but unfortunately Elmer Colby was just beyond the north wall. Elmer was a hulking thug who'd joined the army to stay out of jail after one too many bar fights back in West Virginia. He was a heavy drinker and a nasty one. No one was willing to share quarters with him and even the officers avoided him.

One night the three of us were sitting around talking. I had broken down my M-16 and was cleaning it—this section of the coastline was all sand and dust and M-16s tended to malfunction if they weren't pristine. Someone was fumbling around on the other side of the north partition. We didn't have walls, just eight foot high barriers separating each hooch from the next. We heard a sudden scratching sound and a moment later were reeling from the latest onslaught of Iron Butterfly played at maximum volume.

I don't have anything against Iron Butterfly. After I got back to the States, and a decent interval had passed, I picked up my own copy of *In-a-Gadda-da-Vida* and I still play it occasionally. But Colby had bought himself a cheap turntable and speakers by mail order and he only owned two albums, the other being *Abbey Road* by the Beatles. I like them even better, but when you hear the same two albums played over and over again, day after day, with the volume turned all the way up, even good music gets old very quickly.

Russell sighed and stood up. "Guess I'll go over to the chapel and catch up on my paperwork."

Chapman was a short-timer, due to go home in another two weeks. Not much bothered him anymore, but he swore under his breath and started for the door. "I'll be back in a while."

I would probably have followed except that I had a disassembled weapon spread all over my bunk. Doggedly, I finished cleaning the components as the album ended. There was a brief moment of blessed silence, then the Beatles began exhorting us to "come together". I winced and began reassembling my weapon.

All might still have been well if Colby hadn't been so thoroughly drunk. I had just locked a magazine into the M-16 and was putting my cleaning supplies away when a half empty can of beer arced up over the partition and came down, with a splash, in the middle of my bunk. Why Colby would throw away a nearly full can of beer was never clear to me. Maybe it was too warm, or had gone flat, or he was just being more ornery than usual. In any case, it was very hot and humid, I had been on guard duty the night before and hadn't slept well, and I snapped. I picked the can up, rotated my body, and tossed it back where it had come.

There was the brittle sound of impact and the music died. With deadly if inadvertent accuracy, I had scored a direct hit on *Abbey Road*, right in the middle of "Maxwell's Silver Hammer." There was sudden, palpable silence from Colby's hooch.

I was, frankly, befuddled. I had acted without thinking, and now my mind refused to consider the potential repercussions. I was still a bit dazed when Colby appeared at the door.

"Kramer, I'm going to rip you a new asshole." No matter how much he drank, Colby never slurred his words, and always seemed calm and unemotional. He could be falling down, semi-conscious, threatening to kill someone, but he would still speak clearly and without heat. And he didn't make idle threats.

My M-16 was lying on the bunk and I picked it up. "Take one step inside that door and I'll shoot you through the kneecap."

I know he heard me because his eyes blinked and his mouth tightened. He raised one foot and placed it deliberately on the threshold. "You ain't got the balls."

I looked into his face and knew I wasn't going to be able to talk myself out of this. What I didn't discover until later was that not only had my return volley broken the record, but the still half full beer can had splashed down inside the turntable and shorted it out. "Try me," I said, hoping that I sounded more sincere than I felt.

Colby stepped through the doorway. Without hesitation, I turned the weapon in his direction and pulled the trigger. The round passed him at hip level and buried itself in the sandbagged bunker just beyond.

Colby froze where he was. "You're lucky I'm a bad shot," I said quietly, pleased that my voice remained level. "But I probably won't miss the next time."

The only way to frighten off a madman is to act like you're madder than he is. Colby's face registered doubt for the first time and he stayed where he was. "You'd better watch your back, Kramer, because I'm not going to forget this."

Somehow I managed not to shake visibly. We stared at each other for a few more seconds, and then he was gone. I was so relieved that I nearly passed out.

There was a good chance that Colby would have forgotten the entire incident once he'd sobered up if it hadn't been for the broken record and turntable. I figured, rightly, that he'd be watching for a chance to get even. Or better than even. So I had to be circumspect. He wasn't due to rotate out of our battalion for almost six months, so that was no solution. I might have requested a transfer, but I had a comparatively soft job in a helicopter support unit, well away from combat, shielded from attack by a large Korean contingent whose encampment surrounded our base. I alternated between clerking for the colonel and for the battalion intelligence officer, typing and filing rather than sweating in the field or helping to maintain the aircraft or dodging bullets. I liked it where I was.

The alternative was to stay out of Colby's reach, at least when there weren't other people around, preferably an NCO or an officer. Colby was nuts, but not completely nuts. He wouldn't assault me if it would clearly result in disciplinary action. He could be patient when necessary, and I knew he was sly as well as violent.

For the next couple of days I spent a lot of time in my two offices, "catching up" after everyone else was off duty. Actually, I always smuggled in paperbacks and read until late in the evening, then made my way circumspectly back to my hooch, lurking long enough to be certain Colby wasn't lying in wait. Several days passed in this fashion before I realized this couldn't go on. Sooner or later he'd outsmart me, or I'd be careless, or coincidence would put us together without witnesses. I could have gone to one of my superiors to complain, or maybe the chaplain, but they weren't likely to do anything except yell at Colby and make the situation worse. Apologizing and offering to pay for the turntable was not really an option. It would only have told Colby how much I feared retribution.

If I wasn't going to leave, then Colby would have to go, and I'd have to help him along.

Like I said, I did the clerical work for the S2 office. S2 was intelligence, of which we had very little, of the military kind anyway. Most of the documents in our files concerned members of the battalion rather than the Vietnamese. We had information on their criminal records while in the military, disciplinary histories, and other things you'd expect to find. We also had information I wasn't supposed to talk about. There were presently mail covers on half a dozen of our personnel. A mail cover is when they keep track of how much mail you get and record all the return addresses, but don't actually open anything. We also had a few pieces of actual correspondence that had been discarded and later retrieved. They were pretty much what you'd suspect, letters criticizing the war or President Johnson or the military authorities. There were typed reports from officers and enlisted men who had witnessed, or professed to have witnessed, disloyal or dubious acts. A lot of the smokers had notes about their drug use, although I noticed that no one bothered to report the heavy drinkers. There were also summaries of rumors, observations, even unsubstantiated opinions. I'd read all of them, and had yet to find a credible account suggesting disloyalty. Nevertheless, these files were reviewed on a regular basis and personnel were reassigned based on their contents.

Clearly it would not do to add suggestions that Colby was a communist sympathizer, an anti-war activist, or anything similar. No one would believe it. So I had to be more subtle. I checked the activity log and confirmed that Colby's file had not been reviewed since Captain Wescott became our new S2 Officer, so I could add as much as I liked without raising suspicion. I could also alter the schedule so that it would be on his desk anytime I wanted. But what could I add to his file—currently empty of prejudicial material except for notes about three Article 15 disciplinary actions for missing roll call?

I would have to become creative. Using his service record to make sure I had times and places recorded correctly, I composed observations by completely imaginary officers who suggested that Colby was selling government property on the black market, that he'd assaulted an officer under cover of darkness, and a couple of similar peccadilloes while stationed at Fort Dix and Fort Lee. Colby had briefly been assigned to a unit in Nha Trang before coming to Phu Hiep, and I wrote an official sounding report advising against charging Colby with selling a box of hand grenades to suspected enemy agents because there was insufficient evidence. "Subject should be closely watched, however, in view of the severity of the situation should the charges be accurate." As an afterthought, I included a handwritten note to the effect that the two witnesses to this imaginary transaction had both been seriously beaten by an unknown assailant and had recanted their original testimony.

Our previous company commander had finished his tour, so I used his name to append a note to his most recent evaluation. "There are persistent rumors that Private Colby has been seen fraternizing with the locals in unsupervised situations. Recommend that the situation be monitored." A few other, more subtle alterations were designed to suggest that Colby would sell equipment, ammunition, even information without a second thought, which was probably true, although I didn't think he was bright enough to actually do any of the things I ascribed to him. It was enough to mark him as potential trouble, and support group commands like ours routinely provided involuntary reinforcements to the grunts in the field, or in this case, jungle.

I also looked at his personnel jacket and noted his hometown, Walnut Falls, West Virginia. We had a form letter we used to request background information from civilian authorities and I ran one into the typewriter and filled in Colby's name. It wouldn't hurt to have something genuine in the file and Colby made no secret of the fact that he'd enlisted to avoid jail. I forged Wescott's signature and put it in the mail.

Nothing happened for several days and I started to relax. Then I was careless one night and went out for a smoke without checking the lay of the land. Colby seemed to materialize out of nowhere and I was about to bolt when First Sergeant Grimes showed up, staggering drunk. I took his arm and offered to help him back to his quarters. Colby never said a word, but even his silence was eloquent.

Two days later my request for background information came back. No such zip code, no such town. The information in Colby's jacket was wrong. I wasn't about to be defeated that easily, however. I faxed a request up the chain of command for a corrected jacket. Someone was on the ball for a change because a return fax was waiting for me when I got to the office the following morning. To my dismay, it also listed Walnut Falls as his home town. But then I read the rest and my day brightened. Upon arriving in Cam Ranh Bay, Private Elmer Colby had been assigned to the 312th Support Company based in Tuy Hoa. Not only was Tuy Hoa not far away, but I knew Brian, their company clerk. I rang him up on the field phone.

"Hey, Brian, I think I found a glitch. One of your guys got sent over here somehow."

Since the support groups were always undermanned, Brian was immediately enthusiastic. At least, he was enthusiastic until I told him the name.

"Nuts! It's got to be two different guys with the same name. We've got our Elmer Colby and frankly, we'd all be happier without him."

My spirits plummeted. "Yeah, I was kind of hoping to get rid of ours. He's nothing but trouble."

"They must be related. Ours is an ugly drunk and a troublemaker. Sorry, can't help you."

I rang off and turned back to the paperwork, was just about to file it all away when I noticed something. Our Elmer Colby's service number was RA52903257. The one assigned to the 312th was RA52903258. Probably one or the other was a typo, but it was still a pretty big coincidence. So I read further. They both had the same date of birth, both enlisted on the same day, and their social security numbers were only two digits apart. That was stretching coincidence, or bad typing, beyond the limits of probability.

It bothered me so badly that the next day I hitched a chopper ride up to Tuy Hoa. In addition to my two main jobs, I was also the PIO clerk. That's Public Information Office, which was supposedly an internal news service run by the Army but which was actually designed to produce puff pieces, human interest stories, and mostly profiles of soldiers that could be sent back to their home town newspapers. I was supposed to turn in one story a week, and the officer in charge—a second lieutenant who got stuck with all of the annoying little jobs—gave me a free hand so long as I kept him out of trouble. So I told him I was running up to Tuy Hoa to do a couple of stories about how units in the field were supplied and he nodded and approved my request without even listening to it.

The Huey that brought me was going to return in about four hours, so that's all the time I had. I stopped to see Brian, told him my cover story, and asked for suggestions. He gave me some names.

"What about that Colby guy you were telling me about?" I tried to sound casual.

"Him? Trust me, you don't want to interview him. He's a jerk." Brian expanded on the subject, and mentioned that his Colby helped maintain their fleet of trucks.

I had to ask someone else for directions to the motor pool, a sprawling area behind a low hill nestled up against the corner of the local minefield. There were a dozen or so mechanics at work, but I didn't have to worry about identifying which one was Colby. He looked just like mine. I figured that was the explanation. They were identical twins and had the same birth date. Of course their social security numbers would be almost consecutive, and if they enlisted at the same time, their service numbers would also be close.

I returned to my own unit, resigned to the fact that coincidence had been playing with me, but coincidence wasn't quite done. One of my duties was to process service awards and in the batch that arrived the following day was an Army Commendation Medal for Elmer Colby. Except it wasn't my Elmer Colby, nor was it the one working at the 312th. This one's service number was RA52903255, and his social security number was only a couple of digits away from the two Colbies I already knew about. I called my contact at awards distribution, gave him the RA number, and he apologized.

"Sorry, some kind of mix up. Colby is with the 14th Armored Brigade. Just send it back to us and we'll forward it."

Up until now I'd been doing my utmost to avoid Elmer Colby. My Elmer Colby, that is. Suddenly my attitude changed. I was so curious about him—and his alter egos—that I decided to investigate. I didn't throw caution to the winds, exactly, but I did let the breeze push it around a little. I sat near him in the mess hall, trying to eavesdrop on his conversation. Unfortunately, there wasn't much conversation to overhear. My Colby worked as a menial in helicopter maintenance, so I asked some of his co-workers about him. They didn't know much more than I did. "He's okay, I guess. I never really talk to him." "Colby? I try to stay out of his way. He's got an ugly temper." He had no close friends, drank alone, had no obvious hobbies or interests, never went to the enlisted men's club. I also found out that he had never once received mail since joining our unit.

Then I got careless. I spotted Colby from a distance one evening, walking along the company road from the PX toward Hooch country. Curious, I decided to follow him. This part of the compound was generally deserted in the early evening; the last seating was still underway in the mess hall, the enlisted men's club had just opened, and tonight's sentries had already been trucked out to the guard towers along the perimeter. Most of the time it was clear at night, but there'd been a storm that day and the clouds were still pretty thick overhead. Thick shadows washed over the buildings, barely retreating before the handful of subdued and very widely spaced lights strung from our generators.

I looked away at just the wrong moment and Colby was gone. I was stupefied for a second or two; it was as if he'd melted into a shadow himself. I quickened my pace and closed to where I'd last seen him.

Colby stepped out of the darkness. "Thought that was you, Kramer. You and I have unfinished business."

The worst part was that there was absolutely no emotion in his voice.

Now this might have been a very bad few minutes for me, but I got lucky, though at someone else's expense. Down at the end of the unpaved road, another uniformed figure stepped out into the dim light, an M-16 held at his side, muzzle pointing toward the ground. I didn't recognize him, but there was something about his stance that set off alarms in my head. Involuntarily I turned and looked behind me. Still another figure, similarly equipped, stood at the opposite end of the street.

I was smack in the middle of an imminent gunfight. Like I said, more of us were killed by fellow GIs than by the Vietnamese. I was facing Colby and I started in his direction. Better a beating than a bullet. Colby smiled and stepped forward. Much of what happened then I only reconstructed later. The two strangers were PFC Manuel Cristobal and Specialist Fourth Class Arthur Rand. Rand didn't like Hispanics, words had been exchanged on several occasions, and something had triggered this confrontation. No one ever did find out exactly what. All I know is that I heard both weapons start up simultaneously, the chatter of semi-automatic fire, and I ducked and ran for cover. Colby smiled and reached for me.

Several rounds hit him, walking up his chest, making a small, dark hole in the center of his forehead. I guess it must have been Rand's errant fire, because Cristobal's burst castrated the hulking Spec 4 and sent him flying backwards, screaming in agony. Cristobal himself was never touched.

Colby staggered back a step, looking vaguely surprised, then collapsed without making a sound. I passed him in a running crouch and kept right on going. There were shouts all over the encampment and I knew the MPs would be there within seconds. I had no intention of letting them find me. Witnesses to fights inside the compound often had "accidents" if they talked too much.

I hid in my hooch and pretended to have slept through the whole thing.

Cristobal was shipped off to Long Binh Jail the following morning. Rand had been medevacced out during the night. No one said anything about Colby and I was afraid to ask directly, so at lunch I wandered over to the maintenance hangar to see what I could find out. Colby was there, lugging boxes into one of the storage sheds. He looked just as he always did.

I requested a transfer that afternoon and left Phu Hiep two days later.

No, I didn't say anything to anyone. Look, I was nineteen years old, working with people I didn't like and who didn't like me, surrounded by others who spoke a foreign language and wanted to kill me. I'd been taught by experience to avoid officers whenever possible, and senior NCOs as well, and never to volunteer. All I wanted to do was forget all about Elmer Colby. I ended up at a small Signal Corp outfit in Da Lat. They had no one on the roster named Elmer Colby, no Colbies at all in fact. I spent the rest of my tour with them, then a year at Fort Sill winding up my enlistment. I thought about Colby at times, sure. I wondered if it was some kind of secret government project, robots maybe, or if they'd cloned a whole bunch of him and had replacements stockpiled somewhere. But who and how and why weren't any of my business.

—•—•—

About twenty years later, I was living in Wallingford, Connecticut. My neighbor was a really nice guy named Romeo Bolduc. We had almost nothing in common but somehow we managed to enjoy each other's company. Romeo worked in a foundry and spent most of his leisure time hunting, fishing, and playing cards. The only time I went out into the wilderness was with paint, canvas, and easel, and I wasn't sure if a straight flush beat a full house. Romeo had never married, which was probably just as well.

He invited me over one day to take some of the venison out of his freezer. "I'll never eat half of it and I hate to have it go to waste." I knocked on the screen door and heard him yell a welcome from somewhere in the basement. I walked downstairs and found him painting wooden ducks. Well, they looked a little bit like ducks anyway. They were roughly duck shaped and duck sized and even pretty close to duck colored.

"I didn't know you were into art," I joked.

"Yeah, I'm the Picasso of duck lures."

I squinted my eyes. "I guess if the duck was really nearsighted and wasn't paying attention, he might think this was another duck."

Romeo kept a second fridge in the basement. He opened the door, extracted a beer, and tossed it to me. "Danny, my boy, you look too close at things, that's your problem. Most of us, we don't sweat the details, and that includes ducks." He picked up the nearest, smearing still wet paint all over his hand. "See, I float a string of these babies out on some likely piece of water and sit back and wait. Now from way up above, they look like they might be ducks, and if they're safe, then it's safe to come down and join them. But maybe we have ourselves a really careful duck. It circles a little lower. The shape is right, the color is right. It doesn't have to walk like a duck and talk like a duck to be a duck, at least not to other ducks it doesn't."

"So it settles down in the water, but it doesn't get too close to my ducks, because that would be rude. Maybe it does notice that these really aren't exactly ducks, but whatever the hell they are, they aren't getting shot at. So the duck relaxes and I stand up and POW! Fresh honker for supper."

I shook my head and drank some of the beer. "I guess ducks just aren't long on brains."

Romeo laughed. "Oh? You think you're so much smarter than a duck? Let me tell you something, Danny. People are just the same. They don't look close at the people they follow, and sometimes they follow them into some pretty nasty scrapes. That's how most wars get started, you know?"

I hadn't thought about Elmer Colby for years and I didn't think about him in Romeo's basement, but I did think about him about two months later, and Romeo's little lecture rolled back into my mind about the same time.

Politics bore me, frankly. I vote in the general elections, most of the time, but I've never bothered with the primaries and I'm not a member of any party. I've always thought they were all pretty much the same, when I thought about it at all. But I was waiting for a football game one Sunday and I turned on the television early because Doreen was visiting her family for the weekend and I was feeling lazy. I sat on the couch, drinking fresh brewed coffee, and watched as one of the talking heads introduced their next guest. I wasn't really paying attention until I heard the name. It was Elmer Colby, senior senator from West Virginia and one of the leading candidates for his party's nomination as President of the United States.

I sat up and the coffee grew cold in my cup. The commercial break seemed to stretch on forever and then they were back and a man about my age was sitting at the table and it wasn't hard to recognize my old nemesis. He rarely smiled and answered in short sentences. At times he seemed almost angry. He wasn't a candidate, he insisted, but if he decided that he should be, it would be because he felt an obligation to help lead the people of the United States into a new future.

I couldn't help wondering just what kind of future he had in mind, and who or what might be sitting out there waiting for us to come into range.

Chronic Pain

When I stumbled across Peter Nicholson while he was torturing a cat, I immediately assumed that he was also the one who had fed ground glass to Mr. Turnivale's dairy cows. It was impossible to prove, of course, and no one was going to take the unsubstantiated word of one twelve year old boy against another, even or perhaps particularly when the two were known to be long time enemies. My six suspensions from school since second grade had all involved fights with Peter, although in my defense he earned at least that many again without my help. But the casual and pointless cruelty of the two separate acts linked them in my mind.

I'd been hiking through the woods up behind the Stanton farm. No one had lived there in years; the barn was little more than a pile of twisted lumber, and the house was not much better preserved. Part of the roof had collapsed, the windows were all empty shells, and the porch was overgrown and crumbling. The dissolution was so nearly complete that the place didn't even hold the romantic attraction that abandoned buildings usually have for the young, and I only approached it in the first place because it was the shortest way back.

The sound that caught my attention was a squeal rather than a scream. I suspected rats and was intending to move on, but then I heard the unmistakable sound of a human voice. Curiosity overcame common sense, never a serious struggle at that age.

I entered by the front door, open now that the hinges had pulled free from the rotting wood, leaving a gap I stepped through easily. It was dim inside, but not dark, and it only took a few seconds for my eyes to adjust.

Peter was at the far end of the room, crouched over the cat.

For the first few seconds, I stood dumbly, not really comprehending the situation. He'd nailed the cat's paws to the floor, slightly spread, but its head was held high by a thin wire wound around both jaws and secured to another nail driven into the wall. It was mewling constantly, eyes wide and glittery, but I could tell it was near death even before I recognized that the colorful coils looped below its abdomen were intestines.

"What the hell?" My voice was a hoarse croak, but Peter whirled around at the sound.

"Scapelli! What are you doing here?" The way he said my name irritated me, as always. There was a contemptuous loathing that rasped along a raw nerve. I hated Peter Nicholson with that degree of fanatic devotion only possible to the young.

"Kill it, Nicholson," I spoke to him but my eyes were locked on the cat, whose agony seared me from across the room.

"What d'ya mean, kill it? I'm doing an experiment. You're the one always talking about how great science is and all that crap. So I'm doing science."

I walked forward slowly, still not meeting his eyes, and truthfully I think I was in a mild state of shock. If Nicholson had made any attempt to stop me, I don't know what I might have done. But he actually stepped back once I had closed the gap separating us, made no effort to prevent me from snatching up the long bladed knife that lay on the floor and plunging it deep into the animal's body, into what I hoped was its heart. I must have been close enough, because it gave a short convulsive shudder and died almost immediately.

"You're a goddamned monster!" I turned on Nicholson, the knife still clutched in my hand, and if he had said the wrong thing at that moment, I think I might well have struck again, but at a new target, and this would be a considerably shorter story. In retrospect, I probably should have. But the disadvantage of civilization is that its rules and restraints often work in favor of the uncivilized.

After some indeterminable time, I let the knife fall to the floor and turned away without speaking, so filled with unsettling emotion that I could not find the strength to speak. But just before I left the decrepit building, Nicholson called out a parting taunt.

"Just remember, Scapelli. Scientific research has to be confirmed by further experimentation."

Nicholson continued his warped experiments and occasionally made certain that I knew what he was up to. Mutilated cats, dogs, rabbits, squirrels, and birds punctuated the eight months that followed. Sometimes the mangled corpses were left in my front yard, sometimes they lay strewn along the path I followed to school. Once a skinned, eviscerated squirrel showed up in my gym locker. But never in such a way that I could point a credible finger and cry foul.

During summer vacation, Nicholson apparently grew bored and overconfident.

Dawn Rayfield was a year older than Nicholson, and considerably more athletic. She played basketball and baseball, went backpacking with her parents, and had taken a short course in self defense. Nicholson was a little bigger than average for his age, but not a particularly good fighter; even though I was—and still am—a spindly bookwormish type, I was able to hold my own during our periodic entanglements, primarily because Nicholson seemed to lose all resolve as soon as he received one good blow. His fondness for pain was in the infliction not the actual experience. Dawn matched him physically, and overwhelmed him in skill, and when he provoked an incident at the athletic field one bright August morning, Dawn sent him running home with a bloody nose and bruised ribs. If I'd been present, I might have fallen hopelessly in love with her on the spot.

But Nicholson was not a good loser. He never referred to their confrontation, but he never forgot it either. Unbeknownst to anyone, he began studying Dawn's habits, waiting for his opportunity. Two days before school started, Dawn went out for her morning jog; she was planning to try out for track that year. While cutting through the woodlot that separated her apartment complex from the highway, someone threw a blanket over her head, wrestled her to the ground, and beat her savagely with feet and fists. The broken ribs and limbs eventually healed, but one blow to her head caused permanent damage, and she was never able to walk properly again.

There was no proof that Nicholson was responsible, of course, and in fact his mother insisted that he'd been home at the time of the assault. But I knew with utter certainty that he'd done it and most of the other kids shared my belief.

The animal mutilations stopped at the same time, apparently no longer holding any interest for their perpetrator. Nicholson was ostracized by those of us in his age group, but he seemed more interested in playing with the younger kids and showed no distress at his isolation. Although there were some suspicious incidents, bruises, black eyes, Tommy Galloway's broken finger, there was never any strong evidence that Nicholson was preying upon his newfound playmates, and none of the injuries were serious.

The following spring, a party of hikers found a dead man not far from the reservoir.

He'd been there about a week, according to the police reports. Approximately forty years old, he was assumed to be a vagrant. There was no identification, his clothing was non-descript, and even after reconstructing his jaw, the authorities had been unable to find matching dental records. The condition of his fingers made it impossible to raise prints.

Whoever he was, he'd been tied by wrists and ankles to nearby trees and put to death quite methodically. The details were suppressed, of course, but my father was the investigating officer and I learned some of the highlights by eavesdropping when the state police liaison came to the house to discuss the case. The dead man had been flayed alive, his finger and toe nails ripped off, eardrums punctured, sexual organs burned away. You get the idea. Some of the mutilations were apparently post mortem, but he'd survived for at least several hours of excruciating pain.

To be honest, it never occurred to me that Nicholson might be responsible. Even if I'd been willing to accept that his fascination with inflicting pain could have risen, if that's the right word, to such new levels, I saw no way he could have waylaid and incapacitated a grown man in good health. And in any case, the Nicholsons moved to Providence a month later and I put Peter and his idiosyncrasies out of my mind for what I hoped was forever.

Fat chance.

Several years passed. I graduated and went on to MIT and a year later, my sister Pam won a scholarship to Brown University. The independent work I did during my junior year attracted some favorable attention, and I was offered a one year internship at the new International Quantum Physics Institute in Volgograd. The single year stretched to two and I completed my undergraduate degree in Volgograd rather than return to Massachusetts. At the urging of my professors, I applied for and was accepted into a special fast track doctoral program.

I was twenty-three years old when I returned to New England for a brief vacation, during which visit I discovered that Pam was engaged to be married. To my utter horror, her fiance was Peter Nicholson.

I'll give him credit for having cleaned up his act. Peter had matured into a handsome, well groomed, and frequently charming person. He deferred to my parents, catered to Pam's every whim, and even greeted me forthrightly and with a firm handshake.

"Never expected to be meeting up with you again, particularly under these circumstances," he admitted. "But we've both changed a great deal."

Perhaps I had. At least, I couldn't muster the same degree of resentment that had previously boiled to the surface automatically when Nicholson was present, although I did not entirely trust this new manifestation. Peter had spread a fancy polish over the old surface, without doing anything to change the grain of the wood beneath. None of which I realized until much later.

When it was too late.

The next few years went by quickly and with no hint of danger. I received my degree, but remained in Volgograd for two more years working on the prototype for the Timetap Project. It's entirely possible that I might have remained even longer, if we hadn't realized the potential advantage of relocating closer to the quantum multi-accelerator recently brought online in Groton, Connecticut. Under the auspices of the International Coordinating Committee for the Sciences, I was installed as Assistant Director of Research for Timetap with a salary that would have allowed me to live quite luxuriously if I'd been willing to spare the time to do so.

I rarely saw Pam and her husband, but she called frequently to keep me abreast of family matters. She always appeared upbeat and positive about her life and the future, and if there was a brittle hollowness there, I missed it. Or chose to miss it. Self recriminations are pointless now, but perhaps I should have realized something was amiss when Kevin, their eighteen month old son, fell down a staircase by "accident", and never regained consciousness. But at the time, Peter seemed to be expressing honest grief, and Pam was in such a self accusatory state, it never occurred to me to draw a parallel with anything from our mutual past.

The Nicholsons moved to Seattle and I saw them in the flesh only two or three times over the course of the next ten years. Pam still holophoned me from time to time, but at much greater intervals than formerly. Their daughter, Lucy, was born shortly after the move, and she did not fall down a staircase. I wasn't used to dealing with children, so the impressions I carried away from those widely scattered visits were fragmentary and superficial. Lucy was demonstrably bright, but where Pam had been a vivacious, extroverted youngster, her daughter was withdrawn and solemn.

My own life grew progressively busier. My parents died tragically in a tubecar accident. Dr. Singh retired on disability and I became Director of Research, essentially the project director although nominally subject to the Chief of Administration. We had already achieved and in fact surpassed our original goal, although not quite as we had expected.

Time travel had, despite the arguments and equations offered by skeptics, proven to be possible after a fashion, but not into our own true past. We could transmit recording equipment into an indistinguishable, exact duplicate of our time line, even alter the course of events there, then retrieve the instruments, but without in any way changing the present in our own reality. It appeared that the branching theory of time was correct after all, and while it was possible to assassinate a young Hitler or Stalin, there would be no impact whatsoever on our own world and time. There were, admittedly, a few anomalies as yet unresolved, so we had refrained from sending back a human being, even though we knew it was the next logical step. It appeared that we could have the best of all possible worlds, that we could go back and even experiment with the course of history without risking our own existence, but the scale of what we were playing with kept us relatively humble.

My first suspicion that something was wrong with Pam came when I found myself rerouted from Greater LAX to Seattle International Aerospace following the first of the long series of major earth tremors in 2031. Impulsively I decided to pay my sister a surprise visit. It was a surprise, all right, for both of us.

Pam was quite obviously distressed to see me when I arrived at their apartment, and almost wouldn't let me in. The damage was still recent enough to be lurid, bruises, both eyes blackened, the unmistakable pattern of laser stitching on her jaw and across one cheekbone.

"What happened?" I asked instinctively, but I think even then I knew the truth.

Pam denied it at first, insisted that she'd been mugged on the tubeway, but she couldn't meet my eyes. I had caught her off guard and unprepared, and she finally admitted that Peter was responsible.

"It's never happened before and he's almost as upset as I am. There were some problems at work," Peter was employed as a maintenance supervisor in the orbital platform support group, "and I was acting real bitchy when he came home and things just kind of got out of hand."

I pretended to be mollified, but I was seething inside when I left the house. That night, I holocalled Nicholson from my hotel room and threatened him in the only way I could think to. "I can pull strings in every space related facility in the world through the Institute," I told him. "If you so much as slap my sister's face, I'll see to it that you'll never work again."

It was a hollow threat. I had no such influence, wouldn't have had the faintest idea of how to go about blackballing anyone, if it could be done at all. But Nicholson didn't know that, and when he was fired two months later for entirely unrelated reasons, it was only logical for him to assume that I was involved.

I was frankly not surprised that he'd lost his job. A little discrete research had uncovered the fact that he was an unpopular, authoritarian shift supervisor, and that his crew had the worst performance record in North America. What did surprise me was that he immediately uprooted his family and moved to Groton, where he took a job as a tubeway mechanic. My delight at having my sister and niece close at hand was short lived, however, because his physical abuse of Pam grew more brutal and more regular, although he seemed not to have touched his daughter. Obviously he had come to Groton to flaunt his power over Pam under my virtual nose.

There have been laws against spousal assault since the last century, of course, but they still cannot be enforced without the cooperation of the victim. And despite everything, including my constant urging that she terminate their marriage under the Adult Consent laws, Pam refused to leave her husband.

Six months later, she was dead.

Officially, it was an accident. The police suspected suicide. Pam died of electrocution when her hand came into contact with an exposed power conduit at a relay station several blocks from her home. Her fingerprints were found on the crowbar that had been used to break the locking latch on the door. Her body bore signs of a fresh beating and Nicholson confessed to having had a violent argument with her that morning. His reputation as an abuser was a matter of public record, which automatically made him a prime suspect. Nicholson himself had been on an inspection tour that morning, unaccompanied, and had no alibi, but without some substantiating evidence, there was nothing to link him to the death. Results of a polyencephalograph were ambiguous, which I'm told is not unusual with psychopathic personalities.

For weeks, I couldn't concentrate on my work. If anything, it was even more devastating knowing that while I could go back in time, after a fashion, and discover the truth, it would be inadmissible in a court of law. And I already knew Nicholson was responsible. More frustrating was the knowledge that while I could change the outcome, the results would only be apparent in the newly branching universe that my act created. Nothing could restore Pam to life in the "real" world.

I think that was the point where my unconscious mind began to work subliminally. My dreams were frequently filled with violent images, memories from childhood, wish fulfillment fantasies in which I beat Nicholson to death with my fists. But consciously, I was resigned to the situation, and might never have acted if it hadn't been for Lucy.

Nicholson never made any objection to my frequent visits following Pam's death. Sometimes he'd even make feeble attempts to start a conversation, until my lack of cooperation caused him to smile and turn away. Then I arrived one Saturday morning to find Lucy sitting on the front porch, a few feet away from her father, with her right arm in a sling.

"What happened?" I tried unsuccessfully to conceal the anger in my voice.

Lucy looked away and answered me solemnly and without conviction. "I fell off the swing and broke my arm."

I didn't believe it. Neither of them thought I believed it, nor did they believe that there was anything I could do about it. They were wrong.

I laid my plans that very evening. Access to the laboratory was less of a problem than you might suspect. As Director of Research, I was responsible for equipment and supplies and had the necessary authority to implement my plan. It was a simple matter to input a bogus requisition for some additional monitoring equipment, and I stenciled the appropriate code numbers on an empty crate from a previous shipment after salvaging it from the trash dock.

Scheduling a late night test run for the Timetap equipment was even easier. Although solo operation of the main unit was technically against policy, I'd done so a few times in the past without arousing comment. I logged in my power request on a standby basis; unless the rest of my plan went as devised, there was no point in diverting the resources.

Before leaving the Institute, I paid a brief visit to the lower laboratory, where we house the animals who had so far been the only living creatures to travel through "time". It was fairly easy to locate the equipment I sought, and I left quickly, my small theft witnessed only by an insomniac rabbit.

Nicholson was still up when I reached his house, and when he answered the door, I could smell alcohol on his breath.

"Well, if it isn't my erstwhile brother-in-law. What brings you out to the slums on such a nice evening?"

I didn't trust myself to speak, rather, I withdrew the anaesthetic gun from my pocket and pressed the trigger. The dart struck him in the left cheek, and he collapsed before his upraised hand could reach the tiny wound.

He was heavier than I thought and I used up most of the slack time in my schedule wrestling him into the cargo hold of my floater. It would hardly do to be stopped by a traffic monitor on my way back to the Institute, so I forced myself to stay just under the legal limit for the entire trip. Nicholson wouldn't recover consciousness for at least twelve hours without the antidote, so he wouldn't mind the wait.

Everything after that went right on schedule. I manhandled Nicholson's inert body into my prepared crate and sealed it before calling for a service-bot. It was a fairly sophisticated, voice activated model we'd just acquired, and it followed docilely as I led the way to the Timetap complex. The guards knew me by sight and checked my ID and materials requisition more as a matter of form than of substance.

As soon as the servicebot left the main lab, I uncrated Peter Nicholson, emptied his pockets and removed his watch.

He slept peacefully as I dragged him into the transmission booth. The settings I needed were already calculated and programmed into the main terminal. When everything was done, I would have to subvert the catalog program to cover my tracks, but I would have at least three days to do so before the next mandated audit took place. I doublechecked the snapback remote, strapped it around my waist, and activated the Timetap.

The transition was virtually instantaneous. We had suspected as much from our experiments with live animals, none of whom had displayed any signs of distress even after being transmitted through a span of hundreds of thousands of years, then snapped back to the present.

Nicholson and I were in a wooded region in southern New England, twenty five years in the past.

He groaned in his sleep when I tied his wrists and ankles to the surrounding trees, so that all four limbs were stretched far apart, but he didn't stir until I used the anaesthetic gun to inject the antidote. I changed cartridges when his eyes fluttered open, but he had managed only a single indistinct syllable before I placed the gun against his throat and fired again, this time a local that would paralyze his vocal chords.

Then I stood up and walked slowly away from the recumbent man, counting my steps until I knew he was well beyond the outer perimeter of the snapback field. Judging by the position of the sun, it was mid-morning.

I almost touched the device at that moment, propelling myself back to the present, leaving Nicholson stranded forever in an alternate time track, unable ever to harm his daughter again. But the accumulated resentment and hatred of years was too strong to be shrugged off, and instead I found a sheltered spot where I could watch without being seen myself.

It was not until a thirteen year old Peter Nicholson walked into the clearing and crouched over the prostrate man with a bright, feverish hunger in his eyes and a switchblade knife in his hand, that I pressed the toggle.

Curing Agent

Morocco didn't seem a likely place to find a miracle cure, and that first night Masterson wondered if he was wasting what little time remained to him.

When he'd arrived in Rabat, he'd been vaguely disappointed to discover that the capital city of Morocco was almost indistinguishable from those of southern Spain or France. The flags were different and the buildings weren't quite as tall, but most of the population had adopted western dress, and he'd seen almost as large a proportion of veiled women in the streets of Madrid as he had during the cab ride from the airport.

The hotel clerk had welcomed him to Al Maghrib rather than Morocco, but otherwise had spoken nearly accent free English. The accommodations were slightly old fashioned, but clean and comfortable, and he'd eaten a quite excellent fish dinner at the hotel's restaurant. The walls were covered with posters advertising the romantic splendors of Marrakech and Casablanca, the latter of which had just opened a Humphrey Bogart based theme park, but Masterson wasn't in Africa for entertainment.

The virulent, mutated cancer in his body was spreading quickly. Implants could retard its advance for a few weeks, perhaps even a few months, but they were fighting a desperate rearguard action against an implacable enemy.

Hakim Rashid had met him for breakfast the following morning. Over spiced tea and breaded fish, he produced a series of maps, tickets, and other documents designed to speed Masterson on his journey. Both men spoke Arabic, but Rashid's Berber accent sometimes confused his companion, who was forced to ask him to repeat himself more than once. When they were done, money changed hands and the two half bowed to one another, then

Rashid disappeared into the street while Masterson collected his one suitcase and checked out of his room.

The journey that followed was loud and dirty most of the time, and tedious throughout. He traveled by rail to Azrou in relative comfort, although there were two significant delays because of obstructions on the tracks. At Azrou he transferred to another line and found himself standing in a space crowded well beyond capacity, the railcar itself sandwiched between cargo carriers filled with iron ore and manganese from the north. There had been a series of major earthquakes earlier in the year, and the mines had been closed for a long time, seriously impacting Morocco's balance of trade.

At Khenifra he changed modes and actually managed to sit down on the bus as far as Ben Mela, but he surrendered his seat to a pregnant woman for the balance of the journey to Azilal. There was supposed to be a car waiting for him there, but the agent's office was closed and dark. Masterson inquired at the leather shop to the left and the pottery maker to the right, but either his Arabic was less fluent than he had thought or they simply chose not to understand the impatient foreigner. He wanted a drink badly, but alcohol was only openly sold in the tourist centers, which this decidedly was not, so he made do with a cool but not cold citrus concoction hawked by a young woman who stood hunched over because of an enormous wen on the side of her neck.

The agent showed up two hours later, relaxed and unconcerned. Masterson knew better than to let his anger show, even when the rental fee turned out to be twenty percent higher than he'd been quoted. Money was the least of his worries. To his surprise, the vehicle was only three years old, a rugged Eurojeep landrover that looked to have been well maintained. He returned to the office to demand a full tank of fuel, not because he had already paid for it but simply because he didn't want to be stranded somewhere between Azilal and Quarzazate. The agent blamed the problem on his unreliable and probably nonexistent assistant and a few minutes later stood waving as Masterson pulled away in a cloud of flying sand.

It was a track rather than a road, sometimes so windblown that he was afraid he was drifting off his route and would end up lost in the desert. Twice he passed the rusting hulks of tanks, one Moroccan and one Algerian, relics of the war for Western Sahara back in 2009. UN peacekeepers were still stationed in the disputed territory, but the turmoil following the drought in 2020 and the overthrow of King Mohamed VII the following year had given Moroccans other matters to occupy their minds. The Algerians had reverted to their own civil war now and no longer had leisure to cause trouble outside their borders.

There was a hotel of sorts in Quarzazate, but when he saw the condition of its exterior, Masterson felt no temptation to go inside. In the rear of the landrover lay a bundled tent and other gear, along with enough food and fresh water to last him two full weeks. He refueled before leaving town while two barefooted boys about ten years old stared at him with impossibly wide eyes, and a wizened old woman stood under a ragged awning muttering angrily under her breath and watching him suspiciously.

He'd thought the road from Azilal was primitive, but the next leg of his journey was even worse. The landrover bucked and tossed, its suspension complaining loudly, and fine red sand covered his windshield unless he ran the wipers. A scratchy soundtrack accompanied him from that point onward. When the sun started to go down he reluctantly pulled into the hollow between two hills for the night. His implants must have been silently active, however, because he felt unusually weak when he stepped out of the landrover, and he ended up sleeping sprawled across the seats, too tired to set up the tent.

Early the next morning he saw the low buildings of the town of Tuvaresh, nestled up against the side of a low hill.

When his doctors first delivered their pessimistic diagnosis, Masterson had refused to accept it. "You must face the inevitable," insisted one specialist after another. "It is almost unheard of for anyone to survive once it has spread this far."

Masterson snatched hold of the word "almost" and demanded clarification. He learned that only six people were known to have survived an advanced case of Glastonbury's Disease since its identification in 2013. Two had been young children whose immune system had been strong enough to win the battle, although at the cost of years spent on life support. "The techniques that were used in their cases would be incompatible with an adult. Mature organisms are tougher but less flexible." Of the remaining four, two had subsequently died of unrelated causes and two were still alive, but neither of them would speak to Masterson, nor was there any record of their having been treated by any known medical facility between their final diagnosis and subsequent miraculous cure.

"They must have been spontaneous recoveries," suggested yet another specialist. "I admit it would be unusually extraordinary in these instances, but as you can see from the dossiers we've prepared, all four terminated active treatment prior to remission. The human body still holds surprises for us, Mr. Masterson, but it would be disingenuous of me to suggest that your prognosis is anything less than grim."

Dissatisfied, refusing to accept that his future was in the hands of blind fate, Masterson had used part of his fortune to buy information that he felt should have been offered freely. Within weeks he had accumulated more information about the four survivors than they probably knew or had known about themselves. Human investigators and artificial intelligence programs sifted through the data, searching for patterns, commonalities, and found several, the most interesting of which was that all four had visited Morocco at least once in the months preceding their extraordinary recovery. The first two cases were unremarkable in that regard; one had been a Moroccan national working in the embassy in Washington, and the other was a Spanish military officer who had been stationed in one of the coastal enclaves still administered by Madrid. The latter had recently died in an air crash.

Masterson searched for more linkages and found them. The Spaniard had twice visited the small village north of Naples where little Maria Tomassi, survivor number three, lay on what was supposed to have been her deathbed. Her family had taken the terminally ill nine year old with them on an unlikely trip to Morocco between those two visits, after which she had recovered her full health. He had yet to find proof of a direct link to the fourth survivor, the wife of a Jordanian translator who had worked at the United Nations for two years, but the Moroccan diplomat might well have known the couple socially if not professionally. She had refused his request for an interview, and the Tomassi girl and her family had all perished when their village was virtually swallowed by an earthquake.

It had proven more difficult to track movement inside Morocco, particularly since more than a year had passed between each set of visits. Although the major cities of North Africa had all become reasonably cosmopolitan, the system broke down quickly as one moved into the interior. Two of the four subjects had visited Marrakech, and all had stayed in Rabat for at least one night. Hotel reservations and credit card payments had been saved electronically and were therefore available to be clandestinely retrieved and analyzed. In the interior, records were generally hand written, if they existed at all. Masterson liquidated more of his assets and his hirelings spread out into the desert villages seeking information. As his days of comparative comfort dwindled toward their ultimate end, Masterson teetered on the brink of despair, and was contemplating suicide when he had finally received a report that held promise.

All four had visited the same nondescript southern village.

He passed several pedestrians as he slowly advanced into the town. Most of them glanced disinterestedly in his direction, a few waved angry fists at the dust he stirred. Tuvaresh was a backwater community, existing precariously on what it could farm from the reluctant soil or fashion by hand from crude raw materials. Masterson's spies had told him there was no local gendarmerie. If the police were needed, there were radios in the village by which they could be summoned, although that didn't necessarily mean they'd actually make an appearance. There was no hospital, just a medical station with a single physician, a local man who'd been trained in Europe but who had turned down a position in Rabat in order to return to his home.

Masterson drove around the perimeter of the village until a hill blocked his way, so that he had a good idea of its general layout, then retraced his path to a small, open plateau and parked the landrover in plain view just above the marketplace. He locked the doors and set the alarms and electronic wards, making sure that the young boys who watched him saw what he was doing as well as the revolver he slipped into his jacket pocket.

The market was a study in contrasts. Much of it was straight out of a travelogue, booths whose owners hawked colorful swathes of cloth or wood carvings or pottery or some form of food or drink. Most seemed very traditional, as though they had been swept forward from centuries in the past. But there were others with a distinctively modern aura. Portable electric generators hummed or spluttered beside some of these, where customers could choose from a variety of electronic games, pirated western videos or music CDs, or connect to the internet via radio to look at pornographic images.

It only took a few minutes to walk through the market, and he saw nothing of particular interest. He tried his Arabic on a young girl, who either couldn't understand him or was too shy to answer, then bought some fruit from one of the vendors, who stared at him with open curiosity. "Can you tell me where I could find Dr. Massoud?" he asked, speaking slowly.

The merchant, a thin but robust looking man of middle age, nodded slowly. "Two streets past the mechanic's shop, monsieur," he replied in passable French, obviously mistaking Masterson's nationality. "There is a red crescent over the door."

Masterson thanked him and returned to the landrover, which had been left undisturbed, although there were now nearly a dozen youngsters sitting or standing about. Masterson realized that he hadn't been approached by any of them for a handout yet, which was most unusual. They watched as he disabled the anti-theft field and showed neither pleasure nor disappointment when he drove away.

He found the clinic with no difficulty and parked in front of it. This was the outer limit of the village, and in fact the clinic was built up against and partly into the side of the same hill that had blocked his way earlier. It was in somewhat better condition than the rest of the buildings in town but that was far from a testimonial. The roof looked new and tight, the shutters for the windows were modern and in good condition, and an electrical generator purred quietly in a prefabricated metal shed to one side, but the stucco walls were pitted and crumbling in spots, and there were irregular stains that vaguely suggested thunderclouds. A small electric lamp had been installed over the door and there was a lighter glow from inside, obscured by gauzy curtains.

Since there was no bell, Masterson knocked, wondering if he should just open the door and walk in.

He was about to do just that when he heard a sound from within, and a moment later the door swung away to reveal a cadaverously tall man with a long, gray beard wearing a western style flannel shirt that clashed incongruously with his baggy silk trousers.

Masterson got a quick once over and the man addressed him in Spanish. "May I help you, Senor?"

"I'm looking for Dr. Massoud," he replied in Arabic. "And I'm not Spanish. My name is Carl Masterson and I'm from America." The Spanish were none too popular in Morocco at the moment because of their intransigence about surrendering their last few small enclaves on the mainland as well as a handful of islands in the Mediterranean.

"I am Massoud." The man's expression remained wary but was a trifle less unfriendly. "Are you in need of medical help?"

"Yes I am. May I come inside?"

"Be welcome then." Massoud stepped back and Masterson entered the clinic.

Contrary to his expectations, the clinic appeared to be empty except for Massoud himself. It wasn't just that there were no other staff or patients, but rather a pervasive sense of neglect. The beds were bare, no sheets or other coverings, all of the medical instruments were apparently shut away, and in general things were dusty but otherwise remarkably well maintained and tidy. It was possible that he'd come at just the right time, but when he thought about it, he realized that all of the inhabitants of Tuvaresh whom he had seen so far appeared to be healthy, which had not been true of the other towns and villages through which he'd passed. Nor had he noticed any street beggars, neither elderly unemployables nor children deliberately mutilated by their parents to make their appeals more compelling. In Tuvaresh people might have tightened their belts because of the poor economic conditions that prevailed in North Africa, but they were free of the endemic diseases that troubled their neighbors. Realizing that, Masterson felt his first rush of optimism since deplaning in Rabat.

He was ushered into a small, dimly lit office that didn't look particularly welcoming, although at least here there were some personal touches that indicated human habitation. Massoud waited until he had settled onto an unbalanced wooden chair before speaking.

"In what way may I be of assistance?"

"I have an advanced case of Glastonbury's Disease. It's a new form of cancer in which…"

Massoud waved his hand impatiently. "We're not so isolated here that I haven't kept up with things in my profession. You have my profound sympathies, Mr. Masterson, but surely you realize that there is nothing that I can do for you here. Perhaps in Rabat? There is a fine hospital there, one of the best on the continent."

"I'm not interested in conventional hospitals, Dr. Massoud. They've already failed me. Your services were recommended to me by Sarina Farouk. I believe you treated her for the very same condition just a few months ago."

Massoud blinked but his face remained immobile. "I am afraid you are mistaken, Mr. Masterson. There is no one in Tuvaresh of that name, and I have not traveled further than Taroudant in over a year, and that was to visit relatives."

"I know she doesn't live here, but she came to this clinic last November. She was in the terminal stages when she arrived, and shortly after her return to Cairo she made a complete recovery."

"Allah smiled upon her, no doubt. It is entirely possible that this woman visited Tuvaresh as you have indicated, although few have any reason to come to such a remote place. But I assure you that I did not treat this woman, an Egyptian I assume, for any condition whatsoever, let alone so serious an ailment." He made an elaborate gesture to indicate his surroundings. "Surely you can see that we are a poor community with only the most basic facilities. I cannot imagine why this woman would send you to us."

"She was quite explicit," he answered firmly. He was willing to pay a quite large bribe to get what he wanted, enough in truth to raise the standard of living for the entire community, but none of the four survivors had been remotely wealthy. Masterson was sure that this was one of those few things he'd wanted in life that he couldn't buy. At least not directly. "And I'm quite desperate."

"As I have already said, I am very sympathetic, but there is nothing I can do for you. It is out of my hands." He held up his palms with fingers spread to illustrate his words.

"Then perhaps someone else?"

"Not in Tuvaresh, Mr. Masterson. It will serve no purpose for you to remain here." He rose to his feet, an obvious gesture of dismissal. "I can offer you something for the pain if necessary, but beyond that, I am powerless."

"I've had blockers implanted," he said impatiently as he stood up. "I need a cure, not a palliative."

"You will not find it here."

"Perhaps not. Thank you for your time, Dr. Massoud."

⊢•◦•○•◦•⊣

Masterson set up camp back where he'd first parked. The rear of the landrover unfolded into a small sleeping compartment. He didn't bother to start the generator for the air conditioning, but he was fastidious enough to assemble the chemical toilet rather than use the communal facilities at the corner of the market square. A handful of young boys watched him but lost interest once it was obvious that no new wonders were to be revealed.

He spent that evening walking around the small village, speaking casually to anyone who seemed willing to tolerate the presence of a foreigner. Many moved away without responding to his greetings, but others were curious and willing to talk, particularly once he'd made it clear he was not French and, even better, not Spanish. He was careful not to mention his illness or his reason for being in Tuvaresh. It was difficult to resist the temptation to probe for information, but Masterson had amassed his fortune because he was patient and methodical, and he would not allow even the threat of imminent death to deprive him of his best weapons.

But by the afternoon of the following day, the sense of urgency had begun to gnaw at him and he found it increasingly difficult to ask insincere questions about an artisan's methods or to sympathize with an ex-soldier's tirades against the Spanish. He started to drop hints about the real purpose of his visit, watching to see if anyone would react. To his surprise, they all did. Adults and children alike, they became cool and distant and sometimes visibly disturbed when he mentioned that he had come to Tuvaresh seeking treatment for his illness. He had thought that someone locally was concealing a miraculous secret; he hadn't anticipated that it might be the entire community.

As his questions became more insistent, the responses grew less friendly. No one threatened him, no one shouted angrily, but by the third day he was clearly unwelcome. The merchants in the market would sell to him, but they made no effort to entice him with their wares, and their haggling was perfunctory. Some of the children were actively afraid of him.

Masterson had learned the name of the village's folk healer before his current ostracism, and knew that she was held in at least as high regard as Dr. Massoud. On the third evening, she returned to Tuvaresh, riding in the oxcart beside her two grandchildren, a boy and a girl both in their early teens. Rhaliyah sold charms and herbal cures and dispensed advice, apparently welcome or not, and was certainly a figure of more authority than the town's ostensible administrator, Mohammed Bin Dayoud, an overweight, elderly man whose waist length beard was so full of sand fleas that it sometimes seemed to move of its own accord.

He waited until late in the evening before visiting her, rapping lightly on the door of her small house. An impudent wind had sprung up, and he kept his face averted. He had just raised his hand to knock again when the door opened.

"Come in, Senor Masterson. I have been expecting you."

He brushed sand from his clothing and stamped his feet before stepping inside. The interior was relatively dark, lit only by a pair of small oil lamps, but it looked to be surprisingly clean and orderly. There were piles of cushions scattered about the room, but no chairs, and the door leading to the rest of the house was covered by a beaded curtain.

He apologized in Arabic for intruding, but she continued to speak in Spanish throughout his visit, perhaps as a sign of distrust. Masterson launched into essentially the same story he'd used with Massoud, but Rhaliyah cut him off quickly.

"I know why you are here and what you seek. You are wasting your time. You should not have come. There is nothing here for you. We cannot help you. It is best that you go home. Stay with those you love for as much time as remains to you."

"I can't do that." He was silent for a few seconds, having realized that he'd misjudged the situation. "I will do whatever is necessary to find the answer. I am a wealthy man. I could help you, or your people."

She shook her head. "We are content with what we have. Allah provides. What you seek is beyond our power to give even if we sought your wealth. Go home, Senor Masterson. There is no help for you in Tuvaresh."

Masterson sighed and reached into the pocket of his jacket, removed the revolver without pointing it at the woman, but making certain that she could tell what it was. "I am dying, old woman. I will do whatever it takes to save my own life."

Neither her expression nor the tone of her voice changed in the slightest. "I am too old to fear death and I could not help you even if I did. So do what you wish and leave for I have had a tiring journey and I wish to rest now, in one fashion or another."

His hand tightened around the grip of the revolver, but he'd sat through enough board meetings to recognize her determination. The revolver went back into his pocket and he left without another word.

~―•―0―•―~

Masterson spent the next day wandering the streets as before. The adults continued to avoid him, as did most of the children, but he brought gifts with him this time, a bagful of treats including handheld computer games he'd bought for an exorbitant price in the market square, chocolate bars from his refrigerated larder in the landrover, a few other items he'd selected from among his equipment. The girls and older boys were still wary, but some of the younger ones surrendered to temptation and let themselves be approached. Masterson carefully avoided saying anything that might alarm them, asked instead about Rhaliyah and her family and by early afternoon he had the information he sought.

He returned to his encampment and took a long and refreshing nap. It was going to be a busy night.

~―•―0―•―~

It took longer for Rhaliyah to respond when he knocked this time, and he thought she looked surprised as well. She did not invite him in until he asked to speak to her, and then did so grudgingly. The room looked exactly as it had the night before.

"You have not taken my advice." Tonight she was speaking in Arabic.

"I told you. I'm desperate. I have no other place to go."

"And I have told you that I am unable to help you."

"Unable? Or unwilling?"

"Does it matter?" Her expression puzzled him. Was it contempt that he saw, or anger, or fear, or actually sympathy? It seemed to him an amalgam of them all, but it didn't matter. Nothing mattered except escaping the trap that resided inside his body.

"I want to show you something. I think it might convince you to help me." His hand slipped into his jacket pocket.

Her eyes widened slightly and he realized she thought he was going to threaten her with his revolver again. But his fingers slid past the cold metal and gripped something else. He handed it to her.

Rhaliyah accepted it reluctantly and squinted to see the details of the photograph in the poor light.

"Alina," she whispered.

"Yes," he said quietly. "That's your granddaughter. Don't worry, she's a bit uncomfortable and very frightened, but she's not in any immediate danger. I've locked the rover and set up the defensive field. Anyone who tries to get in will get a painful electric shock unless they have this." From his other pocket, he withdrew the control wand.

"You should not have done this." Her voice was still pitched low, but he heard anger in it now, and a threat.

"This is actually a very sophisticated device." He tossed the wand up into the air and caught it. "That bundle between her legs is a bomb." Her head jerked and he spoke quickly. "Don't worry. Unless it's disturbed, it won't go off for almost twenty-four hours. Plenty of time to disarm it." He held up the wand. "I just need to key in the right code and touch the transmit key."

"She is only thirteen, Mr. Masterson. She has her entire life in front of her."

His own voice hardened. "And all of this wouldn't be necessary if I had more life in front of me. I don't want to hurt anybody, but believe me I have nothing to lose. If it takes a death to bring me life, then that's an arrangement I'm willing to make. I'll kill your granddaughter and you and everyone else in Tuvaresh if necessary until one of you gives me what I want. Life from death; it has a kind of poetic balance."

"Flies from a corpse," she responded.

"Remember, it will be your granddaughter's corpse. And before you decide to try anything, the defensive field is tied into the bomb as well. I'm the only one who can save her." He leaned forward. "Or perhaps I should say that you and I are the only ones who can save her."

She didn't argue any further and Masterson decided he was glad she wasn't working for one of his competitors. Rhaliyah knew when to fight and when to surrender. She wrapped herself in a cloak without saying another word and gestured for him to open the door. A moment later they were out under the stars.

Much to his surprise, she led him directly to Dr. Massoud's clinic. She opened the door without knocking and disappeared inside with a perfunctory glance back over her shoulder to see if he was following. Masterson kept his hand in his pocket, fingers curled around the revolver, and cautiously entered.

A flickering fluorescent light from another room was the only illumination. Rhaliyah moved through the darkness with easy familiarity, but Masterson bumped his hip on the side of a gurney and cursed softly. Her voice seemed unnaturally loud when she called out. "Ebiran, we have a visitor."

There was no answer and she continued through the next room, then turned left into a narrow corridor. Masterson's nerves were taut but he told himself not to be foolish. He was in command here; he had his weapon and the girl.

At the end of the corridor were three doors, and Rhaliyah paused, then produced a key from somewhere within her clothing. She used it to open the middle door and led the way inside. Masterson hesitated, blinking to let his eyes adjust to the dim light.

He stepped forward into a fairly large room incongruously mixing the modern and the ancient. There were two small computers at matching desks to his right, not state of the art but clearly operational. A row of filing cabinets extended away on his left and a table and four chairs sat in the center of the room. The far wall was completely covered by three tapestries, and there was another to his immediate right. They were in good repair but looked to be very old. Rough cushions were also scattered across the floor.

Masterson stepped forward and slipped the revolver out of his pocket. "All right, it's time for an explanation."

Rhaliyah smiled unpleasantly and her eyes flicked to one side. It wasn't quite enough of a warning. He heard the tapestry move behind him and half turned, then felt something hard pressing against the small of his back.

"Please drop your weapon, Mr. Masterson. I would regret having to shoot you but I will not hesitate if you disobey." It was Massoud's voice and he was speaking nearly flawless English.

Masterson did as he was told.

"Take a seat, if you will. And no sudden or unexpected movements, please."

He walked slowly to the nearest chair and turned to face the doctor. "I told you I was desperate," he said simply.

"And I told you that I could not help you." Massoud sighed. "Now I shall have to radio for the gendarmes."

"There is more," interjected Rhaliyah, speaking Arabic. "He has Alina." She explained quickly about the bomb.

Massoud's expression darkened. "You are not an honorable man, Mr. Masterson, but I will bargain with you. Release the girl and we shall forget what has happened this evening."

Masterson smiled and crossed his legs. "You know what I want, Doctor. It's the only thing you have to offer me. Heal me, or the girl dies."

Massoud sighed. "I could kill you where you sit and take the device from your pocket."

"Without the code, she will certainly die. I'm a dead man in any case without your secret, so it does no good to threaten me."

Massoud and Rhaliyah exchanged a few quick sentences that Masterson couldn't follow, apparently in some Berber dialect. It bothered Masterson not to know what was happening, but only a little. He still held all the trump cards.

Their conference ended, Massoud seemed more saddened than angry. "All right, Mr. Masterson. We can tell you what you want to know in exchange for the girl's life, but it will still do no good. That is beyond our power."

He hesitated only a second. "I'll take that chance. I don't have any other options left to me."

Massoud had entered the room through a doorway concealed by a small tapestry. Now he lifted aside another, revealing a much wider passageway that immediately angled steeply down. With a gas lantern in one hand, Rhaliyah led the way, Masterson following close behind, Massoud bringing up the rear with his weapon pointed directly at the center of the American's back.

It wasn't a long descent. The floor of the earthen tunnel was hard packed, as though it had seen a great deal of traffic. After a hundred steps, it leveled off for half that distance, then ended at what appeared to be a solid wall. The wall was dark and oddly textured, and it wasn't until Masterson was within reach of it that he realized it was some form of metal.

"Please use caution. There are sharp edges." Massound was close behind him.

After another few paces, Masterson saw what he was referring to. Part of the metal wall had been ruptured, and the metal had split along jagged lines. Rhaliyah was already gingerly climbing through the rent.

"What is this thing?" Masterson tried to estimate its size, but there wasn't enough light to see how far it extended.

"A messenger from Allah, bearing a gift for the people of Tuvaresh," answered Rhaliyah.

Masterson noticed a faint glow as he negotiated the tight, ragged passage, a glow that seemed to strengthen with each passing second. At first he thought that his eyes were adjusting, but then he realized that large sections of the walls around him were lightening, as if responding to the comparatively weak glow from the lantern. In less than a minute the entire chamber was illuminated and Rhaliyah set the gas lamp down.

The walls were metallic, inset with what appeared to be scores of small instruments or displays, none active insofar as he could determine. There were strange symbols inscribed in various places, but he didn't think they were Arabic.

"Is this what I think it is?" He wasn't sure whom he was asking, but Massoud answered.

"Yes, a voyager from another world."

"A goddamned flying saucer!"

Massoud gave a thin chuckle. "More like a flying sausage, I think, although we cannot tell for certain. Most of the forward compartments were crushed and buried. It is only the rear portions of the vessel which were not destroyed."

Masterson felt a sudden, immense sense of satisfaction. "And you found something here, something which cures people."

"It is better that you see the Healer for yourself. Please follow Rhaliyah."

The passageway to the next compartment had been twisted by the impact, but remained otherwise intact. The threesome continued until they reached the next compartment. There had probably been a hatch or doorway here at some point, but it was missing now. They stepped through into a much larger, almost spherical space, and Masterson saw something moving on the opposite side, something alive.

It looked like a cross between a spider and an octopus and it was enormous, its body spread across a third of the chamber's inner walls. There was a bulbous shape up near the ceiling with dark markings that might have been some kind of sensory organs. Gelatinous extrusions spread from below its mantle, covering a significant portion of the wall, and dozens of impossibly thin legs or tentacles or something like a hybrid of the two were busily moving back and forth across the body, performing enigmatic tasks. A portion of the chamber wall had been torn open, split into a wide grin, and tuberous appendages snaked down to that area and disappeared into the packed earth like questing roots.

"What is it doing?" Masterson watched the constant movement as though hypnotized.

"The Healer is healing itself." Massoud stepped away from him, but kept the weapon pointed in Masterson's direction. "You see before you the most precious secret of our people."

"I don't understand."

"The Healer was the only survivor, or perhaps the only passenger. I am not sure that it is even intelligent in any human way. It may have been the ship's physician, or perhaps it is just an organic machine designed to cure illnesses." Massoud shrugged his shoulders. "It does not matter. The people of Tuvaresh have concealed its existence for generations. We extract certain fluids from its body, the Tears of the Healer, and use them medicinally. They help with both infectious diseases and physical trauma."

Masterson nodded. "I could pay you for enough to cure my cancer. I could pay you very well, enough to help everyone in the village."

Massoud shook his head, and his gun hand wavered as well. "If the people of Tuvaresh were suddenly to become wealthy, questions would be asked. People would come and eventually they might discover our secret and take it away. If the authorities in Rabat knew of this," he gestured toward the pulsing body of the alien creature, "do you think they would allow us to keep it here? It is a great gift Allah has given to the Tuvareshi, and we will protect it as well as honor it."

"Then we're back to trading a life for a life. Mine for Alina's."

Rhaliyah's breath was a hiss and Massoud sounded immensely sad. "I have told you, we cannot help. The Tears might prolong your life a short while, but they will not cure the cancer. For that you would need the Embrace." Massoud looked suddenly uncertain and Masterson realized he was upset to have revealed so much. He might otherwise have traded the Tears for the girl's life.

"Dr. Massoud, I know that you can cure Glastonbury's. I regret putting the child's life at risk, but I will do whatever I have to do in order to survive."

"Can you come back in six months?" Massoud sounded suddenly tired.

"I will be dead by then, and you know it."

"Yes, and I am powerless to prevent it. Look." Massoud walked closer to the alien and Masterson followed him, suppressing a wave of revulsion as he saw in closer detail the way the living flesh seemed to swarm with interior life. The doctor pointed to a shallow depression carved into the wall of the ship. Pulsing, dripping flesh had grown down to cover the upper third of the declivity, and that portion of its body seemed to have taken on a different texture, becoming fibrous, almost matted.

"What is this?" asked Masterson.

"We call it the Embrace. Only the most desperately ill receive this gift. They are placed in the Embrace for the space of one night, their bodies are united with the Healer, and in the morning they are whole again."

"Then all I have to do is lie in this thing for a few hours and the cancer is gone?"

"Yes, but it is impossible now. You can see that barely a third of the surface is covered. The Healer must be complete in order to perform its miracle, and you are six months too soon for that. It takes more than a year after each treatment before it is ready for another. You see, Mr. Masterson, even if I wished to help you, I am powerless to do so."

There was a long silence before Rhaliyah spoke.

"The girl, Mr. Masterson. Let us save the girl."

Absently he pulled the control device from his pocket and tossed it to her. "Here. It doesn't matter. I'm not the monster you think. There's no bomb. I certainly wasn't going to blow up my only transportation out of here."

Rhaliyah gave him a look of mixed pity and contempt and started toward the exit. Massoud glanced after her, and let his arm drop to his side. Masterson didn't hesitate for a second. He drew his second weapon and shot Massoud in the middle of the chest. His second shot hit Rhaliyah in the back of the head; she fell to the floor and never moved again.

"It may not be much of a chance," he said quietly, "but it's better than no chance at all."

He should have waited until he'd extracted more details, but he was afraid that Rhaliyah would send reinforcements and that had forced his hand. The prospect of immersing himself even partially in the viscous muck of the Healer's body revolted him, but he was prepared to experience far worse if necessary. After stripping off all of his clothing, he climbed down into the depression, lying back slowly until his head and shoulders were pressed against the alien flesh. It was warmer than he'd expected and itched a little, but then a sense of well being began to spread through his shoulders and he felt immensely weary, closed his eyes, and drifted off to sleep.

⊢•◦○◦•⊣

Masterson woke suddenly and without disorientation, but feeling an unprecedented lassitude. Everything that had happened was clear in his memory, and he could still feel a faint warmth at the back of his neck and across his shoulders. His fingers and toes tingled and when he couldn't move any of his limbs, he wondered if he was paralyzed. For a split second, there was the acid taste of panic at the back of his mouth but then a wave of well being neutralized it and he felt relaxed again.

I just have to wait until the process is over, he told himself.

He dozed for a while, occasionally opening his eyes and letting them wander around the chamber. Time passed, but he had no way to measure it. Nothing changed, not even the pattern of light and shadow. Was it day now outside? Or still night? He had no way of knowing.

And then he opened his eyes and saw another face.

It was Dr. Massoud, looking pale and strained. The front of his shirt was dark where blood had dried. I shot him, Masterson told himself. He should be dead, or at least too badly injured to be up and about. This anomaly puzzled him without bringing any distress. Masterson tried to sink back into sleep, but an incessant buzzing disturbed him, a sound which eventually resolved itself into a voice. Massoud was talking to him.

"Can you hear me, Mr. Masterson?"

Masterson thought he might be able to talk. Experimentally he opened his mouth and tried. He very distinctly heard the word "Yes" but it didn't sound like his voice. It was very thin and high pitched and it trembled.

Massoud's face changed, relaxing slightly. "Very good. You have survived, despite my expectations, Mr. Masterson. And I have survived despite yours, no doubt." He looked down at his chest. "Your aim was poor or I would be dead. As it is, I am only experiencing a great deal of pain. The healer's blood will speed my recovery but I still face several days of discomfort." His face hardened. "Rhaliyah was not so fortunate."

Masterson tried to lift an arm, aware that he was at the mercy of a man he'd just tried to kill, but he couldn't summon the necessary strength, and almost immediately felt that it wasn't worth the effort. The anxiety was still there; he could feel it. But whenever he slipped toward panic, something yanked him back.

"I have some good news for you, Mr. Masterson. The Healer has managed to rid your body of the cancer after all." He laughed unpleasantly, and came closer, lowering his face to within inches of Masterson's. "I admit that I am quite surprised. The process is even more sophisticated than I had imagined. Since it lacked the resources to effect a cure in its usual fashion, it improvised." He leaned back. "Of course, that required some sacrifices. Wait, I'll show you. I think you'll be quite excited."

Massoud was gone for some undetermined period of time, and Masterson had almost lapsed back into unconsciousness when he returned. "I think I can manage something more satisfactory on a long term basis, but for the moment at least this is the best I can do. It should prove adequate." He raised his hand, and Masterson saw that it held a sheet of thin metal, polished mirror smooth. His face was a blurry reflection and he squinted, trying to focus his eyes.

"I believe that when the Healer realized that it was unable to heal your entire body, it identified and isolated the most vital portions and sacrificed the rest."

The image became clearer and Masterson saw at last why he could not move his arms. His body was only intact from chest level up. Below that, his exposed organs were encased in a transparent sheath that expanded and contracted in place of his missing lungs. His arms and legs were gone, along with his entire skeleton below the heart.

Massoud put his face in front of Masterson's again. "Your body appears to be self contained. I wonder if it will be able to survive outside the Embrace." He smiled warmly. "Let's find out, shall we?"

And he reached out toward Masterson.

❖

The Natural World

"I really think you should consider getting an aquarium, Miss Wilson. Then you would be able to enjoy the beauty of God's creation without having to submit to these tedious and unsanitary excursions. These are the 1870s, after all. One doesn't need to be discomforted while viewing the natural world."

Emma sighed and wished once again that she'd been able to find the right words to dissuade Jared Rackham from accompanying them this morning. She and her younger sister, Virginia, were quite capable of looking after themselves and in fact they were both more at ease covering the rough terrain along this part of the shoreline than was their ungainly companion. Ever since their arrival from London, he had been appearing with distressing regularity at the cottage. It would not have been such a trial if he'd been content to abide by the customs of decent society and depart promptly after paying his respects and remaining away for a decent interval between visits, but he was clearly enamored with her, although he had not said as much, and returned with distressing regularity. Her polite but firm refusal to respond favorably to his veiled advances had so far made no inroads on his enthusiasm.

"Perhaps you are right, Mr. Rackham, but one can only stare at the same pressed leaves and flowers for so long, after all, and the fresh air and exercise is good for the health."

They had been picking their way across a fairly steep, rocky slope and Rackham had managed to stumble over every third irregularity, giving his progress an erratic, uncertain quality. "There is no end to the wonders imbued in even the simplest of His creations," he answered somewhat breathlessly. Rackham had recently been promised a living as curate of Merrivale when the incumbent retired, and had discovered within himself a previously

173

hidden piety. "As to the value of fresh air, I must say that I fear it is most over-rated. I find settled air much more conducive to my own health and have not suffered the ague or similar ills since mending my habits."

Emma turned away to conceal her annoyance, raised a hand to shade her eyes. Virginia had run ahead of them, her long legs covering ground quickly and effortlessly. She would be a stunning young woman once her body had regularized its proportions, but at the moment she seemed even younger than her thirteen years. "Ginny! Please wait for us to catch you up!"

But if Virginia had heard her sister, she chose to pretend otherwise and a moment later had disappeared from sight, having reached the crest of this particular rise and descended beyond it. This was the farthest they'd come along the coastline since moving to Seamouth, and the difficulty of the walk had taxed their resolve, but not even this hardship had dissuaded Rackham from accompanying them.

Emma picked up the pace although the backs of her legs were aching and she was breathing heavily. She used a handkerchief to wipe beads of sweat from her forehead before Rackham could see them and launch into another panegyric about the ill effects of over exertion. Given the man's indolence, she was amazed that he had reached the age of thirty without spoiling his figure. He was still quite a handsome man, she admitted, although the effect was quite spoiled whenever he chose to speak.

They reached the crest almost simultaneously, and Emma suppressed a smile when she saw that her companion was mopping his own brow now, apparently too breathless to speak. That suited her own mood precisely, because the vista that opened before them deserved at least a brief moment of silent, appreciative contemplation. The land fell away spectacularly, revealing a narrow defile that seemed to cut down directly into the Earth. From the opposite side, a narrow brook rushed to the brink and toppled over, sending light spray sheeting down over a riot of wildflowers, bracken, various ferns, and twisted vines that seemed to gather all the rest together. Emma experienced a sudden, but brief alarm because it looked as though there was no place Virginia could have gone except a deadly plummet into the depths, but then she heard her sister's voice from quite close at hand, calling to her.

"Emma! Come down! You must see this!"

At first, she had no idea how to comply. She appeared to be faced with an impenetrable wall of thorn bearing shrubbery. A brief investigation revealed this to be an illusion, however. There were overlapping ramparts of branches and stems, but it was a simple matter to move among them once the trick of perspective was revealed.

"I say, Miss Wilson, is that wise?" Rackham made as though to take her arm, thought better of it and hesitated with one hand half raised. "The footing here appears quite treacherous."

"Please don't fret, Mr. Rackham. I shall take care. Please make yourself at ease here until we return." She thought she might escape him at last, if only briefly, but before she'd taken a dozen steps, he stirred himself to follow.

Twice more she had to pause and search for a way to proceed, and on several occasions she'd been able to keep her footing only by grasping sturdier branches or gnarled saplings growing out of the cliff wall. It was, indeed, a cliff face they were descending, crumbling and treacherous, and she would have turned back if Virginia had not continued to call from below, even if that had meant admitting defeat to the odious Mr. Rackham.

But at last she reached bottom and saw her sister, crouched at the edge of a pool of water only a few steps away. The hem of her skirt was heavily stained and Emma felt momentary irritation before glancing down and noticing that her own clothing, snagged by thorns, brushed by damp soil, appeared nearly as disreputable.

"Come over here, Emma. Look at this!"

Waves crashed against rocks only a few meters away, but the sound was muted by the convolutions of this sheltered cove. There were several brackish pools near at hand, and occasional droplets of sea spray speckled their surface. The foliage above them had formed into a canopy, and it was almost as though they'd stepped forward through time into dusk.

"Oh, there you are!" Rackham came up behind her so precipitously that he brushed against her arm, perhaps inadvertently, and she instinctively drew away. But for once she wasn't irritated by his advent, because she was so overwhelmed by the new environment in which she found herself. It was like a great, natural cathedral, the riotously colored plants mimicking stained glass, the filtered light from above, the muffled sounds of the outside world. "I don't look forward to ascending again," said Rackham, apparently unaffected. "The footing is quite treacherous. I should think the local council would have erected some sort of barrier, or at least a warning sign."

Emma refused to let his tedious chatter spoil her mood. She moved toward her sister, picking her steps carefully. There was water everywhere, and any solid ground was covered with delicate plants which she did not want to crush under her feet. Fortunately, a scattering of smoothly worn rocks was profuse enough that she could pick her way from one to the next.

Virginia was still crouched in the same spot when Emma joined her, and at first the older sister failed to see what was so interesting about this particular location. It was the largest of the pools, certainly, and the deepest as well. Although the others had irregular, amorphous outlines, Virginia's pool appeared to be an almost precise circle three meters in diameter, as though something small but very heavy had fallen from above, creating a shallow crater upon impact. There was no shore on the far side, which butted up against a nearly vertical fall of rock, but the near side was bordered by fine sand of a sort not in evidence anywhere else within sight, at least not in such quantity. It might have been a miniature of a wading beach.

But the most striking sight was the object at the center of the pool. "What is that?" asked Rackham, following in her wake.

"I'm sure I don't know." It might have been a lump of earth except that its shape seemed too regular. There was a central cap, its highest point, extending a hand's width above the water, surrounded by a spiraling series of tubes that wound around the core, extending its circumference until it displaced fully a third of the pool. The entire visible surface had a dull, red tint so unvarying that it seemed impossible for it to be natural. "It looks like an oversized sea shell."

Virginia gestured impatiently. "Come here, please, Emma. I think it's almost done."

At last Emma crouched beside her sister and saw what it was that so fascinated her. A narrow finger of that same odd hue ran along the floor of the pool, emerging from the water where it lapped against the sand, then extending across it in a straight line toward a stand of ferns. A jagged rock had fallen from somewhere above, severing what Emma could now see was a hollow tube. "What is it? Some kind of pipe?"

Virginia shook her head. "No, I think it's a tunnel. Look there."

Emma hadn't noticed the secondary line, two of them actually, originating on opposite sides of the obstruction, now very close to meeting. Something glittered and Emma blinked, then focused and saw a jewel spill out of one end. No, not a jewel but an insect of some kind, a beetle perhaps, which sparkled red and purple and green as it moved. One end of the insect's body dropped to the sand, which stirred as though touched by the faintest of breezes.

"What in the world is it doing?"

"Just watch!"

It only took a few seconds. The insect straightened up and then pressed its opposite end—Emma couldn't see a distinct head—against the opening of the tube. Slowly, but visibly, a red hued paste emerged, clung where it was applied, and almost immediately hardened. The diminutive engineer then disappeared inside the open end, presumably to make some modification inside. A second, nearly identical creature had emerged from the other termination point and was performing identical duty there. A few more applications and the tunnel would be restored, bypassing the fallen rock. The newcomer varied from the first only in that one of its hind legs was missing, although it seemed to get along on five just as well as on six.

"That one appears to be injured," she said quietly.

Virginia nodded vigorously and pointed. "Look there, at the edge of the stone. Do you see? There's a leg, or part of one, caught beneath it."

Emma leaned forward, squinting, and confirmed her sister's observation. "Indeed, it must have been caught when the stone fell and perhaps gnawed its own leg off to get free."

"What a horrid thought, Miss Wilson!" Rackham seemed positively repelled by the idea. "But I suppose God spares these lesser creatures the pain and anguish that are our lot."

"Whatever could they be, Mr. Rackham? I've never seen their like before and I've read all the natural histories."

Rackham leaned forward, peering myopically. "Some sort of beetle, I'd say. Or a water insect related to the pond striders."

Emma clucked her tongue impatiently. "I wouldn't imagine that a water related creature would take such great pains to keep its feet dry, so to speak, Mr. Rackham. This seems more akin to the termite or the common ant, although its appearance is certainly uncommon enough."

Rackham sniffed to convey a sense of his bruised dignity. "I wouldn't pretend to understand God's purposes in these matters, Miss Wilson. I'm sure that whatever this creature is, it fits into His plan as perfectly as does the moth or the caterpillar. The role of the naturalist is to observe and appreciate, not to presume to explain Creation, Mr. Darwin notwithstanding."

Virginia turned away to conceal her distaste for Rackham, rising slowly to her feet and stepping away from the water. "It leads back in this direction." She tentatively pushed a branch out of her way, but the undergrowth was much thicker here, virtually impenetrable. "We have to find a way around this lot."

"Whatever for?" asked Rackham, who had grown somewhat agitated. "I think we should go back. We wouldn't want to try that ascent in the darkness."

"Calm yourself, Mr. Rackham. We've barely digested our mid-day meal. We surely have time to indulge ourselves and I for one would like to rest a bit before any further exertions."

"I suppose a brief respite would do us all some good," Rackham admitted, but he was sulking.

With the same instinct that had led her down to this place, Virginia had found a circuitous but relatively accessible route around the obstruction to another clear space deeper in the chasm. At first it appeared that she had gone too far and outstripped the beetles' construction project, but then she spotted the thin red line running along an eroded notch before it disappeared into another bush.

Emma was close behind with Rackham reluctantly bringing up the rear. Tiny flying insects buzzed around them now and Emma waved them away, consoling herself with the knowledge that Rackham was similarly encumbered. Even so, she almost called on her sister to stop when Virginia began pressing herself around this latest obstruction, smearing her dress with fresh daubs of dirt as she brushed against the cliff face. But before she could do so, Virginia was gone again, passing through into a natural chamber so murky that when Emma followed she could barely make out her surroundings until her eyes began to adjust.

When she could finally see, she gasped.

The two sisters stood side by side, Rackham a step behind them. Directly in front of them, and nearly as tall as they, stood a dull red pyramid. The sides were cut up into tiers with ramps connecting one to the other like a giant model of a ziggurat, and at numerous points there were dark recesses, presumably access to the interior. The jewel-like beetles swarmed over its surface, engaged in enigmatic tasks, many carrying leaves and twigs and flower petals, dragging them inside the pyramid. It was too dark to see much of the base of the structure, but there was at least one connecting tunnel on this side, probably the one they'd been following, and one or more additional tubes beyond, stretching back into the farthest recesses of the chamber, which appeared to have no other exit.

"This is most extraordinary," said Emma. "I do believe we've happened upon an entirely new species."

"I don't think that's possible," said Rackham dryly. "I'm sure that our English naturalists have them catalogued and dissected somewhere. One can't just meander about discovering new insects, you know."

"Are you trying to say that there is a limit to God's creation, Mr. Rackham?"

"Certainly not, but we know the size of the Ark and common sense tells us that there must have been a finite number of animals which could have been accommodated."

He seemed prepared to lecture on this point indefinitely, so Emma took advantage of his momentary pause to change the subject. "What's going on over there?" She pointed past Virginia to where a particularly heavy congregation of the beetles had gathered. They edged around the corner of the pyramid, stepping deeper into the shadows.

The beetles were having to deal with another obstruction. Climbing vines had pulled down part of a dead tree, one branch of which had come to rest on the edge of one of the tiers. It would have been a simple matter for a human to shift the weight of the branch, which was only as big around as a human thumb, but for the beetles, it was a major obstruction apparently beyond their capacity.

A small contingent labored for quite some time without making any progress. The three interlopers watched for several minutes as the beetles jostled about, apparently undiscouraged by their failure.

"Can they possibly move it? Let's help them," said Virginia, but Emma grabbed her arm.

"Wait! Let's see what they decide to do next."

Rackham made an annoyed sound. "Really, Miss Wilson. They're only insects. They're not capable of deciding anything; they act entirely on instinct."

She ignored him. So did the beetles.

It was obvious that the work team lacked sufficient mass, which failing they somehow managed to communicate to the rest of the colony. Most of the tiers were relatively empty of traffic, but suddenly they were overflowing with tiny glittering bodies. Beetles emerged from the openings in the pyramid in a fluid rush, hundreds at least, more likely thousands, all streaming toward a single goal. The movement was so sudden and massive that all three of the humans backed away, although there was nothing to indicate that they'd even been noticed.

The swarm reached the broken branch and congealed around the original work team. There was a sudden light scratching sound and the obstruction began to move and was soon pushed over the side. It fell to the ground and bounced away.

As quickly as the horde had appeared, it dispersed, leaving behind only a small crew who methodically began to secrete a sticky substance with which they began patching the small scrape marks visible on the pyramid's exterior.

Emma and Virginia clapped their hands together in applause, but Rackham had grown jealous of the beetles for gaining the attention he would prefer directed toward himself. And then he made a terribly unwise decision. He snapped off a piece of a dead branch and began poking it into one of the openings in the pyramid. The sisters both called for him to desist, but he had grown increasingly miffed at their indifference to his presence.

At first it seemed that he would provoke no response, but then one of the beetles emerged, others following, some of them mounting the stick and rushing along it toward Rackham's hand. Their speed and purposefulness caught him by surprise and he backed away, but he still held the stick and the first of the beetles had nearly reached his fingers. With an inarticulate cry of disgust, he threw the stick down at his feet and, before the sisters realized what he intended, had raised his foot and brought it down squarely on top of his diminutive enemies. There was a faint popping sound and when Rackham stepped back, they could see the ruined body of at least one beetle lying in his boot print.

Something changed around them. There had been an almost inaudible susurration, so low that they hadn't been aware of it until it ceased. Emma glanced toward the pyramid and saw that all movement had stopped as well. There were scores of beetles in sight, but they were uniformly motionless. She had a sudden presentiment of danger but before she could put voice to it, the movement resumed.

Beetles streamed from the pyramid, heading toward the threesome.

Emma and Virginia pushed their way through the leafy barrier, heedless of the damage they were doing to their clothing. Virginia stumbled and fell to a knee and Emma hastened to help her up. She turned to see Rackham follow in their wake, but it was a strangely altered Rackham. Scores of beetles clung to his clothing and his face was twisted in an expression of horror and loathing. He opened his mouth in what started as a scream but which turned into a horrible choking sound as several of the beetles raced up his chest and swarmed over his face. Rackham's look of surprise was almost comical as he staggered forward a few steps, then fell full length.

The sisters were transfixed, too startled and fearful to intercede for the first few seconds. Emma finally rallied, ordered her sister to remain where she was, and cautiously advanced. Rackham lay prone, moving his limbs slightly though to no great purpose, and moaning ever so softly. She had no clear plan to drive the beetles away from his body, but that proved unnecessary. They were already leaving, streaming back toward the pyramid.

"Are you all right, Mr. Rackham?"

There was no answer for several seconds and she was about to address him a second time when he slowly raised his head, then pressed his palms down and lifted his upper body. His expression was still anxious but he was no longer ruled by panic. "What happened? Are they gone?"

"I think so. Have they done you any injury?"

Rackham rose to his knees, coughed, cleared his throat, then examined himself critically. "Only to my dignity. Mrs. Nelson will never be able to clean this suit adequately, I'm afraid, but I seem to be uninjured." He glanced around nervously. "Are they entirely gone?"

"I think so, but we should probably leave now. Are you up to it?"

Rackham waited until he was standing before answering. "I think so, yes. They took me by surprise, you know. Silly of me to become so rattled by one of the least of God's creatures."

Emma bit her lip. "Least or not, I really think we should absent ourselves before they return. Are you certain that you're all right?"

"Quite, my dear. A tempest in a teapot."

The return trip was uneventful, but Emma had never felt so tired and dispirited in her life, and the sisters confined themselves thenceforward to more conventional adventures and shorter excursions. Virginia mentioned the beetles from time to time, but Emma had no wish to be reminded of them, agreed that they had been quite beautiful, and quickly changed the subject.

Rackham seemed fully recovered, and resumed his regular campaign of visitations. His resistance to any outside excursion strengthened and he began to complain that direct sunlight disagreed with him, but Emma saw nothing extraordinary in this. In the past, he had tried similar ploys to discourage them from venturing away from the house. He had always enjoyed a delicate complexion, he explained, and Emma did notice that he seemed very pale, so much so that she inquired after his health. "Quite good, my dear. The spirit of our Lord lends me some of its vitality."

Midsummer passed and Virginia was sent off to spend two months with their mother's sister, who had had a difficult pregnancy and needed help with the infant. Emma had been so far unable to make any friends among the local youth—in part because her father frowned upon most such associations—and her parents were so much taken up in their own affairs that she was left to her own devices almost every day. She began to feel so lonely that even Mr. Rackham's visits became welcome distractions from her growing malaise.

And eventually she felt a quite surprising unhappiness when they began to decrease in frequency and eventually stopped entirely.

Emma felt no attraction to the man, and counted him not even as a friend, but she had been flattered by his infatuation and felt a sense of distinct loss when it was withdrawn. On those occasions when she could find an adequate excuse to visit the village, she made painfully casual inquiries about his welfare, but elicited no intelligence other than that he spent a good deal of time by himself in his cottage and that Mrs. Nelson, who cleaned and cooked for him, said that he had become more studious and reclusive than ever.

She asked about this one day when she encountered Mrs. Nelson in the market.

"Yes, lass, he's a very changed man of late, he is. Keeps to himself, though, and doesn't find fault with my work. I have nothing to complain of." Emma could tell that Mrs. Nelson wished to speak further but required prompting.

"I imagine he's preparing for his curacy. That must take up a good deal of his time."

The older woman nodded. "He tells me all the time that he feels the presence of God within his breast. He's righteous enough, I suppose, though a bit Popish in his practices."

"Whatever do you mean, Mrs. Nelson? He seems quite a proper churchman to me."

It required a bit more enticement, but Mrs. Nelson was clearly primed to tell someone of the strange goings-on at Rose Cottage, where Rackham was ensconced. She had noticed a slow evolution of his behavior during the past several weeks, the individual increments of which had not been alarming but which were, when taken as a whole, somewhat troubling.

"I can understand him locking himself in his study for hours at a time, studying on his books, what with the responsibilities he'll assume within the year. But I'm not so convinced that what happens in the root cellar is entirely respectable." Emma was forced to prompt her again at this point, and their conversational tug-of-war continued until she had the outline of Rackham's strange behavioral transformation.

Mrs. Nelson had arrived one day to find the door to the root cellar reinforced and padlocked. As it happened, her duties did not require that she have access to that portion of the property, which was used only to store wine and a few odds and ends, but she thought this new security unusual enough that she remarked upon it to Rackham, who assured her that it was simply a safety precaution. "Those old steps were rotted through and might collapse at any moment."

Although she had accepted his explanation, subsequent events contradicted it. "Sometimes while I was cleaning up, Mr. Rackham would come out of his room and go into the cellar. He told me that he was repairing the steps, and that he was barring the door from below so that I wouldn't fall to my death in a moment of forgetfulness." She leaned closer and gave Emma a conspiratorial look. "But I never heard no hammering or any other sound, for that matter. And he always wore the same thing, a raggedy old robe like those monks up at Christwarden Abbey wear. I think he was down there kneeling in the dirt, saying prayers, and if that ain't Popish, then I don't know what is."

Emma admitted that it sounded odd. "But I'm sure Mr. Rackham is entirely orthodox, Mrs. Nelson."

More days passed. Emma finally made a local friend, Mary Waddell, the mayor's niece, and through her Mary's fiancé, Roger Hornby, and several other young men and women. A few of the men were interesting, but otherwise committed, and others seemed to find Emma's company appealing, but they were uninteresting. This unhappy state of affairs was still preferable to her former isolation, and her new social life was sufficiently engaging to take her mind off Mr. Rackham until late in the fall.

She was in the market again, running an errand for her mother, when she saw Mrs. Nelson at a fruit vendor's stall and recollected her former acquaintance. "And how is Mr. Rackham doing these days?"

"And how would I know that, Miss, seeing as I've not set eyes on the man for these last eight weeks?"

Emma's brow wrinkled. "But aren't you his housekeeper still?"

A vigorous shake of the head. "He sacked me, lass, and without a hint of a warning. Told me to get out and never come back."

"But why? Was he unhappy with your work?"

Mrs. Nelson looked affronted. "He had no reason to be, and I've not had a complaint out of him or any who came before him. One morning I came to his door just as I always did, and he was waiting for me. My services are no longer required, he tells me, and other arrangements have been made." She grunted heavily. "Other arrangements indeed. There's not a working woman in the village gives as good service, if I do say it myself. And he's not had in any other help either. I'd have heard."

"But surely someone must cook for him, clean his house? Mr. Rackham is not the sort of man who could do for himself."

"Can't say that I would have thought it myself, Miss, but there it is."

Emma decided that she must find an opportunity to call upon Mr. Rackham personally and find out the truth of the matter. He may have made a pest of himself in the past, but he'd never done her a disservice and it was her Christian duty to inquire further as to his welfare.

But then Virginia returned from her brief exile, and Emma was introduced to Thomas Wallenby, son of Sir Arthur Wallenby, and more time slipped away with no investigation of Mr. Rackham's odd behavior.

⊢•◦•⊣

Emma Wilson gave no further thought to Jared Rackham until the day her father mentioned the new curate in Merrivale, Robert Bowlby.

"But I thought that position had been promised to Mr. Rackham?"

Her father had shaken his head. "Strange situation that, Emma dear. It seems that he turned the post down at the last minute."

"Then perhaps he had a better offer."

"Wetancourt says otherwise." Wetancourt was the innkeeper. "Apparently Rackham spouted some nonsense about serving God more efficiently right where he was. Sounds a bit daft to me, but there's talk in the village that he's gone Romish and is set to enter a monastery or some such."

Her father had no further information, which did not prevent him from expounding on the subject for several more minutes, but Emma barely heard what he said from that point on. She had silent resolved to herself to pay a visit to Mr. Rackham and learn the truth from his own lips.

⊢•◦•⊣

The opportunity to follow through on her promise did not present itself for several more days. First she was required to accompany the family on a brief but tedious visit to her father's brother, a tiresome man who had never married and who still treated Emma and her sister as though they were children. Then they returned to discover that the servants had quarreled in their absence and it required a firm hand and some understanding to restore peace and efficiency to the household. And there were various other social obligations that must be satisfied.

But at last Emma found herself left to her own devices for a day and, with nothing to compete for her attention, she set out alone and on foot to visit Mr. Rackham, an impropriety which would have shocked her parents but which, in these modern times, seemed to her quite acceptable. Her parents were visiting the Wheelers and would not be back before dark, and Virginia was off somewhere with her newest companion, Evelyn Lane.

Emma had never actually been to Rose Cottage before, although she had certainly passed it often enough. The name came from the climbing roses that swarmed over its walls, so profuse in growth that only the roof of the cottage was visible from outside the property. There was a gate, of course, but it was open. Emma noticed with growing dismay that the grounds had not been tended in some considerable time. The modest gardens were overgrown, and a sizable branch had fallen from a tree and partially blocked the pathway to the door. She stepped around it and continued, determined to discover the truth of Mr. Rackham's situation.

The door stood slightly open, a circumstance which caused her some concern. Emma raised one gloved hand to the knocker. There was no response, not a sound from inside, so she leaned forward and called out his name. "Mr. Rackham? Are you at home? It's Emma, Emma Wilson. I came to see how you were faring. Hello!"

She paused, listening, but there was no response. Her first impulse was to leave, but she'd invested considerable time and effort in this venture already and besides, Mr. Rackham might be lying sick or injured and unable to respond. She pushed against the door, which swung further open, and started to call again.

But she stopped in mid-syllable, aghast.

She had a very limited view of the interior, but circumscribed though it was, it still revealed the terrible conditions inside. A table and lamp stood under a large painted landscape, beyond which stood a chair, a mirror, and a doorway. By shifting position slightly, she caught sight of a portion of a tapestry, another chair, and a second doorway. Every object, as well as the floor and walls, was covered with filth. The interior of the house was if anything in worse condition than the grounds. Appalled but fascinated, she deliberately opened the door wide.

Dirt lay everywhere, not the patina of dust left by neglect but a perceptible layer of dirt as though a flood had coursed through the hall, leaving a filthy detritus in its wake. Something terrible had happened here. Emma knew it instinctively, and her concern for Mr. Rackham's fate overwhelmed her sense of caution.

She stepped inside, calling his name. There was still no answer.

The arrangement of rooms was unfamiliar to her, and there was such a thorough application of dirt throughout the cottage that it was sometimes difficult to tell one from the other. Every surface was covered, sometimes with a thin layer, sometimes with actual mounds including a particularly large one in what was presumably Rackham's sleeping chamber. But in due course she found herself in the kitchen, having seen no trace of her quarry elsewhere. Nor was he here, but there was a narrow doorway that did not lead to the outside. This door too was open, and a brief look told her it provided access to the root cellar. Somewhere below, a lamp had been lit, because formless shadows danced on the near wall.

"Mr. Rackham! Are you down there? Please answer me. Do you need assistance?" No one answered, but there was a faint rustling. "This is Emma Wilson. Are you hurt? Can you answer me?"

She placed a foot on the top stair, which creaked slightly but seemed secure. Another call brought renewed muffled stirring but nothing else. Emma bit her lip. Logic told her that she should return to the village and seek help there, but what if she raised an alarm unnecessarily? She resolved to descend far enough to survey the cellar and no farther.

Once the decision was made, she didn't hesitate. She did, however, watch her footing carefully because there was dirt on the stairs just as everywhere else, although it was so hard packed here that it seemed almost like carpeting. Within seconds she had descended more than half way and, by ducking her head slightly, was able to see much of the space around her.

If anything had been stored in the cellar in the past, it had either been removed or concealed under enormous piles of dirt. The top of one mound had been leveled off to serve as a platform for an oil lamp, which accounted for the flickering shadows. There appeared to be a second light source further off, but the cellar was L-shaped and she could not see around the corner. Beneath the staircase, wooden boards, an old barrel, broken glass, and other debris had been piled together in a chaotic mass. Rackham was nowhere to be seen, but there were signs of excavation and, not far from the foot of the stairs, one of the supporting beams had apparently fallen. There was a hint of color to one side of the beam and a shape which she recognized with sudden shock as the ankle and heel of a human leg. Emma promptly forgot her resolve not to descend all the way and hastened to investigate.

It was indeed exactly what she had feared. The beam lay across the knee and lower thigh, pinning them to the earthen floor. It didn't seem possible that the rest of Rackham's body could possibly fit into the shallow space beyond, but she didn't investigate. The condition of the flesh of the foot was sufficient to convince her the accident had occurred some considerable time in the past, and that there was nothing she could do for Rackham now.

But if that was the case, who had lighted the lamp? The rustling she'd heard might well have been rats or other vermin, but the lamps would not have lasted the day without being refilled. With the thought came another brief, furtive sound, from the pile of trash behind the stairs.

Although she was badly shaken by what she'd already seen, and certainly had no desire to encounter a rat in its lair, Emma found herself moving not to the stairs but instead toward the hidden branch of the cellar.

Even before she reached it, she noticed something familiar, and disquieting. The walls had changed color, slowly becoming a uniform red, a familiar shade which she could not immediately place. Then she was around the corner. The second lantern was set in another column of dirt near the far wall, but the wall was no longer the delimiter of the cellar. A circular hole had been excavated through it, descending at a modest angle into the earth, and the walls of that hole, and the tunnel beyond, were covered with a smooth, almost ceramic layer of red hued material. It was then that she found the elusive memory and realized that it was the very same color as the tunnels of the beetle colony they'd stumbled upon the previous spring.

Emma knew that she should leave, but her curiosity was too great. She must know what lay within that tunnel. If she simply bolted and raised the alarm, she would certainly never be allowed to re-enter and see for herself. Drawing a deep breath, she stepped forward, caught hold of the lantern, and passed through the entranceway.

The slope descended only a few steps before leveling off, then debouched into a circular chamber where, to her amazement, she found a third lamp, also burning. But unlike the rest of the cottage, this space was almost immaculate. The walls, which curved into a domed roof, were smooth and red and seemed to be highly polished, as was the floor beneath her. But the real source of wonder was the structure that dominated the center of the room.

It was a perfect pyramid, constructed of the same material, with a single dark opening just large enough that she might have crawled inside if she'd been so disposed. But even Emma's curiosity had its limits. Without taking her eyes off the bizarre structure, she took a step backwards, intending to retreat.

"Beautiful, isn't it?"

Emma spun around, nearly dropped the lantern, and caught her breath when she saw Jared Rackham standing just out of reach. Her first reaction was astonishment that he was alive; her second shock because he was completely naked, although his body was so heavily encrusted in filth that in the dim light it almost seemed that he was clothed.

"Mr. Rackham! I thought some harm had come to you!" In fact, she still did. He was certainly not in his right mind. The fact that he kept his distance did not appreciably diminish her alarm at his appearance.

"Harm! No, of course not. I am perfectly all right. More so than ever, my dear Miss Wilson." He casually lifted his hand and filled his mouth with a handful of dirt, swallowing it almost immediately. "I am filled with purpose. I feel God moving within me every minute now. My life has direction and I have penetrated the fog of ignorance and seen the truth. For years I longed to understand the nature of the Creator and it is only now that I have come to realize that I was lost in a search for myself." He stepped forward and swept his arm out, indicating the pyramid, or perhaps the chamber as well. "I am the Creator, you see, and this is my Creation."

Emma had retreated instinctively although Rackham did not seem to mean her any immediate harm. She also noticed that he lurched rather awkwardly when he moved, and she observed belatedly that there was something slightly wrong with his legs, which were both covered with a red hued encrustation. The temptation to avert her eyes was strong, because he was altogether indecently exposed, but she persevered and realized that his right leg was noticeably shorter and more slender than the left. How could it have withered so when he looked otherwise hale and hearty?

And then she remembered the crushed leg at the other end of the cellar and realization made her heart race. The leg had not withered; it was being re-grown. Rackham had been caught by the collapse and had somehow severed his own limb. But how was this regeneration possible? Emma had no idea, but she knew that whatever mechanism might be involved, it was certainly no holy miracle.

"I must be going now, Mr. Rackham. I just stopped by to see if you needed anything, but I'm expected home." She caught her breath and stepped forward, but Rackham continued to stand in her way. "Let me pass, please."

"The work has taken much longer than I expected, but now that you've come to help me I'm sure that it will go much more quickly." His expression changed. "You are here to help me, aren't you?"

"Yes, of course I am. But not just this moment. I will return in due course, Mr. Rackham. Now please let me pass."

For a moment she thought he would do as she bid. He nodded, but it was to some inner voice that was audible only to him. "You must stay and help me."

"And I will do so, at the proper time. I have other responsibilities to attend to first." Her voice sounded wrong and she realized that she was afraid.

Rackham seemed to be considering her words, but only for a moment. "There is nothing in this world more important than the Creation. Perhaps when it is complete, there will be time for other considerations, but nothing must interfere with its progress." He raised his arm, perhaps to point to the pyramid once more, perhaps not, but Emma interpreted it as an attempt to restrain her and she responded without thinking, turning to one side and swinging the lantern with her arm fully extended.

Rackham managed to duck away, leaving a gap through which she attempted to escape, but Rackham caught a fold of her dress with one hand and she staggered, nearly lost her footing. He would have had her then, but the dress ripped and the disparity between his legs proved his undoing. He stumbled, off balance, and lost his concentration as well as his grip as he tried to recover. Emma swung the lantern a second time; it barely grazed the side of Rackham's head, then struck the wall of the tunnel. Glass shattered, metal tore, and flaming liquid splashed out like fingers of fire.

Emma ran up the sloping tunnel into the cellar and then to the stairs, stumbling in her haste to ascend. She didn't stop until she was out of Rose Cottage and off its grounds, then collapsed under a tree not far distant, exhausted both physically and emotionally. When she glanced back the way she'd come, a thick column of black smoke was already rising above the wild roses.

>–•–0–•–<

She stopped by a brook to wash her face and repair as best she could the damage to her clothing. The dress was no doubt ruined but it would pass muster from a distance and if she was lucky, she'd have time to repair the situation before she was found out. It had already occurred to her that no one would ever believe her story, and that it would be best not to be connected in any way to the fire which had presumably destroyed Mr. Rackham, or whatever he had become, and Rose Cottage.

Arriving home, she quickly changed clothing and dropped what was not salvageable into the rag bin. Then she made herself some tea and sat quietly, waiting for the trembling to leave her hands and the images of Rackham to leave her mind. She was still sitting there when Virginia arrived.

"Oh, tea! Is there more? I'm quite famished."

Emma was relieved to discover that she could carry on a normal conversation and inquired about her sister's day. Virginia had taken Evelyn on one of her famous nature walks, apparently, but Evelyn was not used to such exertion and confessed herself quite "fagged out". She'd gone home to soak her feet.

"Oh, I almost forgot." Virginia's hand plunged into the pocket of her sweater. "I brought you a present." She brought out a small, ornate box and set it on the table.

"What is it?" Emma peered down, wondering whether or not she was meant to take the box.

"Well, open it, silly. I know you'll be surprised."

With a faint smile, Emma picked up the box and shook it. There was a rattle, as though some small, hard object were imprisoned inside. The clasp was brass and rather stiff, but she pushed it up with her thumb and it opened.

"Be careful! Don't let it get away!" Virginia shouted.

But the belated caution did no good. The moment the lid popped up, the jeweled beetle inside leaped from inside the box to the back of Emma's wrist. Emma's mouth opened wide in surprise, and then shock, and the beetle jumped again, searching for the nearest place where it might be sheltered from the abrasive sunlight.

Emma choked and swallowed and felt God moving within her.

About the Author

Don D'Ammassa was born in 1946 and was reading adult fiction by age six. He has been accumulating books ever since and his library is now approaching 60,000 volumes. He began reviewing science fiction and fantasy in the 1960s and sold his first novel, *Blood Beast*, in 1988. Since then he has sold well over one hundred stories, six more novels, and three reference books. He currrently lives in Rhode Island.

www.ingramcontent.com/pod-product-compliance
Lightning Source LLC
Chambersburg PA
CBHW060936180626
46817CB00004B/1568